ZANDROS RISING

Jeane Moore

CALUMET EDITIONS

Minneapolis

CALUMET EDITIONS

SECOND EDITION DECEMBER 2022

ZANDROS 2,

ISBN – 978-1-960250-30-8

10 9 8 7 6 5 4 3 2

Book design by Gary Lindberg

To Alice Phoenix, my daughter.

I think of her every day.

Also by Jeane Moore

Zandros in Love

ZANDROS RISING

Jeane Moore

2012
Tuesday, April 24

1

We had supper at Tomato Red. Later that evening, I parked Clare's car in the lot behind Vincent's, leaned forward to rest my head on the steering wheel, and sighed. I was tired. The last few weeks had been a strain and I thought I should be able to let down now but I couldn't, not yet.

"What is it?" she asked. "Are you okay?"

"Don't do it again," I said. My voice sounded thick. "Don't leave me."

"No. I won't. Never, ever. Under no circumstances. Never. It was awful without you."

"Even if I beat you?"

"Are you planning to?" She sounded somewhat tentative. "Does that go with the Greek wedding and the babies?"

"No." I lifted my head and turned to face her and rested my left arm on top of the steering wheel. I attempted a smile, but I wasn't sure if it was working. I reached out and wound a finger in her dark curls. "No, but I do have a temper. I have to tell you about this. I wish I didn't but I do. Have to. If I ever completely lost it—God, Clare, you know how I'd feel if I ever hurt you. I think I've learned to control it, but what if I haven't?"

"Maybe I'd deserve it."

"No no no. No, never. No wife ever deserves it. Or child." I took a deep breath. "My father hit my mother." I was watching her face and saw it stiffen. Maybe go a shade paler if that were possible. Saw those blue eyes slide sideways to look out the window. "Not regularly. Nothing like that. Maybe three or four times that I know about. He had a ferocious temper. He didn't beat her up, just slapped her. No punching. But when you are a young child and you see something like that, it's all different then."

She nodded. "Paul took the brunt of it for the rest of us. Got slapped around. Philip was pretty much left alone and Catherine was a girl and I was the baby. And I had my own ferocious temper. I hit him back once when he spanked me. He laughed at me. So it's there. In the blood? I don't know. But it's there." My face felt hard and hot. "I loved my father, but I hated him when he hit her. I think I knew how hard he had to work to control himself. But I still hated him at those moments. And you—are you thinking I'll never make him mad?"

Her face said yes, guiltily.

"A *thousand* times no. Don't you see where that goes? I get my way all the time by threat. You've got to let me walk my own tightrope."

"But now I know."

"Yeah," I said. "The worm starts crawling toward the apple. Sorry about all the metaphors."

"But really, I already knew. I never saw it, not first hand, but things you've said, and other people have said, and, you know, the thirty-five centuries of getting your own way. I just knew there was *some*thing."

"You've never been afraid? Of me?"

She shook her head.

I looked at her. "It's not real to you, is it?"

She shrugged. "No. It never has been, not with you."

"And you're willing to live on the side of the volcano?"

"If I get to be the maiden sacrifice."

I laughed and opened the car door.

"Wait."

I put one foot out on the asphalt and sat back and waited.

She took a deep breath and said, "When did you start carrying a gun?"

"I got a concealed carry permit several years ago. We handle a lot of cash and sometimes I'm out at night with a lot of money."

It was legal, more or less. A very large fee was paid to a clerk in the office that issues the permits. All the right papers are in the files. It was just that a few minor steps were actually missteps. It was quite possible that the wrong prints were in the files, for instance—like Andy's in my file and mine in his.

I said, "I keep the gun at the office because of the kids. They generally stay out of my stuff, but who's to know when they'll start hunting for Christmas presents. Thomas probably already knows how to open my safe. Or Ioulia. She likes puzzles. Yeah, probably Ioulia. Stephen wouldn't be interested.

"Does Catherine know that?"

"I think so. She's pretty good about knowing what's going on. And the kids are good at keeping on her right side. And mine. Anyway, I've been wearing it since we told Paul to leave. I thought he might come after you. Or me. He carries a gun. Does it bother you that I do?"

"I don't know if it *bothers* me. It makes me... curious."

I said, "I know how to use it. You don't need to worry about that. Every month I go to the gun range and shoot to stay in practice." I smiled. Philip had this one. We had a standing reservation time, all the adult male Zandroses and some cousins, at the range each month, fourth Tuesday, and on the third Tuesday I get a text reminding me. "Same as I go three or four times a week to the gym. Stay in shape. Stay sharp."

"What do you do at the gym, exactly?"

"Weights. Hit the bags, jump rope, maybe get in the ring with Andy. We're pretty well matched."

"You should be. What kind of gun is it?"

"A Walther nine millimeter."

"Is that an automatic?"

"People call them that but it's a semi-automatic. Full automatics are illegal."

"Not a revolver."

"No."

"The flat kind, not the round kind."

"Yes."

"Will you show it to me someday?" she asked.

"Sure. I'll take you to the range. You can shoot if you want."

"Oh. Well… maybe."

"Let's go in."

2

She moved closer. She needed my warmth. Not sex this time, but she slept cold, and she told me once that when I slept I was a nuclear reactor. She burrowed in. I drifted into sleep—and got jolted out of it.

Someone was screaming. Clare was. In a child's voice. Not me, Mama. Not Clare! Nooooo! No not me! Stop stop! No no no. Hurting me! Mama, make him stop! Mama!

She hit me and I yelled. "Clare! Clare!"

She hit and kicked and screamed. Rough, rasping, horrible screams. "Clare!"

She opened her eyes. She was stiff, shaking. "Sam!"

"Yeah, me." I had her pinned under me. She went limp. I said, not gently, "What the hell was that?"

"Dream."

"Yeah?" I shifted my weight off her, and she took a deep, shuddering breath. I saw her come out of her dream-state.

She said, "He hurt me!" She shivered and struggled to turn over. I helped her. "Who?"

"I was little."

I switched on the lamp by the bed and watched sanity move across her face. Reality coming back.

I said, "What's in the dream? Did it really happen?"

She nodded and was silent for a moment. "I have to get up." she said.

I helped her sit up, then stand. She was shivering. Her robe was on the chair, and I held it for her and she went into the bathroom. She came back with her face washed and her hair pushed around, but still looking a little wild.

"I have to go out," she said.

"Now? Where?"

"Out. Anywhere. Just out." She dropped the robe and even at that moment of fear and disorientation her beauty gave me that little punch in the solar plexus. She started dressing—bra, panties, fleecy sweats and jacket, windbreaker, watchcap, socks and sneakers, and gloves. She looked ready for an arctic trek.

"Okay." Putting on jeans, socks, and sneakers. T-shirt.

I gathered up all the stuff that automatically goes into my pockets when I dress, and then the gun and harness. She watched the gun go on. Then the denim jacket.

I said, "Here," and gave her five twenties. She stuffed them into her jacket pocket and zipped it. I said, "Take your ID."

She looked around. Shoulder bag. Dresser. She took her driver's license from her wallet and put it in with the money.

We went down and out onto the porch. It was still full dark, but a few birds were waking up. I took hold of her wrist. She tried to pull away, but I held on and said all I need is you falling on your head. We went down the steps and got into her aging Honda. At night you couldn't really see the decades of rust. Her car, but I got in the driver's seat.

"South," she said.

Four blocks to University Avenue and turn left, east. A brightly lit commercial avenue, no people. An empty, light-rail train passed us, reassuringly noisy. I turned on the heater fan.

Someone waiting for a bus, huddled into a doorway and peeking out.

She said, "This isn't south."

"I'm getting there."

A lone bicyclist, rider and bike covered with reflectors.

Right on Rice Street, where the Zandroses had come from, arced around the Capitol, and right again, south on Wabasha.

Then down down to Shepard Road, then Warner Road. The city asleep. Dark buildings. Bright street lamps. Blinking traffic lights. A cop cruising slowly through Lowertown. A noisy truck heading for the farmers market.

I glanced over. Her eyes were wide, her mouth compressed. The night city was familiar to me, but Clare was a day bird.

I said, "Enough of this," and jumped onto Highway 61, let it out a bit. Good for the car, good for me. I liked to drive fast.

Headlights were starting to appear, coming at us, going into the city.

I looked at her again. Eyes still wide. Mouth still set. Stiff body. Still hugging herself. I pulled off the highway to buy gas at one of those big service stations lit by thousands of watts on high poles. The sun wasn't up yet, but light had begun to show in the east. "Pay and pee," I said. "Right back."

I stood for a moment next to the car and stretched. The bright white, fluorescent light of the station, the yellow dawn light in the black-to-blue sky. We were on an orbital space ship and Earth was just coming over the horizon.

When I came out some fat guy in black denim and shiny rivets, sitting on an idling Harley, was talking to her through the window I'd left open. Five or six more of them were idling near the driveway back out to the highway. She sat and looked straight ahead. I came up behind the visitor and patted his shoulder, surprising him. He damn near dropped the hog.

I said, "Mind moving? That's my spot."

"Huh? Oh. Sure, sure." He wheeled it back, gave me an all-over look. I knew what he saw: I was thirty-two years old. Dark hair, dark eyes, dark face. Mediterranean dark. Five-eleven. Long legs. In shape. He had pounds on me, but I had reach and toughness and speed.

Guys who give me that once-over almost always give up the idea of challenging me. My cousin Andy says it's because they'd lose all their street cred. Clare says it's my doberman smile.

He said, "Just saying hi, you know."

"Yeah, I know." I got in and started the car, asked without looking at her, "Is your door locked?"

"Yes."

She was back to being tense, clenching her teeth, hugging herself.

"I think we'll dawdle a bit more," I said. In my mirror I watched him join the other bikers. They revved up and roared out of the driveway, toward the city.

I got back onto 61 and drove sedately across the river and into Hastings and parked in front of a local-looking coffee shop near a feed-and-seed store.

"Breakfast?" I asked.

A moment as she consulted herself. "Yes."

We went in and the smells of coffee, bacon, and yeasty bread started my mouth watering. I said, "My God, fresh bread?" A gray-haired man setting tables said, "Sourdough," and moved slowly by. Clare smiled at him and he winked back.

The décor was very much décor. A complete small-town scene. Polished wood, crisp curtains, ruffled chair cushions. On the walls, for-sale watercolors of the river and the bluffs. Not too bad. Not real good either, but perfect for the room. Two gray-haired ladies in bibbed and beruffled aprons were waiting on tables. A gray-haired lady cook was behind the pass-through.

We took a table looking out on the street. I wanted to see if anyone was interested in our car. Other customers quickly filled up the tables around us. Eight or nine sat at a round table in a back corner. They wore denim pants and work shirts and rough brown jackets and gimme caps and fluorescent red vests. Weathered faces. Knobby hands. A few were women, mostly the same wardrobe. They were all big and tall, men and women.

Someone pushed aside a curtain. A ray of sunshine shot in and dust motes danced. We listened to a south-bound train run slowly past a block away. I almost relaxed.

We ate pancakes and bacon and real maple syrup. I didn't have to coax her to eat, like I sometimes did. It was good food and she cleaned her plate. The coffee was strong and tasty and I wanted more, but people started to stand around by the door, so Clare used the ladies' and I paid and we left.

Clear sky, sunshine.

At the car I was on the curb and she was in the street and she turned in the vee of the open door and went up on her toes for a long kiss.

I asked, "The dream—did it really happen?"

"Yes."

"Is it gone?"

"No."

"Can you tell me about it?"

She rested her forehead against my chest and didn't answer for a long time. Maybe she couldn't tell me, or didn't know the answer. Finally she said, "Let's go."

She let her arms drop and turned to face the car, then stopped and said, "I don't want to remember it."

I said, "Talking might help it go away."

"It will never go away. It's in me."

"It's a dream. You've had it before?"

She said, "Oh yes. Never when you were there. I sort of hoped maybe you'd—killed it."

"Have you talked about it before to anyone?"

"No."

"Tell me what you remember."

She was silent for a long time again. Then, "No."

"Damn it."

She got into the car and strapped herself in.

I went around and got in. I said, "We are supposed to be about as close as people get to each other. And this is obviously as important a thing to you as it could be, short of major disaster."

She turned inside her seat belt to look at me. "I can't talk about it. You'll just have to accept that. Or walk away."

"Walk away? Don't be foolish."

"Then deal with it."

We started down the river on the Minnesota side. I drove as slowly as the traffic would tolerate. We were up on the bluffs at first, and then, after Red Wing, down by the water. The low sun dazzled my eyes. The water was high and blurring the boundary between land and river. We drove by a marshy place, with red-winged blackbirds balanced on the tips of last year's cattails sending out their long, shrill call. I could feel myself loosening up—face, shoulders—then easing back against the seat, but not yet sleepy. I stopped the car at a turnout between road and river, unsnapped my belt, and turned to face her.

I said, "Please tell me. For your own sake. I can't take care of you if I don't know what happened."

"Take care of me?"

"Fuck. You know what I mean."

"Yeah, I guess I do."

She slumped and her head dropped forward. Her voice was low and thick with tears. "It's always the same. It's dark." She stopped for a few seconds. "Dark. The air is black and whirling around. I'm little. Maybe two, maybe three. I think—three. I remember trying to hold up three fingers."

Clare, little and hurting and holding up three fingers. My throat ached.

She said, "I don't understand anything. There's a man. He—he hurts me. A lot. I don't know why he's hurting me. I'm crying. He grabs my hair and slaps me, hard. I scream at him to stop, but he laughs. Suddenly I—I throw up on him and he shoves me onto the floor. And then he—hurt me again."

I said, "He raped you."

"Yes. But I didn't know. I didn't know what he did. I had no words, no context. I just knew it hurt. And that's the end of the dream."

I said, "Maybe it didn't happen. Do you remember it? Outside the dream?"

"I think—yes. Sometimes, now, I think about it. And it feels like other memories that I know are memories."

"Have you always remembered it?"

"Yes. But that's all. Just what's in the dream. I was so young…"

I asked, "How old was he?"

"How old?"

I said, "Just wondered if anyone was still available to visit vengeance upon. Beat the living hell out of, for instance."

"I don't know how old. Grown up."

"Did he have gray hair?"

"Sam, I don't want to look at him!"

"Okay. Okay. Forget it. Believe me, you'll never see him again."

At Wabasha I turned up through the bluffs and started the drive back. We didn't speak again until we were home.

3

We went back to bed but not to sleep.

Could that man be alive? Of course he could be alive. If she'd been three… twenty years ago… he could easily be less than forty. I should google the average ages of baby-rapers.

Claire pushed covers away and turned over.

For all I knew, her mother was alive. She'd be in her forties, I guessed.

She turned again, onto her back.

Did her mother know Clare was alive? Her photography professor, Jim Cochran, had been in correspondence with Clare's mother when Clare was first at the U, because she was underage and living with Cochran and his wife. But far as I knew he was no longer in touch with the mother.

She pulled the covers back over herself.

I sat up. "Shall I sleep on the couch?"

"No."

"Want some milk?"

"No."

"Want to talk?"

"No."

"Do you want *any*thing?"

"No."

"Go to sleep. He won't get you here."

4

We slept for a couple of hours and then drank our coffee leaning against the kitchen counter.

"Can you converse rationally yet?" I asked.

"Of course. I'm always rational."

"Uh-huh. I want to call Catherine and have the family to dinner to announce this engagement."

My sister Catherine was the strong, warm-hearted, and tough-minded center of our family's cosmos. Where we went for events and the announcements of events. And love and counseling and scolds and advice and family stories.

Clare said, "I suppose we have to tell everyone."

She seemed entirely back to normal.

"They'll already know, but I want to make all the right moves."

She closed her eyes.

I said, "Just the immediate family."

She opened them and said accusingly, "The immediate family is half of St. Paul."

I laughed.

She said, "What a mean laugh you have. Today?"

"If Catherine can. And you're up for it."

"You may have to hold my hand."

I took her hand in mine and kissed it

5

It was a real celebration. Everyone was delighted. They said so. I got to shine. I got to show off Clare in her rightful place as promised bride. My brother Paul and his wife the dreadful Lillian had gone somewhere, I didn't care where, leaving their young son Nicky with my brother Philip and his wife Sofia as usual, so no one threw a drunken pall over my moment.

Catherine's younger son Thomas, who was five and had been fascinated by Clare from the beginning, seemed especially affected and stayed close to her all evening. At one point I saw her get a startled expression and look down by her side where she found herself holding his small hand. She smiled at him, that glorious loving smile. Lucky lucky Thomas.

Later she said, "They all seemed quite happy about it."

I said, "*It*? Can't you even say it?"

"About you and me getting married. I can say it. Piece of cake."

But I knew it wasn't. Wasn't for her. Not yet.

We were standing in her kitchen, drinking the last of half a bottle of a very tasty Margaux I'd brought from Catherine's.

"Of course they're happy," I said. "They've been waiting for this."

She said, "They were so anxious for you to get married?"

"Not anxious, no. But they thought it was a good idea in principle. And then for us, you and me."

"But they didn't know me."

"They knew me," I said.

"We weren't—we were just friends."

"*You* were just friends. I was burning up."

"You never *said*." Her face went pink.

"Maybe you never listened." I'd been looking into my glass, swirling the wine, but now I looked up. I heard an edge of bitterness in my own voice. "Didn't you ever listen? *Hear* me?"

"Maybe I didn't!" She sounded breathless.

I sounded rough. "For a woman who sees through a lens like you do, you sure miss a lot without it."

"I was so afraid — "

"You haven't needed to be afraid for a long time," I said. "Damn it, I've been here for you, and you knew it. You *knew* I was here. When Harry and I took Donal O'Connell out of your life, didn't that tell you…?" I stopped and my voice went to normal. "Were you afraid of *me*?"

"Oh, no! Oh, God, no, never. Never of you. Oh, God, this is my fault, isn't it? These things happened because *I* was here. *I did this.*" She set down her wine glass where it fell into the sink and broke, then threw her arms around me. We almost lost my wine glass too.

I put my free arm around her. "Yes, you did, but not alone." My anger went as fast as it had come. I said, "There seemed to be so many obstacles, and all of them were things I hadn't told you. The family, the family business, the Mr. Blacks and the Kevvy Smiths, dead bodies in your house. I was wrong—*obviously* I was wrong— to say you haven't needed to be afraid. But when I said that, I was talking about all the family stuff. My family. They didn't scare me, so why would they scare you?" I finished the wine in my glass. "My family has been in business for a long time without running into the kind of threats that Kevvy Smith is making these days. And he's been in business a long time without making threats. Lulled into complacency. If I didn't tell you about this stuff, you'd be safe. I can't believe I was such an ass. And what if I told you and you said no, go away? I had something of you. A lot."

"Some gambler you are," she said into my shirtfront.

"Don't bet it if you aren't ready to lose it. I'm thirty-two years old and everything I own fits into one room. Most of what I've hung onto I'm very attached to." I put my glass down and emptied the wine bottle into it.

"If your family knew, who else did?"

"No one. Well, Harry, of course."

"Harry always knows everything." She looked at the shards of her wine glass in the sink, then took a sip from mine. "Harry introduced us. Maybe he even knew *before* that."

"He has his moments. So. 'Sam Alexandros, Clare Russell.

'And there you were."

"You weren't interested."

I said, "What's to be interested? You had on so many coats and scarves, all I could see were eyes. They were okay. In fact, fine. Very fine eyes."

"One coat, one muffler. I just wasn't your type."

"Huh." After a moment I added, "Was I yours?"

"My *type*? You were pretty tough."

"You took off all the coats."

She said, "There was only one coat. Really."

I said, "You were a nice armful and you were wearing patched jeans and some ragged sweater and a Nikon. And suddenly that was my type." I paused, looking at her, remembering. "You smiled at me. Just me."

She said, "Yes, well—"

"Harry thought it was pretty funny."

"What was funny?"

"You and me. Friends. You smiled at me and it was all there, all at once."

"What was?"

"What? Wanting to own you, I think. Wanting to take care of you. Protect you. It was very Greek. It still is."

She said, "You could have—"

I pulled her closer, put my face in her hair. She smelled good. Like some sort of flower. "No, I couldn't. Christ, Clare, you were a child."

"I was *not*!"

"You were an innocent—" I drew back my head to look into her face. I smiled. "—and you still blush."

She blushed and I kissed her nose.

I asked, "Why me and Harry?"

"You and Harry what?"

"You know what. Friends."

I waited while she figured out the words. "Because… because

you both… you were so strong. *Really* strong, not bully-boy stuff. Your *selfs* were strong. You didn't need me to be… weak."

I said, "Wow. A mystery solved."

Saturday, April 28

I played a game for Hugh Black, my regular money-man, on Saturday night in Chicago. He asked after Clare and I heard that note in his voice that told me I'd better take good care of her or he'd take over the job. I wondered idly whether he would actually shoot me.

Hugh and I had a backing arrangement. He staked me, usually the amount of the buy-in, and at the end of the game he recovered his buy-in and took half of my winnings on top of that. He also set up games, private games, with big money. Not every game I played, of course, but I was making a lot more money with him in the picture than I had been on my own. A lot more.

At dinner I told him more about what we'd done, shutting Paul out of the family business which was making book and, peripherally but profitably, playing cards. No more money or connections for Paul. Doing it had taken its emotional toll on the rest of us, but we did it and we were better for it. None of us had seen him or heard a word of him or from him since.

"I did," Black said unexpectedly. "Hear of him. I have some business dealings in Cincinnati. Somebody there asked me about him. About possibly doing business with him. Nothing specific. A reference. I was evasive. I didn't know where your family stood."

"Cincinnati's where his wife's family lives. The Makrises."

"Yes. I called you at your office and your brother Philip told me that you were out to dinner with Clare Russell. I told him what I'd heard, what I'd said. We left it at that."

After a moment I said, "Clare and I are engaged to be married."

He smiled, truly and genuinely smiled, something he rarely did. "I'm happy to hear that," he said.

Tuesday, May 1

1

All my time with Clare I lived in fear of doing something, saying something, that would somehow damage or disrupt her picture taking. I don't know why I believed her talent was so fragile. Maybe because the pictures were so perfect. So truthful. Never dainty. Never just pretty. Never any whisper of holding back or of disavowal. Strong. All in. That level of *audacity* spoke to me the way a six-figure pile of chips on the table did. And maybe to her too. More than once she stormed out of her darkroom and threw herself on me, dragging me to the floor. The beast in me responded in spades and we ended up sprawled on the floor, mostly naked, panting, laughing, covered with rug dust and sweat. I didn't ask questions.

My fear verged on superstition. I didn't cross my fingers or turn in circles, but I watched my tongue. There were only three or four people I ever mentioned it to, taking care to adopt a voice of reason. And the only one of those conversations that I allowed to go beyond a couple of sentences was with Jim Cochran, her photography professor at the U.

He said, "I don't think she's as susceptible to turmoil as you maybe believe she is. She's probably more apt to run over you than to let you run over her. In her work... I don't know why but she shies away from calling it her art, which it most assuredly is... in her work she's very tough, tough-minded. Very focused. Very organized. I'm not sure you *could* disrupt her work when she's in her groove."

I pondered Cochran's comments and decided to ask Clare a question that I'd been thinking about for as long as I'd known her.

2

I said, "Want to walk? Or taxi? Four cars seems a bit much."

We were about to leave for supper with Harry and Karen at a new Nepalese restaurant across the river. Then Harry and I were going in his car to play at a small casino just into Wisconsin, and Clare and Karen were going in Karen's car to a Norwegian movie, hankies included, and then Karen would drop Clare, and after the game Harry would drop me at Clare's. I don't know who came up with that plan. Some ant.

She followed me out of the bedroom. "It does, doesn't it. So… walk, I guess. We better leave now."

It was still sunny, but the day had been cool and wasn't getting any warmer. When we got to University Avenue we got into the wind coming down the river. By the time we were across the river and three blocks farther, the sun was dropping too far down for us to get any rays. I pulled her into a brew pub in the complex intersection known as Seven Corners.

She slammed the door on the wind and said, "Whoof!" Her cheeks and nose were red.

I pointed at a booth and we went for it. I took out my phone, hit speed-dial for Harry, and asked him to pick us up. He said, "Forty-five minutes," and hung up.

I told Clare, "Forty-five minutes. He seemed sort of breathless."

She grinned. "Forty-five minutes! Wow!"

"Never mind. What do you want?"

"The oatmeal stout."

I went to the bar and ordered her beer and a tall fizzy water with lemon for myself.

The bartender was a complete stranger to me and looked barely old enough to be working there, but he took it upon himself to say, "Water, huh. You know this is a beer pub?" There was a bit of a fashion for rudeness in bartenders that year.

I said, "Yeah, well, the old cirrhosis is acting up. War wound, you know." He looked confused and I walked away. "Move over," I said to Clare, and slid in next to her.

She said, "Are we cuddly today?"

"I want to talk to you without everyone in the room taking part. Cuddly is optional."

"Talk about what?"

I took a long swallow of water.

I said, "I want to ask a question but if it's pushing in where I'm not wanted, just push me out."

"Okay."

"Why portraits?"

She said, "Why portraits."

"Exactly."

"As in, why not mountains or kittens or sheep or horses or cars or hot-air balloons or trains?"

I said, "Right."

She was silent for a long time.

Finally, I said, "Hey, you don't have to explain—"

"No, no, I was just looking for the words." She took a deep breath. "I knew when I was still in school that taking pictures was what I wanted to do. The *only* thing I wanted to do. And I also knew that I'd probably have to do other things too… to live. Things I didn't want to do. Maybe things that would involve moral compromises. Like selling fast food. And I would do that. I wouldn't make porn, or S&M, nothing like that, but even kitties and puppies and snow-capped mountains would be a kind of moral compromise. I think. I'm not sure, because I never got that far off the straight path to my goal. And then there are those pictures of babies wearing flower costumes. I didn't want to do those either. I would, to eat, but I put those in the column with kitties."

She turned to face me.

She said, "People have mystery in them. Puppies and horses and mountains—pretty or cute or beautiful, but no mystery. Static. Unless you're Ansel Adams. Then maybe. But I want my clients' secrets, and I want to show them and other people their mysteries, what they're hiding. Is this wrong of me? Sometimes I wonder about that. But still, that's what I have to do."

I said, "I don't see any wrongdoing there. And you are doing it."

At last she smiled. "You're only the second person I ever talked to about this. The other was Jim Cochran, and he says I'm all right, morally. I've seen and studied a *lot* of pictures. A lot. And I can do it. I *do* do it. Not many other picture takers can. I don't think I'm being arrogant or immodest. Or smug or vain. I can do it."

I said, "Yes, you can. You do."

A strong, confident simplicity came through her words. She was right and I knew she was right. And my own resolution, to do whatever she needed to make it happen, was renewed.

My phone sang. Harry said, "Thirty minutes" and hung up.

3

I did very little big-dog-from-the-city playing, but Harry had talked me into this. He knew a guy who owned a small casino in Wisconsin who needed a few good players to lure people in. So we were bait.

A few hours into the game Harry and I took a short break and went to the bar. I asked for fizzy water with lemon and Harry ordered a beer. He said, apparently to his beer bottle, "Still drinking what you drank in the dry cleaner's basement when we were freshmen."

I said, "I know this because you mention it every time. A couple of these guys know what they're doing. Like you."

Harry smiled, saluted me with his bottle, finished it in one pull, and ordered another. "Yeah. And I'm doing fine. I'm up about ten grand."

I said, "You're up ninety-eight hundred."

"About. *About* ten grand."

"I'm up twenty-two-five, and it's a slow pull tonight."

Harry said, "You're better than anybody else at the table. Which one of *them* is going to beat you?"

"The first one that gets lucky on me."

We went back to the table. I was in the five seat, directly across from the dealer, and Harry was on my immediate right.

A different dealer was washing the deck, getting ready to start a new hand. I said, "Hey, Kathy. I didn't know you dealt here."

"I work extra when I can." She grinned. "I actually do have a baby needs new shoes."

I was happy to see her. She was a great dealer. "Andrew's gone home?"

Kathy said, "He's designated parent the rest of the night."

The man in the one seat whined, "Hey, recess is over. Can we get this goddamn game going again? The guy next to the whiner said, "Hey, loosen up, J.D."

Harry muttered, "J.D. ? Juris Doctor?"

I said very quietly to Harry, "Stands for Jelly Dong."

Harry laughed out loud.

I was sure J.D. had heard Harry's laugh but not what we said. We'd spoken too quietly. But the laugh pushed his button, and he started to stand up but was pushed back down into his seat by one of the guys hired to keep the peace.

Al Berg, who was the owner of the casino and in the seven seat, gave J.D. a cold look and said, "Forget it and play poker. Or leave. Shuffle up, Kathy."

After another two hours I'd won a few more pots and had just over sixty thousand on the table. I'd bought in for thirty and had been playing for nearly eight hours, so I was thinking about calling it a night. Harry had been the big blind on the last hand, so it was my turn next. I said to him, "How about we play one more orbit and pack it in before your next blind."

"Fine by me."

I put up my two hundred big blind and, as I always do, placed my card protector on my cards without looking at them. Some players have tells; I don't, but just to be safe I don't look at my cards until I have to. If I don't know what my cards are, I can't let anybody else know.

Of the nine players at the table, six players, including J.D. and Harry, called my big blind. Time for me to look.

I slid my hand toward me, moved the protector aside, and lifted a corner of the two cards. Deuce and four of spades. I checked my option to raise and Kathy put up the flop.

Jesus. Three and five of spades, six of clubs. I'd flopped a straight and an open-ended straight-flush draw.

Harry checked and so did I. Six seat bet two hundred and the eight seat folded. J.D. raised to a thousand. Harry made it two.

Harry must have had a set. Since he was the small blind, he had to put in another hundred to see the flop. He must have been dealt a pair of threes, fives, or sixes and so made the set. What else could he have?

I called the two thousand, and the six seat folded. J.D. called. Seventy-two hundred in the pot.

Kathy put up the turn, and it was a brick. Harry bet five thousand. I called time while I thought about what to do. Harry had a set, that much I knew. But what did J.D. have? Could be a big pair, could be a stone bluff. If the board didn't pair up, I should beat them both.

I called Harry's bet, as did J.D.

Kathy put up the river, and it was another brick.

Harry, who was down to only a few thousand, went all in. I gestured pushing all my chips toward the pot and announced, "All in." J.D. , who had me covered, said, "Call."

Since I was called, I turned up my cards on the table. Kathy said, "Straight to the six."

Harry turned up his cards, and I was amazed to see the deuce and the four of diamonds. He had the same straight I did.

Then I looked at J.D.'s cards, just as Kathy was saying, "Straight to the seven."

Straight to the seven? That fucking idiot played four, seven? Yes he did, and he'd just taken sixty Gs from me.

After sitting for ten or twenty seconds to get a grip, I stood and said, "Goodnight, gentlemen. Kathy." I gave her a nice big tip and Harry did likewise and we left.

"Hungry?" he asked.

"I could eat."

Wednesday, May 2

1

We ate at the Hmong's Silver Dragon diner on University Avenue, the one we counted on to soothe us with jasmine tea, a bowl of wonton soup, and then best burgers ever. I felt the adrenaline receding, and I told Harry so as we mopped our plates. He made a noise of agreement. The Hmong, as usual, slept in a chair behind the counter, always waking at exactly the right moment to flip the burgers. We theorized that he had two or maybe even three jobs, or maybe he just worked the clock around at the diner, and we liked the show, so we tipped him big.

We sat at the counter (no tables or booths at the Hmong's) and watched daylight creep up the street and take hold. I was thinking about falling asleep right there, but the back door of the diner flew open and hit the wall with a loud bang and I was awake. The Hmong leaped from his chair with a big semi-automatic pistol in his hand and started firing. Two guys in unadorned khaki shirts and pants and black watchcaps pulled very low and blotches of green paint on their faces came in blasting away with assault rifles. Harry and I were on the floor, and we had our guns out and started firing. The Hmong went down among crashing pots and pans and crockery and glassware.

Harry duck-walked to the end of the counter, stuck his gun hand around it, and fired five shots. The intruders stopped firing, shouted something, and backed out the open door. We heard a vehicle engine roar and saw the blank back end of a white van. Harry jumped up, dashed to the diner's door, and put three shots into the van, but he was too late to do any more damage than that.

I yelled, "Harry! You okay?"

"Yeah. You?"

"Yeah."

I saw Harry go out the back door. I went over the counter to take a look at the Hmong and called 911. I crouched by him and looked. He had two holes in his left upper arm and a crease across his forehead, but he was awake and tracking. He put up his right hand and pointed to a land-line phone on the back counter and a sign above it that had a phone number printed on it in black marker. Nothing else, just a phone number. Local area code.

He said. "My brother. Call him."

When I was done with 911, I dialed the brother's number on the landline. No answer. No voicemail. Harry came back and sat rather heavily on one of the stools at the counter. I saw him calling someone on his cell.

"My St. Paul cousin," he said. "He's a lawyer." The conversation was short and he pocketed his phone. "He'll come."

First to arrive were the medics. I went back across the counter and sat by Harry and we watched them apply dressings and start IVs and bundle the Hmong onto a gurney. One of them turned off the grill.

The Hmong said, "Wait, wait," and put his right hand into his pants pocket and brought out a bunch of keys and held them out toward Harry and me. "My brother. Give them to my brother."

I was looking at the guy we always called the Hmong. We didn't even know his name. He was sort of a medium-sized guy. Thin. All hard stringy muscles and lots of bones. Older than I'd always thought. Fifty? More?

Harry took the keys and said, "Don't worry. We'll take care of everything." And the Hmong, always a pure stoneface, smiled.

"I know you will."

They took him out.

Three customers were looking in the front windows, which no longer had glass, looking for their breakfasts. Harry went to the door, told them the place was temporarily closed. There was a sign hanging there where the door's window had been, and he flipped it to show *closed*. There was also a shade which he pulled down. And a shade where the big front windows had been and he closed that one too. I watched him do all this while I dialed the brother again and this time got an answer. I explained who the hell I was and why was I calling. There was a silence. Then he said, "I'll come," and hung up. I dialed my cousin Tim, who was my lawyer. He said, "I'll come," and hung up.

The police were next. I opened the door for them as soon as their siren died down and they got out of the car. They came in and talked into their radios for a bit and looked around. Looked behind the counter. Looked at us.

One took out a notebook and pen and we told them who we were and where we lived and what had happened. They looked around some more. One poked at things behind the counter, wrote the brother's phone number in his notebook. There was a printed card, official-looking, on the wall, and he wrote down everything on it.

Tim came, Harry's cousin came, and the brother came. Notebooks were out and pens were going at top speed all over the room. Then two detectives came, and then the forensic scientist crew of three with their masks and gloves and bags of shiny things. Through it all the brother sat silent at the counter.

Harry and I sat at the street end of the counter and watched it all. I'd never met Harry's cousin, but I knew his name was Rory Parker. He had bright brown eyes and brown hair and a very alert face and manner. He and Tim knew each other, and they conferred in low voices and observed while the scientists worked and the detectives stood around. The squad cops were the first to leave, then the detectives revved up.

One of them said, "We need statements from both of you, and we need to do it downtown."

Harry said, "I would like to confer with my attorney."

I said, "Good idea. Same here."

So Tim took me to the back end of the counter and Rory Parker took Harry to the front end.

Tim said, "Tell me the whole story but talk fast." So I did.

He said, "And you're a regular here?"

"We eat here late or early probably twice a month, sometimes more."

"Who were they shooting at?"

That stopped me. I'd been assuming the Hmong was the target. Could it have been Harry? Or me?

Tim said, "They were terrible shooters. Place the size and shape of a bowling alley, and didn't hit you or Harry. Anything you can do to help I. D. them?"

"No. But can I talk privately to Harry for a couple of minutes?"

2

The lawyers conferred in low voices and then said okay, and Harry and I went to a corner by the front door, turned our backs on the room, and talked very quietly.

I said, "One of them said something to you. When they were leaving."

"He said 'Fenian bastard. ' He said it in Gaelic, but I knew what it meant."

"You were the target?"

"Seems so."

"Tell Rory?"

"Not yet. And I really don't want the cops to know. I don't want to go downtown in cuffs."

"Me neither. Would Rory tell them?"

"I don't think so. Maybe he'll think I should. But I think I can find these guys without the cops, and Rory knows it."

"I'm in."

He grinned. "I'll buy your bullets."

We went back to the lawyers and detectives.

Tim said, "Mr. Parker and I have agreed to appointments for you to give your statements downtown."

Rory Parker handed Harry and me each a piece of paper from his notebook.

Tim said, "Tomorrow morning, eleven o'clock. We'll be with you. You may now leave."

I tilted my head at the brother. "What about him?"

Rory Parker said, "I've agreed to represent him and he's agreed to be represented. At least until he has an attorney from his own community if that's what he wants."

Harry and I both turned to the brother and we gave him our cards with our names and numbers. I said, "Do you need help closing the place up?" I gestured at the glassless windows.

He stood and said, "No. I have two sons." He had the same closed-in face and muscle-and-bone body as his brother. He gave each of us a card. His name was printed in Roman letters on one side, Chee Meng Vang, and Asian characters on the other. I went to the counter and looked at the license on the wall. The name typed on it was Yiuiling Vang. I wrote it down on Chee Meng Vang's card.

Then we shook hands with the brother, and I shook hands with Rory. Harry, Tim, and I went out the front door.

We enjoyed the sun for a few minutes and talked about the details of our appointments and the statements we would give on Thursday. Then Tim went off to his office and Harry drove me home.

3

Clare was standing in the kitchen drinking orange juice. We said hi as I went past into the bathroom. I'd been wanting to pee for an hour. When I came back we said hi again and shared a kiss and I said, "You're up early."

"Well, I sort of missed you."

I grinned. "Good to know."

While I made coffee I gave her the whole story of the shootout at the Hmong's while she looked more and more distressed.

She asked, "You're not hurt? Harry's not hurt?"

"No and no. But Harry's in someone's scope. I think it has to do with Irish politics."

She said, "Harry's not political."

"That we know of."

"Yes. That we know of. He has political *ideas,* but I don't think he's in any way an *activist*."

"I guess that's true. He maybe gives money."

She said, "Have you ever met any of his family? Are they political?"

"Never met any. Except now his cousin Rory. And I've no idea of their politics."

"Don't you and Harry ever talk about *anything*?"

"Women and cards."

"Oh, fuck you!" she said.

She went out, and I heard her go up the stairs.

I took a shower and went to bed.

4

"The parts about getting married that you won't like are starting," I said loudly. I was standing in the bedroom doorway, leaning on the door frame, drinking a beer. She was across the hall in the bathroom brushing her teeth and made a foamy noise in response. I said, "It's the party celebrating the betrothal. I'm supposed to ask you for a guest list."

She spit and said,"Do I have to be there?"

"No, I'll go alone and tell them you couldn't make it." She came out into the bedroom in bra and panties. I became a slavering wolf. Just for a moment. Outwardly I held steady.

"You said we could live however we wanted." She pulled on a loose, long-sleeved, pink T-shirt.

"I knew this would come up sooner or later. Are you serious or are we just talking to keep silence at bay?"

"Just talking, I guess. I've been thinking about it." She stepped into black cotton knit pants that draped satisfactorily around her bottom. I checked the fit with my free hand. She said, "Could I look Catherine and Sofia in the eye and say just a quiet ceremony at city hall? No." She picked up her hairbrush, then turned to put her arms around my neck. "You'll be there, I'll be there."

"So biblical." I pulled her closer. "Take off those clothes."

"No. When do we have to do this? Do I bring the dowry with?" She pushed me away and started brushing her hair.

"In two or three weeks, I suppose. Catherine has only just started planning. Tell me about the dowry."

She said, "You tell me. What's in one?"

"The bride's clothing, the household goods. Furniture, pots, pans, that sort of thing. Sheets and towels. Maybe some real estate, like a good pasture or field."

She set down the brush, ran her fingers into her hair, and fluffed up all the curls. "No goats or oxen?"

"I'm not sure where we'd keep them."

She slid her feet into a pair of woven leather sandals. "In my pasture. Maybe I can get a nice piece of land by the river. Someplace pretty to sit and pet my oxen. Scratch their ears. Feed them flowers. What does the groom provide?"

"House, fields, room and board for the rest of her life, and babies. Maybe a flock of sheep. Some goats. A pig or two. What else could any woman need?"

"The sheep sound nice. They're sort of cute, all fluffy like that. You can start with a Chinese dinner. I'm ready and I'm starving."

In her car, she said, "You've never owned a car, have you?"

"No, why should I? I don't want to. That's why God made taxis and feet. You have a car, Andy has a car, Catherine and Philip have cars—why would I need one?"

"You drive them. You're driving mine right now."

"That's different. As your husband, I'll allow you to own a car."

"Husband."

"That's who I'll be, you know. And you'll be my wife." I glanced at her face and laughed. "It's part of the package."

"I never thought about the words, exactly."

5

The back room at Vincent's was crowded. I started edging through the crush of standing drinkers and had to stop every two or three steps to accept congratulations complete with cheers, hugs, kisses, back slaps, shoulder punches, and hand shakes. Clare was getting the same treatment behind me, without the slaps and punches. About halfway across the room I lost her but got hold of her hand again and finally made it past the invisible boundary into the quieter front room. Mike Malloy was behind the bar and he smiled broadly.

"Lookin' good," he said.

In Ireland, Harry had once explained, we would call Vincent's our local. The pub. We drank there, we gossiped there, we solved all the world's problems one at a time there, then started over and solved them again. We didn't watch sports there because Vincent's had no TV, but his jukebox had a great collection of rock, country, R&B, jazz, all of it. Mike and his brother Vincent had opened the place in 1975 and flipped a coin for the naming of it. Mike said he won and so it became Vincent's. And Mike had exactly the pub he wanted and exactly the patrons he wanted coming there.

He'd said he and Vincent were part of the black-sheep branch of their family. The white-sheep Malloys had founded a major health care products company. The pub was Mike and Vincent's brand of health care. Vincent was dead now and there were no other Malloys to follow.

I pulled Clare up to the bar with my arm around her waist.

"She's going to marry me," I said, and Mike and I grinned at each other. He put down the glass he was polishing and we shook hands over the bar.

"Find a booth," he said. "I'll bring the champagne. Gotta get it from the cellar."

We turned and some friends in a booth right behind us, across the aisle, jumped up and bowed us into their seats.

I said into the ear of one of them, "Has any money changed hands yet?"

He said, "I'm starting the baby pool at midnight. Money to the baby."

Clare was still hugging people, but I finally got her into the seat and slid in next to her. Harry and Karen appeared across from us.

Karen leaned forward and said, "Do I get to be the mother of the bride?"

Harry said loudly, "Jesus, I've been to quieter shivarees."

Clare said to Karen, "My new sisters-in-law-to-be had a tea party for me yesterday. One of them is Lillian and it was at her apartment. Lovely blue and white china and silver tea set and blue and white linens. The colors of Greece, they said. Family picture albums, and I got to see naked pictures of Sam when he was six weeks old."

Karen fanned herself with her hand. "Who else was there? No guys, I suppose. No bulls at tea parties."

"They have a sweet little boy named Nicky, but he had to stay in his room." She pulled a point-and-shoot camera from her bag and showed pictures around. Then Mike came with the champagne.

6

All the celebrants drifted back to their own tables and friends and we four drank up the bottle of bubbly and shifted to beer. After my second bottle I excused myself to hit the head and as I got up I saw my cousin Andonios come through the front door and saw his face. Clare turned her head to see what I was looking at, and stood and we turned together to face Andy.

"It's Paul," he said. "Paul's dead."

"Paul," Clare said.

"My brother," I said automatically.

"Yes," she whispered.

"How?" I asked Andy.

"Shot. Two in the chest, one in the head. In his car. In the parking garage under the Foley Building."

"When?"

"Found about an hour ago. They say probably this morning, nine-thirty, ten maybe."

We stopped talking, just looked at each other, a dead spot in the busy room. Then the moment broke and Andy put out his hand to me and we embraced, me still with one arm around Clare.

"Do you need a ride?" he asked. He looked at Clare, seemed to see her for the first time, then back at me.

"No, we have Clare's car. Sofia's?"

Andy said yes, squeezed Clare's arm rather absent-mindedly, and left by the front door. I started toward the back door, taking Clare with me, plowing through the well-wishers who saw my face and held away. At the car I held out the keys to her and climbed into the passenger side while she got behind the wheel and started the engine.

"Sam?"

I looked at her.

"I don't know where we're going."

"Sofia's."

"I don't know where it is."

I told her where, a building two blocks from Catherine's, leaned back, and got lost in my thoughts.

Had we sent Paul off into the wilderness to his death? Out of the family, away from the protection of the tribe, drawing a target on him for guys like Kevvy Smith, our very own St. Paul-grown mob chief, telling them we no longer cared what happened to him? Everyone knew that we took care of our own and had done so since Rice Street was only a little more than a cow path. The family was larger and tougher and more impenetrable than Clare knew, and now she was in and he was—really was—out.

Clare drove carefully, not speaking until she had stopped and parked the car down the block from the building where Philip and Sofia lived.

"Shall I go home?" she asked. "Or would you like me to wait for you?"

That brought me out of it. "Go home? Why?"

"If it's just family, I might be intruding."

"You can't intrude. You're part of it now. And I need you here with me. We all need you."

7

We took the elevator to the third floor. I shook hands with the doorkeepers, cousins Mike and Pete—Michael Zandros and Peter Nikolaou—and introduced them to Clare. Then we went in.

I went straight to the widow Lillian with Clare's hand in mine. Lillian stood and turned to Clare, who took her hand and whispered, "I'm so sorry." Then I embraced Lillian, rather too stiffly. Lillian and Paul's son, young Nicky, was beside Lillian, and Clare reached out her hand to him. He ever so tentatively and shyly put out his. She took it and held it a moment and then let him slide it out of hers. And then Lillian shocked my whole family. She threw her arms around Clare and bear-hugged her and pulled Clare around to her side, put her arm around Clare's waist, and held her firmly.

I embraced Nicky and murmured, "Hang in there" into his ear and asked him where Jamie, Philip and Sofia's son, and Thomas, Catherine's son, were.

He said in almost a whisper, "In Jamie's room."

I took his hand and gently moved him in that direction while Lillian whispered in Clare's ear and patted Clare's hands and Clare nodded and patted Lillian's hands right back.

I came back and gently eased Clare away and Lillian kissed her and hugged her some more and I put my hand under Clare's elbow and walked with her to the side of the room where catherine, Philip, Andy, Uncle Nick, and Stephen were standing together near several tall windows. They greeted us with hugs and kisses, and I watched Clare step into a space in the family that was waiting for her.

Clare turned aside slightly to Catherine and said, "Tell me what to do."

"Don't worry, you aren't expected to do anything. You're here, that's enough. You'll need funeral clothes. Do you have anything?"

Clare shook her head. "I'll get something." She put her hand on Catherine's. "This must be hard for you. Sam told me about your husband."

"Yes. It brings back some bad memories."

She grasped Clare's hand. "Come into the kitchen," she said. "You have to be introduced to some of the family."

I leaned over and looked into the kitchen when they went through the swinging door and saw four or five aunts and female cousins. And Kori and Sofia. Clare would be all right, even though she looked like she was going to the gallows.

8

We five men looked at each other. Finally Andy said low, "What's with the wicked Lillian?"

Philip gave him a repressive look. "Damn it, Andy—"

"Sorry. I'll be back." He wandered off toward the dining room.

Women began to carry platters of food into the dining room and some of them joined the men in the living room and on the sun porch. One of Paul's bottles of brandy found its way into our little family grouping. Clare came back and saw me from across the room. I put out a hand to her and she came quickly. I pulled her up close to me.

Stephen, Catherine's older son, a teenager with no apparent adolescent issues, came over to us. "Would you like something to drink, Aunt Clare?" he asked.

"Oh, Stephen, some tea? I would love a cup of tea."

"I'll get it for you. Do you like cream or sugar in it?"

"No, just plain, please."

We drank tea and coffee and brandy and talked about Paul. Stephen brought everyone plates of food. Once Philip began to cry and my arm was around his shoulders. We were speaking Greek by that point without even realizing it.

I don't think I'd ever told Clare that we spoke Greek at home. Our parents were fluent, but for me and Philip and Catherine and Andy and Paul, it was pretty basic stuff. Enough to have a conversation but little more. Strangely, probably because he was the firstborn and knew a lot more of the old people, Paul spoke it best of us. Had spoken.

The room grew smokier and noisier and occasionally I heard laughter. Philip and I were smoking cigars and talking about our father, telling stories, ones we all knew already. Catherine came back and Philip talked about Stephanios, and Catherine smiled with tears running down her face. Stephen put his arm around her and stood very straight. Tomorrow we would talk about revenge, but not tonight, not here.

Lillian's strident, ear-splitting laugh cut across the room. Andy winced.

"I'll help Lillian make the arrangements," said Philip. "The funeral will be Thursday."

"Who's staying with Lillian?" I asked.

Philip said, "Sofia and I will be there tonight. All the children are spending the night at Catherine's. And Andy's also staying at Catherine's. Lillian's brother Peter, maybe some others will be here tomorrow. After that the Makrises can take care of her."

I said, "We'll leave now, too."

We took our leave of Lillian and Uncle Nick and Uncle Cy and Aunt Ekaterina and about twenty other people. As we walked to her car under the almost dark sky, Clare took a deep breath and said she wanted nothing more in life than to sit down.

"Give me the keys," I said.

"I'll drive. You've been drinking."

"Two brandies, and you don't look like you could drive a straight line."

She handed over the keys and got in and sank into the upholstery.

"Were you speaking Greek in there?" she asked.

I laughed. "We all sort of slip into it at times like these. Amazing what memory cells will do. We spoke it at home."

"I'm terribly impressed."

"I'm an impressive guy. Do you want to go home?" I asked.

"Not particularly, if you have another idea."

"Good. We'll go to a bar I know."

"Not Vincent's."

"No." I put my hand over hers on her lap. "Was it hard for you, the crowd?"

"Yes, but not so much with you there."

"Good."

9

The bar was called the Stardust. It was on Rice Street. It was big and old and well-lit and furnished with large, round, scarred wooden tables and wooden armchairs shaped and polished by ninety years of butts, and high-backed wooden booths with hard cushions on the seats that sat six easily. It had a long bar across the room from the booths and a jukebox and decor provided by beer and liquor companies, and there was a back room with two pool tables and more booths. And another back room with a poker table. And that musty odor of decades of beer being served and spilled. Someone had punched in the Allman Brothers: "No One To Run With."

Clare whispered, "I *love* this place!"

I helped her into a booth and went to the bar. The bartender and several other customers greeted me by name.

"Everybody knows you," she said when I put a glass and a bottle of mineral water on the table in front of her and slid in. Our arms were touching and she leaned against me. I had a Johnnie Black and water to chase it.

I said, "I play cards here pretty often. Been coming here a long time."

"Doesn't look like very much money here."

"Good players and more money than you might think, and I like the company. I more or less learned to play here, me and Andy. And Philip before us. Paul got permanently banned before I ever started coming." I drank some water. I had some talking to do. "There's another bar a block or so down, maybe you saw it. Devlin's. Here, look at me. I need to see your face. I killed a man there, at Devlin's."

She stared at me.

"Listen, Clare, I've already put this off too long. I'm not planning to give you a detailed accounting, but there are things you've got a right to know and this is one of them. I was twenty. Going to the university and learning to play real poker in my spare time. For fun, Andy and I hustled pool at Devlin's, taking money from frat boys down here to experience the lower classes. Once we brought our cousin Irini to Devlin's. One of the frat boys asked her out, took her for a ride in the country, and raped her."

She took in air, fast.

I said, "Andy and I flipped a coin. I won the toss. We found him playing pool at Devlin's. They pulled me off when he stopped moving."

She turned her head away, ran her finger along a crack in the wooden table top. After a while she said in a soft voice, "He deserved it."

I said, "Yes, he did. He took a life, the one she would have had."

"Not her physical life."

"No, but worse. Her—emotional life. Her happiness. She never got past it."

"You know I... " She gulped some beer. "I told you."

I could barely hear her.

She said in a fierce whisper, "I was raped. Not the time when I was little. Another time."

I said, "When?"

"I was fifteen."

I said, "Who was it? Who did it?"

"He was a football player. He was very strong. And he broke my camera." Tears were spilling out of her eyes. "That I spent so *long* saving up for. He broke it *on purpose.*"

I said, "From now on you will have all the cameras you want."

"It's not the same.*"

I gave her a handkerchief. "No, of course not. But you... you took your life back. Irini didn't."

"That's not the same either."

I said, "No, it's not. But Irini didn't have what you had."

"She had you."

I said, "She didn't have you."

She turned a bit and rested her forehead against me. "Did they catch you?"

"Of course they did. I didn't run. I spent almost a year in prison. Eleven months."

"Oh, Sam!"

"That's what happens, and I knew it going in. I got off easy, and it could have been a lot worse. They charged me with the least they could charge me with and we plea-bargained a minimal sentence. I had some acquaintances and a cousin there, in the prison, and I could take care of myself. I didn't have to be anyone's girlfriend."

She shuddered.

I said, "I had to tell you this now, tonight, because the police will be talking to you, and I didn't want them telling you before I did."

"Police? They want to talk to me?"

"Yes, because of Paul."

"I didn't know Paul."

I said, "But you know me."

"I guess. I thought so. Why would they tell me about you being in prison?"

"Because I'm a killer. It'll occur to them that I might have killed Paul."

Neither of us mentioned Donal O'Connell, but I thought I could hear him buzzing in her brain.

"Sam, no!"

"I'm not joking. Denny Linden is very aware of the fact that Paul and I didn't get along. Big time."

"You didn't?"

"It would not be going too far to say we despised each other."

"That seems unbelievable, you know. In your family."

"This is one of the sticky parts."

"Why did you hate each other?"

"For years I tried to convince myself that it was just because he was so much older."

"Does it work that way?"

"No, not really." I emptied my glass. "He wanted to be good at things that I was good at and he wasn't, and it infuriated him. He was a lousy card player and not good in school and most people didn't like him much, especially the people with money who were the only ones *he* really cared about. He should have been a plumber or something. Something he *could* be good at. With people he could be equals with. And he thought I was an unmanageable brat."

"Were you?"

"Well, probably. Andy and I made his life a misery whenever we had a chance. He was a cheater from early on and never a very good one, and we told Uncle Nick when he was cheating customers. Fortunately Andy and I caught on fast. But Paul never forgave us for telling. And he was a bastard to women."

"This is disillusioning."

"Don't idealize us. There's a lot of love in our family, but some hate too. You're too old for illusions."

"Is there an age limit?"

"I'll check and let you know. In the meantime, Denny Linden is searching hard for my footprints. He would love to label me for this."

She nudged my shoulder with hers. "Let me out."

I stood up. "I'm going to have a beer and then take you home. Do you want another water?"

She said yes.

When she came out of the ladies' room and sat down again, I put my arm around her shoulders. "I saw Catherine taking you off to that kitchen full of women. What did they say to you?" I was curious for real because the men didn't ever hang out in the kitchen.

She said they all kissed her cheek and said how glad they were to meet her. "And how good it is that Sam is settling down. And I met Aunt Ekaterina. I guess she's the matriarch."

"If she doesn't approve of you, we'll either have to break it off or flee to Canada."

She was silent for a few moments, looking at her hands on the table. "Some of them were cooking, and some were drinking tea and eating. And Ioulia and Meli and another girl, Mandy, they came in and they were… *petted.*" Her voice broke ever so slightly. "They were petted and… and told how beautiful they are."

I heard the yearning in her voice. I said, "I'll pet you and tell you how beautiful you are."

She said seriously, "I think it's too late."

I said, "Did they set the wedding date for us?"

"No, but they talked about it. They discussed *several* possible dates with Catherine. We apparently have no say in it. How did you know?"

"How could I not know? Sometime in October, right?"

"Yes, that's a good time, they said. Auspicious."

"Is that all right with you?"

"Are you serious?"

"Totally."

She said, "That's four months from now."

"Too soon? Not soon enough?"

"I thought it would be sooner."

I said, "Just what do *you* want?"

"Well, I just want to be there with you. The wedding seems to be something we do for everyone else, so let's do it whenever they want it. Sure, October."

"As soon as this funeral is over, we'll talk to Catherine about wedding plans. This will be great practice for her, in case Ioulia ever gets married."

"You know, usually the bride does the wedding. The bride's family does."

"You don't have any family and you don't have any money and I have both, and my family will be so disappointed if we don't have a traditional wedding. And let's face it, planning large social events is not one of your strengths. Are we being overbearing?"

"Overbearing Greek is redundant." On the way out the door she said, "You and Philip and Andy were talking about whether it's dangerous for the rest of the family, weren't you? Paul being shot."

"Everyone was talking about it."

"Not in the kitchen."

"The women let the men worry about it, of course."

She stopped in the middle of the sidewalk. "Not this woman. *Is* it dangerous?"

"We don't think so."

"Why not?"

"It was too private. If it were meant to be something else, they'd want to send a message. It would have been more public. Like a drive-by. And the way it was done—execution style. Organized crime stuff. But if anyone like that had a beef with Paul, none of the rest of us were in on it. Maybe it was staged."

"Who are 'they'?"

"Don't know. Maybe there isn't any 'they.' Maybe Paul was just unlucky one last time. Maybe someone thought he carried a lot of money. Sometimes he did. Maybe he pissed somebody off. He did that a lot too. But there isn't any hint that it's any more than that." I shook my head. "Maybe it was over a woman. Maybe it *was* a woman. Maybe I've made you part of something you don't want to be part of."

"I don't think there's anything to be done about that now."

We started toward the car. It was around the corner, about a block away. Two men stepped out of a doorway, twenty or so feet ahead of us. We stopped. I said softly, "Go back inside. Now."

You'd think I'd trained her. She just moved, quick and smooth, turned, and ran back to the Stardust. I heard the burst of noise when the door opened, and then I was totally focused on the two men.

I knew one of them. Kevvy Smith's nephew Brian.

I figured I could take them both if they kept guns out of it. They were too young to be fooling with me and I hoped Kevvy would have told them that.

Brian said, "Move aside, asshole."

"Ever the slick talker, Brian. How's your uncle?"

"Says you should stay out of our way, asshole."

"I don't think he meant on the public sidewalks. Just go on by."

Another burst of noise and then there were two men, one on each side of me. I hoped they were friendly.

One of them said, "How you doing, Sam?" and I recognized the voice of a guy I'd played cards with since we were kids. Relief went through me.

I laughed. "Been better, but I think you're just what the doctor ordered."

After a few seconds Brian Smith and his friend turned, shook themselves into postures of 'fuck you,' and sauntered off across the street.

I turned and found I had four guys backing me. I said, "Christ. It's a platoon."

"Beautiful woman comes running in, up to the bar, says to Kyle, 'Sam's in trouble!' We come out to watch you mess'm up. Maybe there's a beer in it."

"There is a beer in it."

We all went back into the bar, and Clare was there in the middle of the room, facing the door, hugging herself. I said, "Don't you dare cry. I'd never live it down." And she didn't, just hugged me hard. I stood everyone in the place a round, and two guys and a baseball bat escorted us to our car.

I hated carrying in the summer, but the gun was coming back on until further notice.

10

And even after all that, it wasn't quite midnight when she unlocked her front door and we went in.

"Are you hungry?" I asked.

"Actually, I sort of am."

"What do you want?"

"I don't know." She sounded a bit fratchety.

"Soup?"

"Do we have chicken noodle?"

"Uh huh."

"And the little cheese crackers?"

"You're into the haute cuisine tonight."

I heated the soup while she changed into a long flannel nightgown. She was into comfort tonight.

She ate sleepily while I leaned on the counter and drank some wine and talked, to my own surprise, about Paul.

Our parents had expected an oldest child who would take responsibilities within the family for the younger children and for maintaining the family structure, who would be a good student and help the family forward, financially and socially.

But Paul was not interested in upward mobility in the neighborhood. He wanted money and he wanted it now. And he wanted a social group but not a family, a gang, where it was every man for himself and he went up by pushing down.

I thought he also wanted family, but I'd only ever talked to Andy about it. When Andy and I were still in grade school, Paul was living in an apartment with a bunch of other members of his gang, a few blocks from the family. Sometimes he'd show up at suppertime, dirty, smelly, maybe ragged, and wedge himself in at the table. Mama would give him a plate and he would start digging in, putting away as much food as he could fit into his mouth, and talking around it about his exploits. No one but Mama would speak to him because he wouldn't bother to answer. After he ate he would shower and dress in clean clothes. He still had his space in the bedroom he'd always shared with Philip. Later Mama picked up the dirty things he left on the floor there and gave him some money on the sly. The rest of us, including Philip, stayed in our rooms to guard our belongings until he left. And Mama would go stand on the back porch to cry.

Clare finished her little meal and stared up at me with eyes that were glazing over.

11

I was almost asleep when she said, "Did you lose your temper?"

"What?"

"In the bar."

"What bar?"

"That other bar, that… other time."

"No." I turned over and pulled her close. "I did what I went there to do."

Thursday, May 3

1

While Clare shopped for a funeral dress, I went to the office to see Philip and Andy. Uncle Cy was in his usual place in the outer office, working. Philip was there looking at spreadsheets as Cy printed them out. Andy was in the inner office, sprawled in a chair at the big conference table. Bright morning sunlight was flooding in through the big windows, and I closed a few blinds before I sat.

"Have the cops found you yet?" Andy asked.

"No. Are they looking?"

"They were at the apartment, talked to Catherine and me, left a card for you to call a number." He took a small white card out of his shirt pocket and flipped it to me. I caught it in the air. "I didn't give them Clare's name or number. I didn't know whether you wanted to try to leave her out of it."

I said, "I don't expect that's possible."

Two of the several cell phones scattered about buzzed and Andy and I answered and took a couple of bets.

I said, "I told her about Irini last night. And the frat boy."

"Yeah?"

"I wasn't happy about telling her I was a felon."

"I suppose not. By the way, dear… how'd she take it?"

"I'm not real sure. Sometimes it's hard to tell with her."

"Yeah."

Philip came in and asked, "Have you told her about the frat boy?"

"I told her last night."

The coffee pot stopped burbling and he poured coffee all around. "What did she say?"

I powered up my office computer and sat down at the second desk. "She said he deserved it."

More phones, more bets.

Paul asked, "Was this... personal? Her reaction?"

"Yes."

Philip opened a tin of fresh chocolate-chip cookies from Sofia and offeredthem around. I took two. He asked, "Anyone you know?"

"No. She was in high school. In San Diego."

Andy said, "She moved *here* from California?"

I said, "Shut up."

"Wanna make me?"

"Don't tempt me."

Andy asked,"When *was* the last time you tried to shut me up? I think we were fourteen."

I swung around in my chair. "Then you're due."

Philip reached out and dug his fingers into my arm. He had very strong hands and he knew where to dig.

He said, "Both of you, back down. This is the time you choose to act like two dogs in an alley? Christ."

Andy grinned.

I shook off Philip's hand and stood and walked across the room to look out the window.

Philip said, "If they talk to her, it'd be good if you can be there."

"If I can."

"It would be easier for all of us if we didn't have to explain Black to them."

I turned back to the room. "I'll do what I can, but I'm not sure how far she'll go for me."

"How far is there?" asked Andy. "That's how far."

Philip said, "I don't suppose she has a lot of experience lying to cops."

I shook my head. "She crosses only on the green."

Philip looked amused. "But she knows what you do?"

"I admit she has gaps." I answered a phone call.

When I'd hung up, I said, "Kevvy's nephew Brian made a move on Clare and me last night, outside the Stardust." I told them what happened.

"Kevvy is a pain in the ass," Philip said. He ate another cookie "Lillian's relatives start arriving this afternoon, and she'll be off our hands. I don't know what else we can do."

He sounds tired, I thought suddenly.

Andy said, "It just doesn't have the feel of being aimed at anyone but Paul. It's too simple-minded. No messages." Philip and I nodded slightly, silently agreeing.

Philip sat down at his desk. "So who shot him?" he asked. Neither of us answered. "Was it business or pleasure? Where do we look?"

Andy said, "I'd done it, it would've been pleasure."

I said, "Two in the chest and one in the head. *Looks* like mob stuff."

Philip said, "But everybody knows that these days."

I said, "TV. The great leveler."

"A stick-up?" Andy asked.

Philip said, "He had eight hundred in his pocket and I think that's likely all he was carrying. The cops said he didn't appear to have been searched. His gun was still holstered."

"Losers?" I asked.

"I haven't heard anything."

"Husbands?"

"Well, you know Paul." Philip shrugged. "I don't know where he was getting it lately, but there must be someone. There always has been."

Andy said, "He was betting outside. Maybe he cheated someone who really didn't want to lose."

"If that's the answer, all we can do is wait for someone to talk about it."

"That may be all we can do anyway," I said.

"They're releasing his body this afternoon. Catherine and I are taking Lilian to the funeral home for all the formalities."

More phones. I took out a quick minute to call cousin Tim and ask him to stave off the cops about the Hmong for a few days. He said he would. We concentrated on work until lunchtime.

2

Andy and I waited for Clare outside a nearby bar and grill, smoking cigars and looking generally disreputable. When she arrived she said, "You never waited outside before. Can't I walk into a bar by myself any more?"

"No." I took her elbow and piloted her to a booth.

She said, "Maybe I'll rethink this marriage thing. How about you, Andy? Want to get married?"

"Not to you. I want to be alive when I get up in the morning. Sam never would share his toys. But it's a nice day and we were waiting for a beautiful woman. So we can enjoy that much for now."

Clare smiled.

I said, "Did you find what you need?"

"Yes, but it wasn't easy. Pink is *not* the new black. Or vice versa." She slumped in the corner of the booth. "I guess this isn't the funeral season. *Is* there a funeral season? Can I get a glass of water or did that go out with walking into bars?"

I waved down the waiter.

"Will you be at Jenneky's tonight?" Andy asked me.

"Too much money to turn down. But I don't think Philip will show up." He sometimes played at Jenneky's. "He needs a vacation," I said abruptly.

He said, "What would we do, close the office?"

I said, "I can run it. Uncle Cy probably doesn't need us anyway, except to answer the phones."

3

Clare was silent through most of lunch, except for a few minutes when she and Andy shared a joke about a pig eating apples. Andy and I made only desultory conversation. Then Clare and I drove back to her apartment. I followed her into the bedroom and pulled her down on the bed.

"If you won't talk to me," I said, "will you take off your clothes for me?"

"No."

I pushed her over onto her back and unbuttoned her shirt, pulled it open, looked at her round breasts caught up in a little black bra that seemed too small, and gave myself over to what? Anger? At the universe? Jealousy? *Of* the universe? I got her skirt up and...

"No!" she said. She shrieked. "*No! No!*"

Somehow, from somewhere deep, I got control of myself. Pulled away. Stood up.

"I'm sorry," she said.

I went into the bathroom and washed my face and came back to find that she had crawled under the cover and had her eyes squeezed shut. I sat down on the bed next to her and she covered her face with the blanket.

"I'm going to Catherine's," I said. "Do you want to come with?"

She didn't move or speak.

"All right." I stood up. "I'll come here after the game."

"No," she said. "Don't come here."

I took a deep breath, let it out, and left the apartment. Later I went with Harry to Jenneky's to play poker.

4

"Look who's at the bar," Harry said.

I said, "The guy who flopped the seven-high straight on us and wiped us both out."

Harry said. "Our guy J.D. Think he'll remember us?"

We stepped up to the bar. J.D. looked at us blankly, then away. Harry said, "Hi, J.D. Remember us? He doesn't remember us."

I said, "Now that hurts."

He slowly turned and looked at us again. "*You* guys. What the hell you doing here? This is where the big boys play. You wanna see the new Lexus you bought me?"

I said, "No thanks, we might miss our bus."

"This time I got my guy with me, and he'd love to have you as a late-night snack."

"See you at the table," I said. "What do we think, Harry? Should we get a guy? They seem to be popular."

He said, "Okay, I'll be your guy tonight."

Jenneky always had a fifty thousand minimum buy-in, but he set the blinds at one hundred to two hundred to nudge up the action.

Harry wasn't playing tonight. Jenneky's games were often too rich for him. He didn't like to tap into his father's money, but he did like to watch the action. The only rule was that he couldn't be in my line of sight so that he couldn't, even inadvertently, tip me off as to the strength of another player's hand. He took a chair against the wall behind me.

And he would watch my back. Be my guy. The money at Jenneky's games was maybe getting a little too well known. J.D. and I weren't the only ones with guys at their backs.

J.D. was in the three seat, and I was in the five, so on the typical hand, I would be acting after he did. Good, because I felt I had lessons to teach him.

The game was about three hours old when I beat J.D. for the fifth time of the night. As I was stacking my winnings he said, "You gotta admit that you got lucky on that one."

Without bothering to look at him, I said, "Name one hand that you've ever played that didn't have an element of luck to it."

"You've got more luck than anybody I've ever seen."

"No, I don't," I said. "I've got the same luck as everybody else. What I have is skill. Your problem is you can't tell the difference."

"Come on. You gotta admit that I play as good a game as you do."

"I will say that you *talk* a pretty good game."

He said, "Your luck is gonna change."

A few hours later, J.D. had beaten me three times, but none of them had gotten to the showdown; I had recognized each time that I was beaten, and had folded early. He was winning chump change and bragging about it. He didn't recognize the chump part.

This hand, it was my button. As usual, I didn't look at my cards until the action got to me. But of the six people acting in front of me, much to my delight, four of them had called. Being on the button with four callers in the hand, I would've played even mediocre cards. I picked up two corners and looked—red queens were looking back at me. While with this strong a hand I didn't want to chase any of the weaker players out just yet, I was too aware that a king or ace on the board could spell disaster for me. Maybe I should thin the herd some. I raised to six hundred. The small blind folded, the big blind and four other players, including J.D. , called.

The pot had 3,700 pre-flop, and I'm on a large pair on the button. Life is potentially sweet.

The dealer burns the top card, peels off the next three cards, and sets them out face-up. Three jacks.

Jacks full of queens. But five other players had called, so I know that there has to be maybe one or two aces and maybe one or two kings in play. And if they're paired, I'm really screwed.

The seven seat, the big blind, bets six hundred. I put him on a pair but probably tens or below. The nine and one seat both call. J.D. 's turn to act. He raises to two thousand. The four seat calls, but reluctantly. I put him on ace king.

Now there's 9,500 in play, six players counting me. After a minute I decide that I've got to make it too expensive for the weaker hands to keep going; I've got to get them out of the hand before they hit their dream card on the turn or the river.

"Raise it to seven thousand," I say, and put the chips in front of me.

The seven seat looks at me as he tosses his hand in, and says, "Jesus, man, you got the fourth jack?"

Under normal circumstances I would get pissed and even vocal if somebody started announcing possible hands while there are other players who haven't acted yet, but not this time. Let them think he's right.

The nine seat folds, but the one seat calls my five thousand raise. Now it's J.D. 's turn again. "Raise it another five thousand," he says, louder than necessary. The four seat folds and it's back to me.

I'm not sure, but I think the extra volume in J.D. 's voice is to cover up being a little weaker than he was trying to make me think.

I call, and so does the one seat.

Three players left, 42,900 in the pot.

The dealer burns a card and puts up the turn. Queen of clubs.

I fight off the urge to jump up and down. As things stand now the only hands that can beat me are the fourth jack or, depending on the river card, pocket kings or aces. But since I'm sure that the four seat already folded ace king, that's one fewer of each to show up on the river.

The one seat is first to act. He bets ten thousand. J.D. immediately says, "Raise, twenty thousand," and puts it out. I decide it's time to flex some muscle and I calmly say, "Make it 30,000."

The one seat has only got 5,200 left on the table, so he goes all in. J.D. calls and puts in the ten thousand to cover my raise.

Still three players, the main pot is locked at 88,500, and J.D. and I are playing for both the main pot and the 29,600 in the side pot.

The dealer burns a card and puts up the river, which is the most beautiful, most welcome brick I've ever seen—the five of clubs.

J.D. is clearly pleased. With a wide, sweeping gesture he says, "All in." I ask the dealer how much has been bet. He counts down R. J. 's chips and tells me, "It's 41,500 to call, sir."

I had him covered, but not by much. I said, "Call you, R. J. Jacks full of what?"

"Jacks full of aces, Buddy! Guess your luck ran out this time."

The one seat says, "Son of a fucking *bitch!*" and tosses his kings.

I said, "I've got pocket queens, *Buddy*."

J.D. says, "Jacks full of aces beats jacks full of queens, sonny boy. Or didn't they teach you that at high school?"

"You don't understand, pinky, I've got pocket queens, which gives me queens full of jacks."

From behind me Harry said, "Queens full of jacks beats jacks full of anything, pinky. Even aces."

On our way out I said, "Jesus, I thought his head was going to explode. Did you see how red he got?"

Harry said, "And how he was shaking so bad? I think we chose a good time to leave."

5

It was almost two-thirty in the morning, and Harry got onto Pierce Butler Road, a long, empty east-west straightaway through an industrial part of St. Paul, and let it go. He was driving a BMW, one of the Zs, and only a couple of years old, and he loved to drive fast. Fortunately he was a good driver. Great reflexes, great eyesight, tons of confidence.

After a couple of minutes I asked him, "Any luck with your manhunt?"

"I've got three cousins who are known to be very efficient at asking questions, and they've been working the bars and clubs in St. Paul. Pretty much established that it wasn't political. Too much amateur hour. And not that many people living here who have the stomach for assassination. And too much shooting for a robbery. Might be from Chicago. That's it so far. Karen's learning to shoot."

"And here I am without my Kevlar undies."

Friday, May 4

1

At three in the morning I opened the door to Clare's apartment. I'd been feeling more and more uneasy about Clare all evening. As well I should, I thought savagely.

Her bedside lamp was on and she lay face down, her arms flung out to her sides. I touched her shoulder and said her name, then shook her when she didn't move or answer. I turned her over. She was breathing but limp. Not moving. Her face was still. I touched it, stroked it. No movement of her lips. But when I bent over her I could hear, so softly, the sound of her breath. She was dressed in gray sweats and a black T-shirt, so she'd been up since I left.

I shook her again, harder. She said something unintelligible and tried to turn her head back into the pillow. I sat down next to her and pulled her up by her shoulders and yelled her name.

She came awake abruptly and pushed me away with a furious strength.

"Clare!" I was shocked by her physical ferocity.

"*Go 'way!*" she shrieked. She pushed at me again, got herself to the opposite edge of the bed. "*Lea' me 'lone! Go 'way!*"

"Are you *drunk?*" I reached for her.

"No, not drunk!" Somehow she got away from my hands and stood, hanging on to the bedside table, bent over as if in pain, her hair wild around her face, a blue-eyed Medusa. "Wish I were!" She straightened and staggered toward the door. "Couldn't sleep… I couldn't… sleep. All I wanted to do was sleep! *All* the pills. Nope, no sleep!"

She staggered into the living room. She stopped when she got to the front door of the apartment and put one hand up on the wall to brace herself.

"You didn't have to… do that. You didn't. You *didn't*. You could just… could… could ask."

"Yes, I…No."

"Fucking bastard." I could barely understand her. She started to laugh. "Unne'sher'ry." She stumbled twice over 'unnecessary. '"All you had do was ask. Tha's all. Jus' ask."

She sagged against the wall.

"You were going to *use* me in *anger?* Get what *you* want? Do you know what that is? Do you know what that *is,* you *bastard?* Selfish *bastard*! That… is… *rape!* God *damn* you!"

I reached for her again, but she batted my hand away.

She said, "Get the hell out!"

"Damn it, you *are* drunk—"

"I'm not I'm not!" She got her hands on the chain lock and got it unhooked and threw the door open and stood in the opening. "Get out! Now! Go 'way!"

"Clare, please, come back in…"

She squeezed her eyes shut and tears rolled down her cheeks. "Can't work."

"What?"

"*Can't work*! Nobody—*nobody* damn you! Nobody ever did this to me before! Nobody ruined my *work* before! My pictures!" She was crying hard now. "My pictures. They were *always* there!"

I put my hands on her shoulders, gently at first, but tightening my grip when she squirmed. She wrenched herself away, tearing herself out of my hands, but she pulled too hard, moved too fast, staggered, lost her balance, lost her footing, went over the railing and down.

2

I vaulted over the rail and down the stairs and got to the bottom almost as soon as she did. I checked her breathing, the pulse in her throat. Yes. I called 911, gave them the essentials, and then punched in Andy's speed-dial number.

"Andy."

"What is it?"

"Medical center. Emergency. Clare took some pills."

"I'm there."

I felt for her pulse again and found it, strong, but other than that I didn't dare touch her.

An ambulance arrived and I met them on the porch. They attached a heart monitor and checked her vital signs. They put a big foam collar on her. They shot questions at me and I answered. They started an IV. They strapped her onto a gurney, put her into the ambulance, and were gone. Before I followed them in her car, I went back upstairs.

'Couldn't sleep,' she'd said.

I went into the bathroom, found the empty pill bottle in the sink, put it in my pocket, locked the doors, and drove to the hospital. Guilt and frustration and despair twisted my gut and shortened my breath and only long hours at the card table had kept me in control, however precariously.

At the hospital they had taken her into an emergency room bay and they wouldn't let me follow. I gave them the pill bottle and I was prowling the waiting room when Andy came in and pushed me into a chair and sat down next to me.

He asked, "Is she okay?"

"I don't know. She's in there. They wouldn't let me in. That security *malaka* over there got quite firm about it." I rubbed the back of my hand across my mouth. "She had some sleeping pills that she took sometimes, not often. There couldn't have been many in the bottle."

"She took them all?"

"I found the… empty bottle in the bathroom. When I came in she was asleep, wouldn't wake up. Then she did. She was walking around yelling at me. I never saw her like that before." I couldn't look at Andy, so I looked at the wall opposite. "I hurt her," I said.

"You hit her?" He was aghast.

"No, nothing so neat and easy." The words were hard, with no breath in them. "I bullied her. In bed."

Andy groaned, tilted his head back to rest on the wall behind him. "Jesus, Sam, how could you *do* that? To *her*. I thought you knew by now how easy it would be to break that one."

"I've been half crazy! Afraid she'd change her mind, go away again, afraid the family, the gambling, the Kevvys would be too much for her, afraid I might lose my temper and do what my father did. Afraid I might step wrong and bring on one of the things that frighten her. I couldn't lose her again." I stopped and swallowed and went on. "And I didn't know what *you'd* done with her."

"Me?" His expression cleared while I looked at him. He sighed and put his hand on my arm. "You were looking like death on toast. I went to see her and I talked about you and I kissed her for you, just once. I figured that if I got some of her ice melted, maybe I could push you in that direction and you'd have sense enough to hang on to her. I hope I wasn't wrong."

I said, "At lunch—you were laughing with each other."

"For Christ's sake, Sam!"

"I know! I was so crazy with it all. Man, you don't know!"

"I think I do know!"

For an hour we sat, mostly in silence, and for a half hour after that I paced the room in a sort of fury. Andy went out for vending-machine coffee and food—peanuts and chocolate and corn chips. Then I alternated pacing and smoldering for two more hours. Andy slept. Bastard could sleep anywhere.

3

At seven-thirty a young doctor wearing a stained scrub suit came in and stood in the middle of the floor looking around at the few people waiting.

"Sam?" he said.

I stood.

He said, "I'm Dr. Dormanen. Let's go in here."

We went into a small interview room.

While we were still walking he said, "She's going to be all right."

I shivered with relief.

He closed the door and we sat down. "You'll want an explanation of what she did. She's obviously in a distressed frame of mind. Let her talk if she wants to, but don't question her, don't scold her."

"Right."

"She says she thinks she took seven tablets. They're fifty milligrams each and the usual dosage is two tablets. So she took three hundred fifty milligrams, which is about a fourth of an acute overdose. She also drank two cans of beer, she thinks, which generally doesn't help matters. But what she took is a form of a barbiturate that acts fast and wears off fast. It was almost out of her system when she got here. Too late for a gastric lavage or Narcan. Some respiratory support and IV fluids were all the therapy she needed. We did an MRI and there were no visible head injuries. A couple of bruises, a couple of scrapes. No other injuries."

"Can I take her home?"

"We'd like her to stay until tomorrow morning, just to be sure all's good. Is she depressed? Has she mentioned suicide?"

I said, "No, nothing like that. We just recently decided to get married and things were good. We had a disagreement."

"Okay. She's in here."

Clare was on a high, narrow bed with metal rails raised on both sides. Her eyes were shut. I leaned over the rail and found her hand and took hold of it.

I said, "Clare."

"Sam." She opened her eyes, licked her lips. "I wasn't sure they'd let you in."

"And they'd keep me out how?"

"People keep asking about my family and they say you aren't it." She grabbed the rails and pulled herself up. I put my hand on her back and leaned forward and kissed her.

"I couldn't work," she said. She sounded a little scared. She turned to lean toward me, holding tight to the rail. Her voice was low and urgent. "My fingers were like sausages and my eyes weren't hooked up to my brain and nothing looked right. I kept spilling things and dropping things and I couldn't focus and nothing *looked* right. It was always so right in the darkroom and suddenly it was all so *wrong*. And you were—I thought I didn't know you any more. And I was so *angry* and I *hate* being angry!"

"Yes, I know."

She said, "I couldn't sleep and I was all itchy. I took two of the pills and they didn't work so I had a beer and *that* didn't work. So I took three more pills. And another beer. Nothing worked! It was awful. I'm so sorry."

I flinched. "Jesus, Clare, it's me who's sorry."

"Are we still friends?"

"Yes. Absolutely. But no more of this. You scared the devil out of me and Andy."

"Well, someone should," she said in an almost normal voice. "Was he there?"

"No, but he's here."

"Can we go home now?"

"Not yet. Tomorrow."

She lay down again and seemed to drift off to sleep, but her eyes opened, and her grip on my hand tightened when I moved. She said, "You look tired."

"I can't think why. I play cards all night to buy milk for the babies and come back to find you climbing into Charon's boat."

Dr. Dormanen smiled and the nurse was giving me an interested look.

After another few minutes she said, "I want to go home."

"Tomorrow."

"Now."

There was a note of panic that brought Dormanen's head up from the notes he was writing, and he walked over to stand next to her. He said, "You really should be observed for twenty-four hours."

"Sam can observe me. I don't want to stay here."

Andy asked, "Hello?" and came in with a young man carrying a clipboard. Andy said, "Does Clare have insurance?" and came across to pick up Clare's other hand and squeeze it and smile at her.

She said, "There. No insurance. I have to go home."

I looked at the young man. "Do you have some sort of form I can use to guarantee her bill?"

He said yes and started riffling through paper.

Andy put his hands on the foot of her bed and leaned forward and said, "That was a really adolescent gesture, you know? Thought you'd be done with that crap. I mean, at your age and all."

I opened my mouth and shut it again.

"So cut it out," he said. "Sam doesn't need it."

She was silent—we were all silent for what must have been almost a minute, which is a longer time than you might think, and she said, "Yes. I'm done."

Clare continued to insist on going home and finally she prevailed. The doctor wrote orders, gave her some pills for the headache she claimed she didn't have, and gave me some instructions on observing her. She signed her name to several pieces of paper that only Andy read, and I signed the form to guarantee her bill, and the nurse and I helped her into a wheelchair. I took off my jacket and put it on her.

In the early morning sunlight her face was white as new snow.

4

Andy gave me a blanket that he kept in his car, and I tucked it around her and fastened her seatbelt over it. Then he followed us to her apartment.

When we got there I steered her straight into the bedroom, into a clean nightgown, and into bed. "Now stay there. No getting up until I say so. If I don't take proper care of you, that doctor is going to hang me by my balls."

"Is today Wednesday?"

"Yes."

"I have clients."

"No."

"I have to earn a living."

"Damn it, Clare, just once, be sensible. You can call them, put them off. How many are there?"

"I don't know. I'll look in my book." She started to sit up and I pushed her back down.

"I'll get it."

"On my desk. And my phone."

Andy was sprawled on her couch reading her morning paper I found her appointment book in a litter of papers, and her phone, and went back to the bedroom. She was sound asleep.

I went back to the living room and pointed out two names in the book to Andy. "Call these people and tell them Miss Russell is indisposed. Be nice. Not too inventive."

Andy agreed to stay with Clare while I went to Catherine's to shower and shave and change. When I got back at eleven, Andy was sitting in her desk chair and Denny Linden was on her couch wearing another cheap suit and another sour look.

Another plainclothes guy—black, younger, bigger, clean-cut and athletic, better suit—who Linden introduced as Sergeant Jackson, was standing by the kitchen door looking at the photos Clare had on her wall. The collection of the week was pairs of old women walking together in parks and on streets lined with stores.

I raised my eyebrows at Andy, who said, "She's still asleep. Denny thought he might find you here."

"You were right, Denny. You found me here." I sat down on a wooden straight chair—Clare had the most uncomfortable furniture—and put one ankle up on the other knee.

"Thought we might have seen you before this, Sam, seeing as how Paul was killed on Monday. This is Wednesday."

"I've been busy."

"And there wasn't much love lost between you and Paul, was there?"

"We had our differences."

"Did you see Paul on Monday?"

"No, not since last Saturday."

"Not Sunday?"

"Nope."

"Sunday night?"

"No." I lit a cigar.

"Where were you Sunday night?"

"In a card game."

"Were you still there Monday morning?"

"Until about six."

"Who else was playing?"

"Ask your chief." I grinned at him. "I don't talk about who I play cards with."

"What did you do after the game?"

I blew a smoke ring. "I went to the apartment of a young lady introduced to me by my host."

"Not here?"

"No."

"Aren't you engaged to Frances Russell?"

My jaw was starting to ache. "Yes."

"But you went home with a whore. What was her name?"

I shrugged. "I don't know. Like I said, ask your chief."

"Did you pay her?"

"For what?"

Linden glared. "For sex."

"Isn't that illegal?"

Andy laughed.

"How long were you at her apartment?"

"Maybe till seven. Then I went home to get some sleep."

"Not here?"

"I don't live here."

"But you sometimes sleep here?"

"Not relevant."

He paused, then asked The cop question. "So where were you between, say, eight-thirty and ten-thirty in the morning?"

"Home, in bed, alone. Until about four in the afternoon."

"Nice life."

"Not bad."

"No one to swear to your whereabouts during any of that time? No sister, no nieces or nephews? No phone calls?"

"I have voice mail. My niece and nephew saw me before I left that afternoon, but I strongly suggest you stay away from them. My sister knows a very good lawyer."

"You have a carry permit." He looked at Andy. "So do you." Back to me. "I'll need your guns. Both of you."

I unholstered the Walther, hoping I'd get it back, and put it into a plastic bag that Sergeant Jackson held out. Andy did the same.

Linden said, "I want to talk to Miss Russell."

"Well, you can't. She's been ill and she's asleep."

"What's wrong with her?"

"Nothing, now. She just needs rest."

"Why? Is she under a doctor's care?"

"Yes she is and none of this is any of your damn business."

"Wake her up or I will."

"Like hell. You have no right even to be in this room except that Andonios here was overly hospitable in someone else's home." I stubbed out my cigar.

Linden stood up and started toward the door to the little hall and I scrambled to my feet, Andy right after me. The door opened and Clare was there in her robe.

"I heard voices," she said, and came into the room. I steered her to her desk chair and leaned on the bookshelf next to her.

"I'm sorry," she said to Linden. "I don't remember your name."

I kept my face straight.

"Sergeant Linden. This is Sergeant Jackson."

"Yes, that's it. I'm usually better at names."

"You don't have to talk to them," I said, but she just shook her head.

"Sam here says you've been ill and needed rest."

She didn't say anything, just looked at him calmly.

"What was wrong with you?"

She said, "I had a headache. Why is this—why are you asking me these questions?"

"Sam's brother Paul was murdered."

"Yes, but I didn't know him."

"You didn't know him? But you met him."

"No. I never saw him."

"Sam must have talked about him, told you things."

"He said once that Paul was twelve years older. Than Sam."

"Paul liked women. Did he like you?"

I came off the wall fast, but Jackson was on me, had my arm before I could get to Linden. I stopped moving.

Clare said, "I just told you, I didn't know him."

"All right," I said to Jackson. "I'm okay."

Linden jerked his head and Jackson let me go. Linden said, "That would give Sam a really good reason to shoot Paul, wouldn't it?"

She stared at him. "Aren't you listening? I just said I didn't know him."

"But maybe he saw you."

"So you think Sam would just shoot any man who saw me?"

"Saw you and wanted you."

She looked at me. "Which Greek tragedy is this one?"

Andy and I both laughed.

Linden's neck was getting red. He said, "Was Sam here with you the day Paul was killed?"

"Monday?"

"Yes."

"He came about four-thirty. Maybe five. We went out to eat."

"But not before that?"

"No."

"When did you last see Paul?"

She sighed, and spoke slowly and loudly. "Are you deaf? I have never seen Paul."

I said, "Are you about through, Denny?"

He stood up. "Let me know if you hear anything."

"Oh yeah," I said, and smiled.

Linden and Jackson walked out without saying anything more, leaving the door open, and Andy shook his head.

"Bad manners," he said as he shut it. "Being a policeman is bad for your manners."

I said, "A headache? As in 'Not tonight, darling'?"

"Well, I thought I had to say something and I didn't want to tell him the truth."

"That's what they do, they ask questions they have no business asking and make you think you have to answer. Here." I handed her a paper bag I'd brought in. "A hard-boiled egg and a sticky bun. From Catherine."

"Good, I'm starving."

The egg was peeled and wrapped in plastic film. She unwrapped it and bit in.

"You have the constitution of a horse," I said. I brought her a glass of orange juice.

Andy said, "Denny thinks he has a good motive for you."

"Denny can think whatever he wants, but he has to prove it in court."

"If he finds out about Clare's little excursion to the hospital, he may like it even more. Nice and lurid, appealing to his prudish sensibilities." I said nothing and he stood up. "I'm going to have lunch with Kori. Want to join us?"

"No, I'm going to sleep."

"Here?"

"Do you really think she can be left on her own? I may have to move in here."

"Then I'll see you at the funeral home tonight."

"If Clare's up to it."

She said, "I'm perfectly all right. We'll be there." She started on the sticky bun.

"If you don't show up," said Andy, "it'll be hell to pay."

5

"If I'm going to be in this family," she said after Andy left, "I'm going to do it right." She went into the kitchen to wash her hands.

I followed her. "Doing your duty by king and country?"

"You being the king?"

"Exactly."

"Am I the queen or the tavern wench?"

"Maybe the milkmaid." I stood behind her and put my hands on her waist. "Am I still welcome in your bed? In your life?"

"Yes." Maybe she was about to say more, but she changed the subject instead. "But you can't move in here, there isn't enough room."

"I know, but the commuting is getting me down."

"I'm going to take a shower."

I followed her into the bedroom. She stopped by the bed and looked out the back window.

"Does liking women run in your family?" she asked.

"It runs in most men's. Otherwise you don't have a family for it to run in. Why do you ask?"

"Because that Sergeant Linden insinuated that I was Paul's girlfriend or something. Is having extra women something that everyone assumes the Zandros men will do?"

I said, "Extra women, huh. I'll admit Paul always had at least one extra woman around. They changed a lot, sometimes daily."

"What about Philip?"

"What about him?"

"Does he have extra women too?"

I said, "Well, it's been known to happen. Not like Paul. More long-term."

"Do Sofia and Lillian know?"

"I don't know what they know or don't know."

She said, "What if Sofia took a lover?"

"*Sofia*? I can't even think of such a thing. It's inconceivable."

"Well, Philip doesn't exactly strike me as the singles-bar type."

I said, "Is there a point to this conversation? I want a nap."

"What if I took a lover?"

"You know, I really don't like this conversation or the direction it seems to be heading."

"Will you have extra women?"

"We will not talk about this any more!" I said angrily.

"Oh, but you can want me to have sex with you whether I want to or not. Damn it, Sam. You made me *afraid* of you."

I was very still. "That's over, done with."

"Is it?"

"Yes. It will never happen again."

"Won't it?"

She started for the bathroom and brushed past me. I caught her arm and turned her around.

I said, "I won't allow something between us that you bring out to stab me with whenever you get angry."

"*You* won't allow?"

"That's right. *I* won't allow."

She said, "Who are you to allow or not allow?"

"I'm half of what we are. There are things you don't allow and there'll be others. This is one of mine."

She said, "What do I not allow?"

"You won't allow me to ask about your family or your childhood."

She glared at me, then started to giggle. She said, "You're right, you know."

I said, "Of course I am. Do you need help showering or can you handle it?"

"I think I can handle it."

I sat on the bed reading the paper until she came out, then I stood up to undress. She dropped her robe on the floor and sat cross-legged on the bed, holding the sheet up to her chin, watching me.

I said, "What are you looking at?"

"You."

"Not looking for the right spot to slip the knife in, I hope."

She shook her head. "Nope."

"So, are you just looking or are you in the market?"

"Are you *on* the market?"

"You're a very wicked woman."

6

We slept all afternoon, ate sandwiches at the deli on the corner, and went to Catherine's so I could change into a suit.

On the way to the funeral home she said, "Tell me what you're going to do with your building. Are you going to fix it up?"

"I don't know yet. Why?"

"No reason."

Philip met us at the door of the funeral home. "You're late. Where have you been?"

"In bed," I said. Clare looked at the ceiling. "Back off. We're here."

In a large room an open coffin was surrounded by masses of flowers and a crowd of people. Clare stopped suddenly and I bumped into her.

"What's wrong?" I asked.

"Nothing." She moved into the room. "It's just that the last time I saw a coffin, I was five years old and my father was in it. It... startled me."

After an hour she disappeared. I was standing in a group of men who were mostly strangers to me but friends of Uncle Cy and Uncle Nick, and I didn't miss her immediately. When I decided to look for her, Andy told me she was outside with Kori.

They were sitting in patio chairs in a screened-in side porch, two beauties in flirty summer dresses. Kori wore her heavy, reddish-brown hair in a high, complicated knot and had made up her face in a vivid, almost exotic style, but her open, unsophisticated smile gave away her youth. Although Clare wore almost no makeup—a little around the eyes—and her hair was just a mess of curls, she was obviously the grown-up. Something in the face. She knew things that Kori didn't. But Kori was two years older than Clare.

"First a boy, of course," Kori was saying as I came through the door, "or maybe two, then a little girl. I already have some little dresses for her."

I saw that Clare looked white and exhausted and cursed myself for not taking her home sooner. She probably had a headache.

Then I saw Young Nicky sitting alone a few feet away, and I went to sit down next to him.

"Pretty rough times," I said.

He nodded.

"You getting through okay?"

He nodded again and said, "Theo?"

"Yeah?" I held out a hand and he moved over and sat on my lap.

"Did it hurt him?"

"No. It didn't hurt him."

He nodded and said okay and leaned into me and sighed.

7

In bed Clare said, "She sounds like a little girl herself. Playing dolls."

"She does rather, doesn't she?"

"I sort of envy her."

"Why?"

"She's so sure about the babies."

"And you aren't sure?"

"Not like that."

"Are you afraid? Of the birth part?"

"Yes."

"I'll be with you." I turned toward her and spread my hand on her belly. "And Catherine."

"I'm still afraid." She put her hand over mine. "And then there's little whoever, all ready to be taken care of, not knowing, poor thing, that all he has is me."

"Ha! You said he."

"Or she."

"Nope. The first one is a boy. Absolutely."

"That part is up to you."

"And I won't fail you, I promise."

"Me? It's not me you'd be failing. Is it really that important to you?"

I hesitated. Was it? "Yes."

"It might as well be a boy. He won't even look like me. Blue eyes are recessive."

"Well, mostly. Poor darling."

"Poor darling indeed. You never would have looked twice at me if I didn't have blue eyes."

I said, "True. I'd have let Harry have you."

"You still can."

"Are you forgetting Karen?"

She said, "I'm sure she and I could work something out. Why don't Andy and Kori set the date? She's panting to have babies."

"It's Kori's mother. She doesn't entirely approve of Andy."

"Who would? Maybe Kori will get pregnant and force the issue."

I said, "Not Kori."

"Why not?"

"Because, my darling, unlike some I could name, she's a virgin."

She said, "You're kidding. Andy's Kori?"

"Yes, that one."

"Andy has depths unplumbed."

I said, "And so does Kori."

She started laughing and I said, "And don't tell him you know."

Saturday, May 5

1

The day of the funeral was warm, bright, and still. Unseasonably warm. I was irritable in black suit and tie. Clare looked very stylish in a new dress but also very tired and she was irritable in long sleeves and pantyhose and shoes with heels. I was busy being pall bearer and brother of the dead man, and Clare was pretty much on her own until I saw Thomas take her hand and stand with her.

The church was gorgeous, awesome, inspiring. I was always exhilarated by being there. But the crowd, the music, the incense, the heat, the gold and bright colors, and maybe death itself overcame her. I heard Catherine, sitting next to her, order her outside in a sharp whisper, and when I looked over I saw Clare's face was entirely too pale. I made a move to follow her, but Philip's hand on my sleeve kept me where I was. At another whisper from Catherine, Thomas followed her out. He looked white and unhappy and even smaller than usual in his black suit.

The service ended and the crowd left slowly and finally we got the casket out and into the hearse, me thinking Paul, you bastard, this is my last favor to you, and I found Clare and Thomas sitting on a bench in the little park across the street from the church. He'd taken off his suit coat and tie.

"You all right?" I asked her.

"I only needed some air. Are you?"

"I'm always all right. You okay, Thomas?"

He nodded energetically.

"We need to get in the cars."

I got them by their hands, one on each side, and we walked back across to get into one of the cars. We were in the third limo with Stephen, Andy, and Kori.

Andy asked, "Too hot in there, Thomas?"

Thomas nodded and put his head down and sniffed.

Clare said, "Too everything."

"I was only at one funeral before," said Thomas. "For my father." He cleared his throat and wiped his eye with his cuff.

"Me too," Clare said. "When I was five."

"I was *almost* five." He sniffed again. She lifted him onto her lap and I handed him a handkerchief.

She said, "Sam always has a handkerchief and I always forget one."

Thomas blew his nose. "Theo said you cry a lot."

"He did?"

"When you were gone away. He told Cousin Andy." He lowered his voice for effect. "'I hope Kori isn't a goddamned waterworks like Frances Clare.'"

She said, "Did he now."

I said, "No talking Irish."

Andy was grinning and Kori was attempting to hide her face.

Thomas said, "Why did your father die, Aunt Clare?"

I opened my mouth but she made a stop-right-there gesture.

She said, "He had cancer… in his brain."

"My father was stabbed with a knife made out of a spoon."

I said, "Thomas—"

"Shut *up*, Sam. Do you miss him a lot, Thomas?"

"He was big and strong and we were all happy." He sighed. "I guess we're sort of happy again. But it's like a long time since we saw him."

Clare said, "I used to miss my father a lot, when I was a little girl, but I got over it. Well, not over it… sort of past it."

"I miss him too," Stephen said in a low voice.

Andy put an arm around Stephen. "And I miss both my parents, and that was a *long* time ago. Aunt Clare's right. You get past the really hurting parts. But you mustn't stop thinking about them. You need to remember them and they need to be remembered."

Andy's parents died when he was six, and he never talked about them. I was never sure how much he remembered them. Apparently a lot.

Andy and I were close as close, but every now and then he showed me something I didn't know.

The cemetery was brightly sunny, but there was an awning and there were trees. Thomas stayed very close to Clare. After the graveside ceremony we all returned to the church in the limousines, and Clare and I got into her car to go to Lillian's.

Another large apartment, like Catherine's and Sofia's, but not comfortable like theirs. I'd never liked Lillian's ideas on interior decoration. Plus she was always redecorating, and the rooms were always some ugly blend of two or three so-called styles. The place was full of people and food and smoke and wine, then brandy and ouzo. I saw Clare go into the kitchen with Kori. When she came out a half hour later, our cousin Mary Christides, Tim's wife, asked when our wedding would be and Clare said October and Catherine said, "Are you serious?" and wrote herself a memo to call the church.

2

On the way back to Clare's I decided to bring up something that I'd been working on for a while. I pulled the car over to the curb, shut off the engine, and turned to face her.

I said, "Just to be sure now, you are going to marry me?"

"Oh, yes, I have to. Catherine is calling the church tomorrow for the reservation."

"Good. Then we have some business to conduct, you and I. Can I have you for a whole business day? You get to choose the day."

"I'll have to check my book. What kind of business?"

"Various kinds. Money business. You'll see."

"I hate business."

"I know. Don't worry." I restarted the car.

"So you say. But I've put off a lot of clients in the last few days. I hope I can pay the rent next month."

"And you still won't ask me?"

She tilted her chin up and pressed her lips together. Her stubborn look. She said, "No, I won't. And I haven't even paid you the money you lent me *months* ago, before the show, though I have most of it saved up."

"You have what?"

Another of her surprises.

"I have it saved up. Most of it. I put it in a special account. I wanted to pay it all at once, not in dribs and drabs. I don't know why exactly. Maybe because that was how I got it. Is that all right with you? I could pay you now what I have."

"That was a gift, not a loan."

"I told you I'd pay it back after the show. But then, what with one thing and another, it took a bit longer than I'd planned to save it up."

I parked the car in front of her house and faced her again, and she unbuckled her seatbelt and leaned over to put her arms around my neck.

"Will you stay here with me tonight?"

I said, "Yes, of course. Stop changing the subject. That money is yours. Your attitude about money borders on the pathological. There is no good reason for you to refuse to let me give you money. Especially now. We're betrothed. In some times and places, that's as close to marriage as makes no difference."

"I want to make it on my own."

Her fucking mantra.

"You've already made it on your own. Doesn't that count?"

She said, "Of course it counts. So what?"

"So I'll admit I'm not offering olives off my own trees, watered by the sweat of my brow, but I am offering you the hard-won fruits of my labors. And you, you fruitcake, you turn me down. We can each only till the fields we have, and I have been tilling the card tables."

She was laughing. "Now tell me about the rich part. How about all the beers I've stood you when you were broke?"

"A relative and temporary condition. You've been broke and beerless and have drunk on my charity. Sometimes I'm up, sometimes I'm down. That's how it is with the action."

"All the more reason I should have a good business. Babies don't wear diapers just on the good days, you know."

"Don't worry, fruitcake. You'll see. In the meantime, can't you let me have some fun with the few dollars I manage to scrape together?"

"Fun like paying my rent?"

"It might be fun. Let me try it out. Maybe I'll like it."

She said, "How about this? I'll pay the rent out of the money I saved up to pay you back."

"You are impossible."

She kissed my chin. "Can I go in and take off this dress now?"

"Yes."

Monday, May 7

1

We were drinking our first coffee of the day on the front-porch steps, and the morning was already pleasantly warm at half past eight, even in the shade.

She said, rather tentatively, "Do you not want that money back?"

"No. I don't. Absolutely not. You're a hard woman to convince."

"Then I know what I'm going to do with some of it. I need an air conditioner for my studio. With the lights, and especially by the afternoon, it's a sweatshop in there. The window fan doesn't quite do the job."

I said, "Get two and put one in your bedroom."

"This is business money, not personal money."

"Do you keep them separate?"

"Well, I try, but I'm not very good at bookkeeping."

"You should let Uncle Cy look at your books. He's a wizard. He can probably save you money on your taxes."

"I wouldn't want to impose. On him or your business."

"I assure you, he would enjoy it, and I'm a partner in that business and I can make that kind of request."

"It's so hard to think of you as a businessman." She leaned away from me and looked me up and down. "Maybe a nice suit. Navy pinstripes. And a navy shirt and white tie."

"You've never been to the office. I'd like to show it to you."

"Yes, I'd like that."

"So, may I put an air conditioner in your bedroom?"

"I thought Greeks were tough and accustomed to hot places. Like Hades."

"I'm only thinking of you, bred from little blue men who lived in cold misty bogs."

"I think you're forgetting the little blue women. And you've gotten us confused with another bunch of refugees from the Brits. You know the closet in my workroom?"

"Mmm."

"I was thinking that, if you like, I could clean out the junk I keep in there and you could use it. For some clothes, I mean."

"I like that idea."

"The attic! I forgot the attic!"

"Jesus, now what are we on?"

"I have things in my attic."

"Bats? Squirrels, maybe?"

"No, no. Things of mine that didn't get smashed. I completely forgot the attic. I haven't been in it since I moved in. Let's go look. Oh, we can't. Here comes my first client."

"Shall I arrive with my suitcase later?"

"Yes."

2

I arrived in a cab with two large suitcases, a duffle, and three shopping bags of groceries. While I put things away in the kitchen I said, "I have had it with bagels for breakfast. No, don't frown. You don't ever need to eat anything but a bagel and you don't have to cook, God forbid I should even think it, but I, unbeknownst to you, you culinary heathen, I know how to poach an egg and squeeze an orange. Do you have a juicer? I didn't think so. May I keep my juicer in your kitchen? Good, I'll get one tomorrow. At least you have a coffee grinder."

3

I helped her to finish moving old photographic gear out of the closet and into boxes for the attic, dusted the shelves, and unpacked my suitcases. The closet had shelves built in down one side, and she surveyed my neat piles of shirts, shorts, sweats, T-shirts, and socks beside my neatly hung jackets, shirts, and pants.

"Do you think I'm a slob?" she asked.

"Well, you do take out your obsessiveness in your pictures. 'Slob' is perhaps overstating it."

"Will we be able to live together married? Me a messy and you a double-neat?"

"We'll get along fine." I took a half dozen books from one of the suitcases and set them on her worktable, shouldered one of the boxes going up to storage, and took up the empty suitcases with the other arm and hand. "Maybe we'll rub off on each other. Let me see your attic, girlie."

The attic entry was up a narrow stairway from her back landing and through a low door. It was hot and the air hadn't moved for years. A single bulb high up in the peak of the roof showed dusty rafters, a rough wood floor, and in one corner a large, old-fashioned, rectangular suitcase and two cardboard cartons.

I said, "This is it? Your past? Two boxes and a suitcase? You travel light."

"I don't have much past. I couldn't afford it. Let's take them downstairs. I feel like Alec Guinness in that movie."

In her living room she opened one of the boxes. It was full of papers and spiral-bound notebooks, some of the papers typed and some in Clare's rather untidy cursive.

I picked one up. "*A Comparison of the Approaches to the Unconscious of Freud and Jung*," I read. "In nine pages, double-spaced."

She took it out of my hand quickly and shut it back up in the box. "We'll just burn this one, sight unseen."

"No, we absolutely will not. We'll put it in our attic for the babies to look through and be impressed."

"The babies had better be smarter than that." She opened the second box. It was full of photographs. "Oh! My réalité period." She started rummaging.

"Harry said you were a menace."

"Here. Here's you." She picked up a photo. "Before I knew you. You were at the Rat."

I looked. "How old were you?"

"Sixteen." She handed it to me.

"Incredible. You really got it. Nailed me. How did you know, at that age?"

"Know what?"

"Never mind. Am I too old for you?"

She looked up and grinned. "Not yet."

"Let me know when we get there."

She riffled through a handful of photos.

"You were extremely sexy," she said.

"Am I still sexy?"

"Not a bit." Looking down into the box she said, "And you never saw me."

"I wasn't seeing young girls. Christ, Clare, you looked about fifteen. The last thing I needed was getting caught in bed with a child. I stuck to women my age. Or older. I didn't even *look* at anything younger."

She looked up at me now. "But then you did."

"You were in a bar, getting served. So I figured you were more than fifteen."

She had another photo of me in her hand. She said, "I think this was the first time I ever saw you. I couldn't resist your face. Who's that with you?" She handed it to me.

I laughed. "That's Andy, when he had his moustache, and long hair. And you said you'd never seen him."

"How would I see past all that hair?"

"Can I have this?"

"I'll let you have it on a long-term loan. Don't lose it. It's nice to know I had such good taste even then."

I asked, "What's in the suitcase?"

"My really deep past." She opened it up. "My California past." She dug into a collection of more spiral notebooks, cassette music tapes, old clothes, a rag doll, a baby doll, a stuffed dog, some paperback novels, some rolled-up posters, some hair ribbons, and several magazines on photography. "Here." She handed me a photo album of snapshots.

I let her open the cover. "My father." A thin, middle-sized, pale-faced man with a shy, crooked smile and straight, dark hair slicked back. "My mother." Blond curly hair, dimples, lush figure, a mocking smile.

"He was older?"

"About ten years."

"What was his name?"

"Liam Sean Russell."

"And what's hers?"

"Mary Elizabeth Midge. Russell."

"Mary Midge?"

"Right. There. That's their baby."

"You?"

"The only child."

"Curly hair, fat cheeks, lower lip hanging out—you haven't changed a bit."

"I knew you'd say that."

I turned the pages, looking at the skinny, dark-haired, two-year-old Clare in a white dress,skinny three-year-old Clare on a rusty tricycle, skinny five-year-old Clare in a swim suit—suddenly she took the book out of my hands and closed it.

"I don't want to see any more of it," she said.

"Another time? I want to see it."

She nodded and sneezed. "I'm hungry," she said.

"Let's go eat."

4

After we ate at a Thai restaurant over on University Avenue we went and sat on a bench by the river. She leaned against my shoulder and we watched the light fade. After a few minutes I said, "I want us to start living together."

"I'd like that, but my place is too small, you know it is. You've got some stuff there now, but that doesn't mean you *live* there. I can still tell you to go home."

"Yeah, I know. But we could live at Catherine's. Or get our own place. Maybe Catherine or Sofia will have a vacancy."

She said, "I will not move in on Catherine like some poor relation from the country."

"Carrying all your worldly goods in a cardboard box and an old valise with a broken strap?"

"Exactly. And I don't want to live in one of those apartment buildings. I'd smother."

I said, "Well, you know, I've been sort of counting on living with you when we get married."

"Well, where then?"

"I don't know." I sounded like a three-year-old.

"It's in your part of the dowry. And what about my work?"

"You could still do that at your apartment. Why not?"

She said, "And drive back and forth to wherever we live? I'd hate that."

I said, "We have to live somewhere, fruitcake."

"Then you make a suggestion."

"I already did. Your turn."

She stood up. "I'm getting cold. Let's go back."

We started walking back to the car.

She said, "Maybe we could get a house?"

"A nice split-level rambler in a suburb with a walk-out basement for your studio and a hand-lettered sign in the front window that says enter studio at side door and has an arrow."

She said angrily, "There are lots of kinds of houses."

"I don't think I'm ready to be a homeowner."

"Well, maybe I'm not ready to be married if we can't even decide where to live."

We were silent the rest of the way back to her place. After I'd seen her up to the apartment I said, "Harry invited me to a game tonight. I'll see you in the morning. Late morning." And I gave her a quick kiss and left.

Tuesday, May 8

1

I walked to Clare's from the office, where not much was happening until later when Philip and Andy and Uncle Cy would handle it. The days were keeping warm and sunny. As I came up her street I saw her sitting on the porch on an old rattan love seat, left there by a previous tenant, drinking cokes with another guy. It was Thomas. I was still two doors down when he started calling, "Hi. Theo. Hi, Theo."

I said, "Hi, Thomas. Hi, Clare."

They watched me come up the steps. Clare said, "Hi, Sam."

"Hi, both of you. Are you visiting by yourself, Thomas?"

"I came on my bike."

"No kidding. That's a long ride. I thought you were with Aunt Sofia this afternoon."

"We called," Clare said.

I said, "Bet you're in trouble when your mom finds out."

"Yeah." He hunched over his knees.

"You didn't interrupt Aunt Clare's work, I hope."

He said, "No, and she took my picture." He straightened up. "And she said I could come again and I should bring some books and leave them here and then if she's busy I can read or watch TV. But she said I can't come on my bike. Someone has to drive me."

"She said all that, did she?" I sat down next to Thomas. "Any more cokes?"

Clare said, "No, we only got two. Drink some of mine. What time is it? I said I'd deliver Thomas by six."

"We'd better go then."

"I'll get my bag and lock up."

When she went in, I put my arm around Thomas's shoulders and squeezed. "You're a lucky guy, Thomas. Clare Russell doesn't hang out with just anyone. Let's get your bike into the trunk."

When we had driven about two blocks I glanced into the back seat. Thomas was asleep in the corner.

I said, "I'm amazed he even found your house."

"He had a map that he got off the Internet."

"Jesus."

"I know. My heart just stops when I think of what might happen between here and there."

"Surprised you, I bet."

"Knock on the door and there he was."

"Wait. Wasn't the lower door locked?" I'd talked the landlord into fixing the lock.

"Probably not. The guys downstairs leave it open all the time."

"I guess I'll talk to them."

"No more bloodshed in my house, please."

"Just a civil conversation. Did he really not interrupt you?"

"Really, he didn't. I was done shooting. I got him to sit on a stool to help me check the lighting, and I got several good shots of him. I'll print them for Catherine."

"And me."

2

If people don't want their conversations overheard, they shouldn't have them in public. So at Catherine's, while I was making phone calls, I was also in the dining room pouring a glass of brandy and listening, at first only incidentally and then with real interest, to Clare and Catherine in the kitchen.

Clare said, "Can I ask you something? It's sort of very personal."

"Go ahead. I'll tell you if it's *too* personal."

"Was your husband faithful to you?" Catherine didn't answer right away and Clare rushed on. "I don't mean to pry. I know this is really personal."

"You wonder about Sam being faithful to you."

"I know he isn't."

"No, I don't suppose he is. And no, Stephanios wasn't faithful. Not sexually."

Clare said in an edgy tone, "What other kind is there?"

"Stephanios never cared about another woman. Our father never cared about anyone but our mother and he loved her very much. Philip has never loved anyone but Sofia and he adores her. Sam has loved only you since he met you. There's never been another woman in his heart, before or since. And they have all given all of us... "

I wondered if the somewhat prim Catherine was turning red.

"They have all been... generous at home. I mean, sexually. Never any reluctance. Sofia and I have talked. They're... oh, damn. They're good in bed. And very loving. I'm assuming Sam is also. Oh my God, he's my little brother!"

I was grinning.

Clare said, "Then why?"

"I don't know. *They* say it shouldn't matter to us. *They* say it's part of being Greek, or part of being male. Or part of being Greek male."

"But it does matter. To me, anyway."

Catherine said, "And to me. And to Sofia. And it mattered to my mother. But we all just live with it, don't we?"

Clare said, "I have to. I agreed to it."

"In so many words?"

"I knew Sam went around with a lot of different women. Went to bed with them. And he told me he wouldn't change. And I said I would accept it. I was just hoping that you could tell me how to... live with it."

Catherine said, "You already live with it."

Clare said, "I mean, so that it's all right."

"So it doesn't hurt."

"Yes."

"Stop loving him."

Clare said, "Is that the only way?"

"The only way I know. It worked for Lillian, though I don't suppose it was so hard for her, Paul being Paul, and really there was no love there to begin with. I've seen it work for other women. But if you love him, it hurts."

"There must be a way. I can't not love him and I can't bear to think about it."

"Clare, listen. There's one thing I can tell you that does make it easier. Not okay, just easier. He doesn't know, he really doesn't know that it hurts you. He knows how much he loves you and he knows that he cares nothing, less than nothing, for those other women, and he truly believes that that's all that matters. To him, it's no different than pleasuring himself. That's what they all believe."

Now *I* was turning red.

Clare said, "I'm not sure if that makes it better or worse!"

I didn't know either.

After a moment of silence, Clare said, "Can I ask you another question?"

"Of course."

"Why didn't you like it that Stephanios was a gambler? Did you think it was immoral?"

"Oh, no, I'm too much Zandros for *that*." Catherine laughed. "No, I wanted respectability. I wanted security and stability and something to talk to the neighbor lady about. I wanted to be able to talk about my husband to someone outside the family."

Did Clare want respectability?

Catherine said, "It's hard to talk about your husband to people outside when what he does is illegal. And even harder when he goes to prison." Catherine's voice was as cool and self-possessed as usual, but I thought I heard a slight tremor. "And hard to know how to teach your children to respect his memory."

Clare said, "Thomas does. He talks about his father with such love. And he knows exactly what happened. He told me."

"Did he?"

"He knew more than I'd have thought he would. About the spoon and all."

Catherine sighed. "Well, I guess that's best. I expect Sam told him. Or Andy. Or maybe he just heard. God. I told him all about sex and babies, but I choked up on that one."

I told him. Andy and I did—told all of them, to make sure they knew.

So that's the advice the women give each other? "Stop loving him" ? Not a comfortable answer.

3

We went to a movie and then to Vincent's where she sat up straight and craned her neck to see over the back of the booth and check out the room and who was there.

She said, "Who's that?"

"Who?" I twisted my head.

"That blond girl waving at... never mind."

4

On the way home, with her head on the seat back and her eyes closed, she said,"Was she . . . ? I suppose she was. Why can't I learn to keep my mouth shut? I will, I will keep my mouth shut, I will."

"Good."

"Was she?"

"Yes."

"Damn. Damn, damn, damn."

"Why don't you just not ask?"

She said, "Why don't you lie?"

"No. Not to you."

"Why not?"

I said, "I don't know."

"Are you punishing me?"

"I don't think so. Me, maybe."

She was silent for a few blocks, then said, "Please don't tell me any more."

"Please don't ask," I said through my teeth.

"Even if I ask, please don't tell me."

"Stop this."

She said, "You will, won't you? *Damn* it!"

I jerked the steering wheel over and came to an abrupt stop at the curb, turned off the engine, got out of the car, slammed the door behind myself, and jogged away across the street. I stopped in the dark between two houses and looked back. I saw her get out and go around the car and after a couple of minutes I heard the engine start and saw the car move slowly away.

Wednesday, May 9

1

I came up the walk in the colorless light of the very early dawn and found her in her nightgown and robe, sitting on the top step, almost invisible in the dimness, leaning up against the porch pillar, hunched over her drawn-up knees, and shivering in the damp cold.

I sat down next to her and pulled her onto my lap and put my arms around her to hug her close. I was warm from walking and she burrowed into my open jacket.

"I suppose you have some explanation for this," I said.

"For what?"

"For being out here."

"I'm watching the light."

It was no doubt true. Sometimes I thought she had an extra eye or saw a broader spectrum than we mere ordinaries.

I nuzzled her cheek. "Is that why you came outside?"

"No." She wiggled closer. "I woke up and came out to see if you would come."

"Of course I would come. I would always come."

"Maybe not."

"Yes, I would. I did. Let's go in."

"Not yet. I want to see the rest of it."

"You're freezing."

"Not now. Why did you go?"

"I was getting angry, so I took a walk."

"You've been walking all this time?"

"Uh huh."

She watched the light and I watched her face, heavy-lidded, pale, sleepy. Finally the light became pink and then yellow and she tilted her face up to kiss my chin. "You're very prickly."

"And getting pricklier. Let's go in."

She got up stiffly and stumbled up the stairs with my arm around her.

"I hate it when you aren't here when I wake up," she said.

"So do I."

2

We got into bed and she snuggled against my side. Her skin was still cold.

She said, "I saw that girl before. That blond girl. Two times. No, three. Well, two."

I sat up. That blond girl was associated with Leo Graff who was, for reasons I had always supposed were financial, associated with Kev Smith. Leo Graff was legitimately rich and well-born and Smith was illegitimate in every aspect and had money but how much was your guess. Yet somehow they were connected. Philip could probably tell me how. As a side note, Paul had been a sort of clown jester for Leo. And how did that fit in?

"Where?" I asked.

She turned onto her back. "The day I was shopping for a funeral dress I saw her in Jo Webster's. That's a shop that sells women's clothing."

"Right."

"She was with a man who looked sort of familiar. He wasn't actually familiar but maybe related to someone I've met. He also looked rich. And about an hour later I went into a shop called Lady Domino and she came in right after me and looked around while I did and then came out right after me."

I said, "We'll call all that one time."

"When we left the Stardust that time, and then I went back in, there was a car at the curb with a couple in it and I'm sure it was her."

I asked, "Who was she with?"

"Don't know. I could just barely see him. And later they were gone."

"Two times. Son of a bitch."

She asked, "Is she following you?"

"Sounds like she's following you."

"How weird."

"Yeah."

3

Two hours later I woke up when I heard her say my name, but when I turned over, she was still asleep. She had pushed all the covers off and was lying on her back, her arms at her sides. Her lashes were wet and she was frowning. I pulled the covers over her and put my arm across her and stroked her shoulder. She shivered and said my name again. Her body was stiff under my arm and I pushed my other arm under her and pulled her close.

"It's me," I said. "I'm here."

She woke up and took in a deep sobbing breath. I held her, stroked her, kissed her face and hair, and she gradually became soft and warm.

"Bad dream?" I asked.

"It was dark and everything was whirling around. I was so dizzy."

I turned onto my back and pulled her over on top of me, found her mouth, and kissed her until I felt her begin to respond. We made love gently, quietly. When we were done, she was satisfied but still caught up in the dream. I pulled the cover around her and held her tight against me. She dozed off and we both slept again. When we woke up the second time she seemed to have shaken off the unreality, but she was tired and quiet. I took her into the shower and held her in my arms under the warm water and kissed her wet face.

We drank our coffee on the porch, where she sat one step down and leaned on my knee.

I asked, "No clients today?"

She shook her head.

"What's wrong?"

She shook it again.

"Was that an answer?"

"It means I don't know."

I said, "Tell me about it."

"Dr. Zandros?"

"The doctor is in."

"If you'll scratch my back."

I did.

"Before, it was just us, you and me. I loved it. I loved it being you and me. Now it's so many people I can't even count them—new clients, Mr. Black and his blackguards…"

I grinned.

"And I love your family, you know I do, it's not them. Mm, that feels good."

I was scratching under her bra. "But I've brought the whole world down on you."

"It's not your fault… exactly."

"But I did it." I stopped scratching and started massaging her neck and shoulders.

She said, "Catherine and Sofia were discussing the guest list and I was thinking about standing in that church in front of half the population of North America. Couldn't we just go to the courthouse and do it?"

After a minute I said, "I don't give a rat's ass about all the rules and I'm not getting married in the church just for their sakes. I want to do this thing the way I think is doing it right. And I want to show you to the world and say this is who I have chosen and this is what she means to me. And I want to bind us to each other on heaven and earth."

"And hell," she said.

"There too."

She sighed deeply. "Okay. I want to do it right too, and to me, doing it right is being with you and if that's how you want us to be together, then that's the right way. I'm not making myself very clear, because that makes me sound like an idiot. But if it isn't right for you, then it can't be right for me. Does this make any sense at all?"

"Yes. And the other way around too."

"Mmm. And it can't be just us any more, can it?"

"It would be... hard to arrange."

She moved up a step to sit next to me and put her arms around my neck. "Well then, in the meantime, can we do something I want to do?"

"Yes. What do I have to do?"

"Just come with me to see something."

"That's it? Sure. Whatever you want. Let me see your face. You're up to something."

She was pink. "I have to make a phone call."

She came back down carrying her shoulder bag, took my hand, and led me to her car. "I'll drive," she said.

4

We went to the storefront office of an architect we both knew named Anson Greeley. It was a few blocks from my building, in an old warehouse that had already been rehabilitated and was an advertisement for the old brick and stone, beamed spaces, brass fixtures, etched and stained glass, and wrought iron that the neighborhood specialized in. I'd known Anson for several years. We'd played poker together many times.

He brought out a big portfolio and laid out several large sheets of drawings on two long tables at right angles to each other. Clare gestured for me to look and I was as intrigued by the excitement in her face as I was by the drawings. I moved slowly past the display she and Anson had made for me, looking carefully at each drawing, saying nothing. Then I took her hand in mine and pulled her with me while I studied each one again.

The first sheet of drawings was several sketches, with little labels and arrows, of my building's exterior, from several perspectives and viewpoints, but reborn, with new windows and millwork all the way up, and a covered walkway on the east side, entered through a large iron gate and leading to a courtyard in the back that was overhung by a large porch on the second floor. The porch was part of the second-floor suite, and it was covered by a leafy trellis that hid it and isolated it from the courtyard below. Anson's excellent sketches were done in hard, sharp pencil and were, some of them, very detailed.

Another drawing showed the west side of the building, which also had a covered walkway, wider, securely fenced in by more wrought iron and welded steel chain-link fencing, even forming a roof, with an Art-Deco iron gate with PRIVATE woven into its design. Halfway down the walk on that side, maybe two-thirds, there was an entry into the rear of the building where there was a door into the first floor, a stairway to the upper floors, and an elevator. At the southwest corner of the building, which faced south, on the front, beside one of the big glass windows, there was yet another, more regulation-size door. This one said, in itty bitty letters, Frances Russell, Photography, and I remembered that that door opened onto a vestibule and staircase to the other floors.

One of the big front windows had penciled on it, faintly, "Rick's," and I tapped my finger on it. "Nice," I said, and Anson smiled.

He said, "It's a bit light on interiors until we talk more, although I'm assuming you don't want a lot of Beaux-Arts kitsch."

I said, "I rather like Mission—Arts and Crafts—but I'm very open."

The second sheet was sketched plans and drawings of the interior of the first floor just as I had described it to Clare. After that the second floor: a photography studio with a large shooting area, a little waiting-and-talking area, an office, a dressing room, and a wc. There was a note in a box that said: Darkroom and Workroom in Basement. The third floor was kitchen, dining room, wc. , and large living area as yet undivided. Fourth and fifth floors were big spaces labeled Bedrooms and Baths, and the sixth floor was a large blank labeled Sam's Space. Two sets of stairs, the elevator, and a dumb-waiter linked all six floors and the cellar.

I looked back at several parts of the drawings and she finally couldn't stand it any longer.

"Well?" she demanded.

I looked at her.

"Do you like it?" she asked. "Is it a good idea? Can we do it?"

I took a deep breath. "Yes, yes, and yes," I said. "My God. I was so—I never thought above the first floor. And now I see that what few thoughts I ever had about where we might live together were all wrong. This is so obvious! This is what you want?"

"Oh, yes, it's *just* what I want."

"It's just what I want too."

"And we'll do it?"

"We'll do it."

She threw her arms around my neck and we both laughed and squeezed each other hard. We talked with Anson for almost two hours about surveys and scale drawings and utilities and structural engineers and contractors and schedules, told him to send bills to Cy, and left his office with a roll of copies of the drawings to study and play with and scribble on. I took her to a nearby deli for a late lunch and sat across the table from her just looking, unable to look away from her face until she dropped her eyes.

"You always have another surprise for me," I said. "This is really what you want?"

She looked up at me. "To work in that space? And live there together? Oh yes. Yes, yes, yes! I'm very attached to that ratty duplex but I know it's just a way station. You're sure we can do it? It'll be a ton of money. Boxcars of money."

"Yes, definitely we can do it. You'll have exactly what you want. And it'll be what I want. What we both want. I've been saving my pennies just for this."

"Why didn't you think of this?" She sounded almost indignant.

I laughed. "Once you said you thought I didn't live anywhere, and you were more or less right. Catherine's is hers, not mine. I was waiting for you to live with before I lived anywhere. And since I got the promise of you, there hasn't been room for anything else but being with you. We hadn't gotten to where yet."

"I was wrong though," she said. "You live wherever you are."

5

We went to Catherine's and Clare sat cross-legged on the living-room rug with a can of Surly in her hand and Thomas hanging over her shoulder and the drawings spread out in front of her. Uncle Nick was there, and Andy, and Stephen and Ioulia, and details were pored over and discussed.

"Can I stay overnight in your new house?" Thomas asked, and Clare said, "Of course you can."

I said, "It'll be huge. Everyone can stay overnight."

After dinner Philip and Sofia and their kids came in, and, surprise, Uncle Cy. Ioulia and Stephen were sent to clear and wash dishes. Meli went with them to keep company, and Thomas went to his hidey behind the long sofa with one of his summer reading books. He'd showed me his list. He had almost finished it and it was only early June. I'd been neglecting the summer library schedule. I took the young kids, Andy took the older kids. Jamie was sprawled on Philip's lap, also reading.

"Lillian has made up her mind," Philip said. "Cy and I saw her today."

Clare started to stand up, but I pulled her back. I said, "I want you in on this."

"What does she want?" Uncle Nick asked.

Philip said, "She wants us to buy her out. Two million."

Uncle Nick said, "Too much."

Philip said, "And she wants it all now."

"She doesn't trust us?" Andy asked, only mildly sarcastic.

Cy said, "She doesn't trust anyone. She wanted a sixth of the business, but we showed her the paperwork that Paul had signed. She claims she didn't know about that. But of course she did and that doesn't matter anyway. It has no bearing on her claims, whether or not she knew. And it was for Paul to tell her, not us."

I said, "What are we buying her out of?"

Philip said, "The family, I guess. The city. The state."

Uncle Nick said, "Technically, under the agreement, her spouse's share stopped when Paul left. But then, of course, her widow's share kicked in, until she'd found some other source of income. Made a new life for herself somehow. We couldn't just leave her and Nicky out in the cold and we couldn't trust Paul to have provided for them. That was the intent of the original agreement, after all."

Catherine said, "She's moving back to Cincinnati, to be with her family. I talked to her today and she said she's decided for sure. She's selling her apartment building and wanted to know if one of us would buy it. It's the only property she owns."

Philip said, "I think someone in the family should buy it. For Ioulia, maybe. Or Meli. It's a good building. Good location."

I said, "I don't want to be short of cash for a while."

"I think you will be," said Philip. "I hear you have plans for a new place to live."

Clare blinked and even I was surprised.

I said, "The rumor channels are running fast today."

"Ioulia called Meli while we were eating dinner."

"You allow that?" I asked.

"Of course not."

Clare asked hesitantly, "Why is Lillian so angry?"

Philip said, "I don't know. She's unfriendly. Verging on hostile. Maybe she thinks we should know what happened to Paul. Maybe she thinks we *do* know."

Andy said, "She's *always* been unfriendly. And angry."

Philip still looked angry.

"What else?" I asked him.

"Lillian told me something else. I'm not sure why. She seemed

to think that giving me dirt on Paul would be some sort of payback."
He drank off his brandy in one quick move and wiped his mouth with
the back of his hand. An unusually inelegant gesture for Philip. He
said, "What a spiteful bitch she is."

Uncle Nick said, "She has a very small heart. Like a walnut."

Clare said suddenly, "No. She doesn't. She's scared."

Everyone looked at her and she lifted her chin and looked back.

After a short silence, Philip said,"Paul had a secret."

I said, "I'm betting he had several, all nasty."

"He told Lillian this one right after you met Hugh Black. In
L.A. She said Paul was boasting of it." His voice was hard and he
talked a little faster than usual. "It was Paul who told Hugh Black that
to get at you he should go through Clare. That you didn't have any
other weak spots but you'd do whatever you had to do to protect her.
He—Paul—told Lillian that he was the one who introduced Black to
the Salters. One of the Salters played poker with Paul. Barry, I think."

I just stared at him. My face felt stiff. Clare's was white. No one
moved.

"Paul didn't want you to quit. He was afraid of losing the money. He asked me once if the cops might come after us if the people
who counted weren't playing with you any more. The people who
counted." He made a spitting motion. "He told Lilian that Black
would make you keep playing."

I still said nothing.

"Black sent one of his men to the office to see you, to invite you
to meet with him. Black. Paul was there by himself, so he talked to
Black's man who also paid Paul some money to be a go-between on
this end. The rest of us never even knew Black's man had been there.
It was I guess two days before you first met with Black here in St.
Paul."

Met with. Black had abducted Clare.

I said, "Paul was supposed to pass it on. To me. The invitation."

Philip nodded. "Yes."

I said, "But he didn't."

Uncle Nick said, "He didn't tell any of us. I'm guessing that after he thought it over he was afraid to tell us about the money. He was always afraid of Sam and Andy. So he took the money and never said anything."

I said, "Did Lillian know how much he sold me out for?"

Philip said, "No."

"You're lying."

"It doesn't matter. He did it, that's all."

Another silence.

I said, "Did Black know this? That Paul never passed it on?"

He said, "I don't know."

Thursday, May 10

1

We stayed the night at Catherine's, in my old room, which was still mine, and Clare slept up against me, her breasts warm on my back, her legs pushed up behind mine, her arm around my waist. This time it was me who had bad dreams, but she didn't know it. In the early dawn I woke her up and we made love and went back to sleep. The dreams stopped.

2

Clare had agreed to spend the morning talking with Catherine and Sofia about wedding plans. I phoned Andy and arranged to meet him at the office.

Philip and Andy were already in the office when I got there. I sat down in my chair, at the second desk.

Andy said, "Where's your lady this morning?"

"She and Sofia and Catherine are making up the master wedding plan."

"She's actually going through with this?"

"So it seems."

"And you're building a tower for your faerie queen."

I ignored the flight of fancy. "You know Anson, right?"

"Yeah. He does nice stuff. And he plays the clarinet rather well."

"And he plays a good game of cards. A Renaissance man."

Uncle Cy came in with a bag full of sandwiches and four bottles of beer.

I said to Andy, "So do we do anything about Lillian's little tidbit?"

"I don't know what to say, cousin. What *can* we do?"

"Nothing, I guess. Paul was scum."

Philip swiveled his chair to face us. "Keep that talk in the family," he said.

I said, "Sure," and he swiveled back. I said, "What he said about his role in recruiting for Black—introducing him to the Salters—that contradicts what I was told by both Hugh Black and his guy Carl Huxley, and I believe them."

Andy said, "Do we have a plan?"

"We find and have conversation with Leo Graff. Leo's handprints are all over everything in this city that smells bad. Have been for a long time. And Paul was Leo's shield against us. Paul's gone and Leo is going to start shying at shadows. After we call at his house, which I consider only a formality, he has a country club, a city athletic club, a marina club and a boat, two or three favorite bars, and a certain apartment building full of working girls in which I hear he has a financial interest and where he likes to check out the staff regularly. After that it probably gets complicated."

Andy looked disgusted. "Does he have an office?"

"Yes. Forgot that. Foley Building." I could hear us all thinking: right above where Paul had died.

He said, "Maybe we should put him on hold and try for the maid."

"Leo might be at Grant Jenneky's game tonight."

Andy said, "True. Okay. The maid. Lillian calls her an au pair. I'll invite her out for a drink."

3

We went to a bar down the street and Andy called and fetched Andrea while I watched a baseball game—Twins and Cubs—on big-screen

TV. Major league pro sports and big-time collegiate teams had never really interested me. Boxing did, some. And soccer. But I needed to be up on the popular sports for the business. So when I was presented with a game, I watched.

Andrea had long, straight, dark hair and creamy skin and dark eyes that slanted just enough to give her a slightly mysterious look. She was very curvy under a pretty yellow sundress. She seemed surprised and disappointed to find me there, but she sat down and asked for a Tom Collins. Andy went to the bar for her drink and beers for himself and me.

I definitely needed it. And I was saying that much too often, even if only to myself. Does anyone ever *need* a beer? Time to drop back on the drinking. I was too old for college-boy excuses and too young for middle-management angst.

We sat silently until Andy came back and handed the drinks around, sat down next to her, and draped his arm across the back of the booth behind her. She sipped her drink delicately through a straw and twirled the little umbrella.

"So Lillian is going back to Cincinnati," he said. "Are you going too?"

She nodded. "I'd rather stay here, but my father won't let me."

A good Greek girl.

"What if you got a job here?" Andy asked. He let his fingertips rest on her shoulder.

She shook her head and shrugged.

He said, "Maybe we can help. What can you do?"

She looked at me. I was saying nothing, and she shrugged again. "Not much, I guess."

"Can you type?" he asked. Just a friendly guy, helping out.

"No."

"Come on, Sam, what do you think? Maybe she could be a model."

I leaned forward and looked at as much of her as I could see. "Hmm. Pretty round to be a model."

She moved uncomfortably and sipped some more.

"Definitely round," said Andy, and stroked her shoulder. "Drink up, honey, you'll get behind."

"Have you ever had another job, something besides working for Lillian?" I asked.

"Oh, no." She shook her head vigorously, like a child.

I took a box of little cigars from my pocket and offered one to Andy. We lit up and smoked a few puffs and looked at Andrea.

"I was going to have another job," she said finally.

"Really?" said Andy. He let his hand move down her shoulder to where the curve of her breast began. She shifted on the seat.

"Cousin Paul was fixing it up. With a friend of his, Mr. Leo."

"Is that so?" Andy said, all friendly interest. "What sort of job?"

"As an entertainer. Mr. Leo knew a girl who would teach me to dance."

I smiled at her and she smiled back. Andy moved his fingers gently and she looked slightly confused.

"I can see," I said, "that you could be very entertaining."

"He said I could make a lot of money and have lots of clothes, really beautiful ones."

"Who said?" I asked.

"Paul."

I leaned forward on my elbows, keeping my eyes on her face.

"So what happened?" I asked.

"I don't know." Shrug.

Andy said, "Oh, come on, honey. Tell us what happened."

"I couldn't do it any more."

"Why not?"

She shrugged. "Because."

We didn't say anything.

"Because a baby," she said petulantly.

Andy set his cigar in the ashtray and ran his hand over her belly. She squirmed and looked up at him.

"Definitely pregnant," Andy said. He picked up his cigar. "Who's the daddy?"

She shook her head.

"We can't help you if you don't tell us," I said. I reached across and took her glass away. "And no more of this. It's bad for the baby."

Andy bent his head and said softly, "Was it Paul?"

She turned red, didn't answer.

"So it was Paul." He nudged her with his chin on the side of her head. "Right?"

"I guess so."

"He ruined it for you," I said.

"No job as an entertainer," said Andy.

She shook her head.

"What did Paul say?" I asked.

"He laughed."

"Did he, honey?" Andy said gently.

Jesus, if I were a woman, Andy's voice could get me to tell him my bra size, my phone number, and the combination to the safe.

"He said he'd give me some money to go to a doctor, but I wouldn't."

"For an abortion," I said.

"So then he said he'd give me some money to go home."

"To Cincinnati," I said. "To your father."

She leaned heavily on Andy and closed her eyes.

I said, "Hey."

She opened her eyes.

"So you shot him," I said.

"Oh, no, Lillian did. When I told her." And her eyes shut again and after a bit she snored ever so faintly.

Andy said, "What now?"

"We talk to Philip and Uncle Nick."

"I'll take her home."

I said, "I'm going back to the office. Do you need any help with her?"

"No. Go on. I'll see you later. You playing tonight?"

I said, "At Jenneky's? Yeah.

4

Philip and Uncle Nick were at the office and I asked Uncle Cy to join us. I told them all about Andrea. Philip looked, I think, angrier than I had seen him look since—when? Maybe since the time he'd found Andy and me cheating at cards when we were seven. Of all of us, he was most protective of our family's reputation, and Paul running a whorehouse was not acceptable.

I also showed them the very official-looking report that Uncle Cy's ballistics guy had sent back.

I said, "The two bullets were from the same gun. Paul's gun. The one he used to shoot at me and Clare in Clare's back yard. And Lillian used to shoot at me, also in Clare's back yard. And the smart money says one will get you a hundred she used it to shoot him under the Foley Building."

Philip said, "I hope you're not wagering your life."

We were all quiet, thinking. But there wasn't much thinking needed.

I said, "So both Paul and Lillian are—were—everything I ever thought they were. Are. Do we go to the cops?"

Philip said, "No."

Uncle Nick said, "We really have nothing to go to the cops *with*. Bullets aside, it's all just talk. Andrea says yes, Lillian says no, then what?"

I said, "I'll vote yes. I saw and heard Andrea."

Andy said, "I'll bet Lillian still has the gun. And we could get it. Then we'd have a chain of evidence."

I said, "We've got *our* chain of evidence. Let the cops worry about theirs."

Philip said, "They can both go to Cincinnati, both Lillian and Andrea, but no money for Lillian. This is now a Makris family problem."

Uncle Nick said, "I'll call old Spiro."

I said, "What about Young Nicky?"

Philip said, "We'll take care of him. She'll know that. I'll go talk to her."

I said, "Wear your bulletproof vest and don't eat or drink anything. And get that damn gun... before she shoots someone else."

Uncle Nick said, "Half a million for Young Nicky. Same as Paul got, and she's probably still got most of that left. She can use Nicky's income from the half million until he's eighteen, then it goes to him. She won't ever have any control over the principal. We keep that until Nicky's twenty-five, then he gets it."

We all nodded.

I said, "What about Andrea's baby? That may be our niece or nephew in there."

Philip said, "When we see the DNA results, then we'll decide."

I said, "Lillian's brothers in Cincinnati will be pissed as hell. I'll bet they were looking forward to her having that buy-out money."

5

At Catherine's I found Clare and Thomas sprawled on the living-room rug playing chess. I looked down at the board.

"Have you ever played before, Clare?" I asked.

"Yes," she said defensively.

"Thomas is wiping you out."

"I know that. Go away. Leave me alone."

Thomas grinned.

I went on through, found Catherine on the sun porch, and told her what Andy and I had found out. We regarded each other glumly.

"What are you going to do?" she asked.

"Take Clare home. Tonight I'm playing cards at Jenneky's. So's Andy. If I see Leo Graff there, I may ask him some questions. Or maybe I won't. Paul was operating outside the family more than we thought. He really was a parasite."

"Well, we knew *that*," said Catherine.

"Yeah."

She said, "He always wanted to be more than he was. What he *thought* was more."

"I wonder what he thought he *was*." I looked out the window at the tops of trees. "At least I don't have to wonder anymore whether I—we—sent Paul off on his own to be killed."

She put her hand on mine. "Is that what you've been thinking?"

"It crossed my mind." I turned my hand under hers, gave hers a squeeze, and stood up. "Did you and Sofia and Clare get all the plans made?"

"Mostly. We have an overall outline and a timeline and a list of assignments. Sofia is so organized. I think Clare's terrified."

"Maybe she'll get over it by October."

She said, "Even if she doesn't, she'll do it. She's doing it for you, and you don't deserve it. I used to change your diapers and you were a spoiled brat then and you're a spoiled brat now."

"I am not."

"You've gotten your own way your whole life."

I said, "What the hell are you on me about?"

"I feel guilty putting her through this."

"She's a grown woman and she can say no if she wants to."

She said, "Would she say no to you?"

"That depends."

"On how you put it to her?"

"Maybe." I grinned. "Entendre intended?"

She picked up her book.

I went back to the living room. Thomas was trying to explain a chess move to Clare, and she was gazing at the board uncomprehendingly.

"Game over?" I asked.

"Yes." She shook her head. "I'll never get it, Thomas."

I said, "Give it up, Thomas. She doesn't think straight ahead. She thinks sideways."

She gave me a fierce frown and he snickered.

6

We didn't talk on the way to her place, and when we got there I dropped onto the couch on my back with my arm across my eyes. If I couldn't look at any of it, maybe it would go away.

"Do you want a beer?" she asked on her way to the kitchen.

"No. Yes."

"Are you sick?" she asked. "Indecision is not one of your strong points." She brought a can of Surly and one of lemonade, opened them, put the beer in my hand, sat down on the floor next to me, and draped her arm across my chest. "What's wrong?"

"Promise me you will never drink a Tom Collins in my presence."

"That's it? I promise."

"No, that's not it. Not all of it." I lifted my head and drank some of the beer. Then I told her about Andrea and Paul and Lillian and Leo Graff. And Andy. "So that's the dark side of the Zandroses." I chugged the rest of the beer and handed her the empty can.

She asked, "Will he hurt her?"

"Andy? No, nothing like that. Maybe he did just take her home. But whose home? If he seduces her, he's taking advantage of her, and she'll think she's in love with him."

"Maybe that's as bad."

"Maybe. I wonder whether she knows she narrowly missed being turned out. Cincinnati and Daddy have got to be better than being a pro in St. Paul."

She got up onto the couch and lay full length on top of me, kissed me gently, then less so, then rested her head on my shoulder.

"What will happen?" she asked.

"I don't know, but I think it's unlikely that the cops will ever know about this. Or the newspapers. Lillian's family will keep her and Andrea quiet." I could feel the beer starting to buzz in my veins. "I'll continue to be a suspect and every five years you'll read a feature article in the Sunday newspaper about unsolved murders in St. Paul that will mention my name. How will you feel about that?"

"I won't care."

"Are you sure?"

"How can I be sure? But I think I won't care."

"I'm going out tonight. I won't see you until late. You going to be okay?"

"Mmm." She was kissing my chin. "Of course. I'm always okay."

"Tell me about my wedding plans."

She stopped kissing me and propped herself on her forearms on my chest. "We had one disagreement. Well, two."

"Which were?"

"First, no wedding showers. Absolutely."

"You're so not fun. What was the other?"

"Catherine and Sofia want me to invite my mother."

"And you said no."

"And they don't say so, but they think—I don't know what they think. Do they think there's something wrong with me? What do you think?"

"There's nothing wrong with you and they don't think there is. It's just… strange to them. No family."

"They asked didn't I have any aunts or uncles? Cousins? Anyone?"

"Did you? Do you?"

"I don't know. My mother was an only child, I'm pretty sure, and my father, I think, had a brother who was in the Navy, but I don't remember ever seeing him."

"Today I almost agree with you about families."

"You *must* be sick. Shall I put you to bed and take care of you?"

"Yes."

7

I felt strangely passive and let her make love to me, undress me, caress me, kiss me, lie on top of me and slide onto me, move on me.

"Will you really be mine?" I asked in her ear.

She said, "I'm already yours."

I lifted my head and she gave me a lovely sleepy smile.

I lifted my shoulders and chest, still on her, still in her, still hard, and put one hand between us, flat on her belly. "I want to make you pregnant. I want to put my son in you, in there. Now."

"You can. Right now." Still that smile.

I laughed. "Darling, I count your pills every morning."

"I know you do. I've been washing them down the sink for a month."

I could only stare at her. "And you didn't tell me?" I said finally.

"I just did."

"When did you decide this?"

"One day when I was tired of having everything decided for me. I know, my fault, letting it happen." She put one hand between us, on mine. "You can have everything but this. This is mine, even more mine than yours. I'm the mother, I carry the child, I give birth. This is my belly. Once there's a baby, you can still walk away, but I can't, not ever. I knew that a long time ago, even when I thought I would never be a mother." She pushed herself up onto one elbow. "I suppose you're angry, but I'm not going to apologize because I'm not sorry." Her voice was urgent. "Because this is the right day. I *know* it is."

"Do you?"

"Yes." She fell back onto the pillow and closed her eyes. "You *are* angry."

"How do you know it's the right day?"

"Arithmetic, and a little pain I get in my side."

I didn't say anything.

She said, "I didn't want to wait any longer, until everyone else said okay, you can do it now, while it's still my decision."

"So it's put up or shut up."

"You can still make me wait."

"Maybe. I may have already put up."

"Maybe."

I said, "Open your eyes." She did. I said, "I am about as mad at you as I've ever been, but that can wait. We can go into that later, be-cause I am also about as turned on as I've ever been, and I am keep-ing you in this bed until you are as pregnant as a woman can get."

I slid my hand into her hair and pulled her head forward to kiss her, kept on kissing her while I touched her breasts, her belly, her thighs. She welcomed me and drew me in as she never had before. Her legs around me pulled me deeper than ever before. Her mouth was more insistent than ever before. Her hands were behind my up-per arms, pulling at me, and my hands were on her breasts, then on her waist, her hollow straining belly, then behind her, drawing her even closer, as if that were possible. We came together, violently, then slowly collapsed.

I was face down on her, and I shifted my weight slightly.

"Sam, don't move."

"I've got no intentions of moving."

"Was that a hurricane or an earthquake?"

"A tsunami at the very least. Sooner or later we have to reach our peak, the ultimate, the Olympic gold of love-making, but so far we continue to surprise me."

She giggled. "Maybe right now the little tadpole—"

"Tadpole?" I muttered.

"—is swimming upstream—"

"Doesn't need to swim tonight. You were sucking me in."

"—about to run head-on into the egg—"

"Hey, sailor, got a light?"

She said, "She's leaning on a lamppost. Wearing fishnet stock-ings and a shockingly short skirt."

I suddenly fell asleep while she was still giggling.

Friday, May 11

1

I got out of bed to go to the bathroom and when I came back to sit on the side of the bed, she followed my example.

"Aren't you going out?" she asked when she came back.

"Uh uh."

She leaned sideways against my shoulder. "Don't they expect you?"

I said, "Andy's there, I think."

"Your replacement?"

"Substitute. I can't be replaced."

She said, "You are so vain."

"Facts are facts."

"I'm thirsty. There's some beer."

"Not for you, cupcake."

"Not even a taste?"

"No alcohol."

"None?"

"Don't blame me. You brought this on yourself." I stood up and pulled on my jeans. "And you can stop trying to con me. You're hardly drinking lately anyway. You thought I didn't notice. All those barely touched glasses of beer you've been shoving at me? I'll make you some nice orange juice."

"No beer?" she said. "Maybe I'll rethink this whole idea."

"Too late. What goes around comes around. This is your punishment for deceiving me."

She put on a pajama top that actually belonged to me—I never used the tops—and followed me into the kitchen. She said, "That doesn't exactly compute. Even if I hadn't deceived you, I still couldn't drink beer. I think. Maybe that's backward."

I laughed.

"I'm hungry," she said. "I don't remember any supper. What time is it?"

"Twelve-thirty. I like that outfit."

The pajama top just covered her bottom—and she wasn't wearing anything else.

"I'm surprised I slept so long," I said with my head in the refrigerator. "I didn't really mean to sleep at all."

"You're always surprised when you aren't perfect."

"Well, you get used to something." I brought out oranges and started cutting them into halves. "I, of course, can drink beer and anything else I want to."

"Maybe not, maybe the fumes or something will get to me. The vibes."

"I haven't seen any research on that particular point."

"Sam."

"What?" I looked up.

"Maybe right now a baby is starting to live in me."

I started to grin and a voice behind her said, "Ain't that pretty?" and her whole body froze and I saw a hand close on her arm, a big, hairy hand.

"Don't. Move." Someone else, not attached to the hand, came from behind her to stand between us. He was tall and very thin, and he had a gun in one hand and a permanent leer from a scar down the left side of his face.

"Put the knife down," he said, and I did. He said, "She's pretty cute." He waved his free hand at me. "My friend here wants to see just how cute she is."

Another hand came around her and she looked down at the hands pulling the pajama top apart. They were large and had coarse black hair all down the backs and fingers and they were reaching for her breasts. She cried out "No, don't!"

Then whoever was behind her pulled her backward, and she struggled and tried to throw herself to the floor. The hairy hands had hold of the pajama top, but she tore away, out of the pajama, and fell into the man with the gun, who was knocked off balance, and I jumped. The gun flew across the room and the hairy man got hold of her again and she shrieked and kicked.

Suddenly Andy was in the room, which was strange, and he had a gun in his hand, which he jabbed into the side of skinny man. Are all the bad guys idiots? I didn't know.

"Go!" Andy yelled and the guy holding Clare tried to put her between himself and me, but I pushed her aside and got hairy guy by the throat with both hands, squeezing so hard my own fingers went white, until the hairy one started to go limp, and then in a sort of frenzy he twisted out of my grip and the two of us scrambled across the floor until I caught him again and lifted him bodily and swung him into the corner of the kitchen counter.

There was a crunching sound when his head hit and I let go and the hairy guy dropped into a heap. Suddenly the room was silent.

2

I reached for Clare, put out my hand to her. She pressed harder against the wall.

She said, "Don't touch me." Said it very clearly.

I stopped and looked at her, and said quietly, "Clare?"

She said, "Don't touch me."

"Uh, oh," Andy said. "She's gone, Sam."

She needed a haircut and her mop of hair was falling over her eyes, which were round and blank. I took a deep breath, straightened up, and let my hand drop to my side.

"I think," Andy said, very quietly, 'that she's okay where she is for a few minutes."

I looked hard at her, but her face didn't change. I leaned over the body on the floor and put my fingers on its neck, checking for a pulse.

"Nothing," I said to Andy and looked at the now-silent skinny one, gestured at him. "Who is this? He looks familiar."

"Dickie Jordan."

"Oh, yeah."

"Kevvy's boy," said Andy.

"Yeah. Kevvy. Shall we do society a favor?"

Andy thought for a moment. "My idea is this. He can carry his friend out to the alley, and he can walk away. I'll call Kevvy and tell him that Dickie blew his little assignment and lost a unit of personnel into the bargain. Bet Kevvy will love that one. Maybe Dickie should be looking for a ride out of town."

I said a word in Greek that my father used to say.

Andy said, "There's that."

"You won't do it," said Jordan. "You're too soft."

Andy said, "Not a matter of soft. A matter of smarts."

Jordan looked at me. "I'll make a deal with you."

I said, "You don't have anything I want." I looked at Clare, but she hadn't moved.

"I do. I'll tell the cops enough to put Kevvy out of the way for a long time. The Feds."

"I'm not a cop and I don't talk to cops. Not even the Feds." I told Andy, "I'm going to get Clare into the other room."

He said, "I can handle this. You handle her."

"Are you sure?"

He looked around and said, "Hand me his gun. Wait. Use a towel. Stick it in my back pocket."

I did as he asked.

He said, "Give me the towel. I'm taking this knife. The better to prod him with. No batteries required."

"Okay."

I turned to Clare. "Come on, Clare. Come in the bedroom. You need your nightgown."

"Don't touch me," she said in that eerily clear and toneless little girl's voice.

"No, I won't. It's okay." She moved away from the back door, took three steps, and stopped by the dead man on the floor.

I said, "He won't touch you."

She finally moved on and went into the dark dining room. Behind us Andy said, "Pick him up," and I followed Clare, shutting the kitchen door. She was standing in the dark.

"Come into the bedroom," I said.

'Don't touch me," she said warningly.

Tears stung my eyes. "No, I won't touch you, darling."

She went into the bedroom, where a small light was on by the bed. I found a nightgown that buttoned up the front.

"Can you put this on? Shall I help you?" I held it out and she took it in her hand and stood holding it. "Put it on. Here, I'll help you. I won't touch you. I'll be very careful." I held it for her and she put her arms in and I dropped it onto her shoulders. I moved around her and she stood in front of me, passive, and I cautiously buttoned it, taking care to touch only the gown.

"Sit down, sweetheart."

She sat on the edge of the bed. I picked up my phone and dialed Catherine's number, shoving my feet into a pair of sandals while I listened to it ring.

"Yes?" she said sleepily.

"It's Sam. We need your help."

"What?" She was awake.

"I can only hit the high points now. First, as soon as I hang up, call Philip and tell him to get Peter and Mike over to stay for a few days, ready for anything."

"Not again!"

"Yes. I'll explain later. Second, Clare has…" I turned away, lowered my voice. "She's lost touch. Suddenly. Traumatically. I'm not sure she knows who I am. She's walking and talking some, but she's skipped town. Nobody home."

"Is she there? With you?"

"Yes."

"Is she calm or agitated?"

"Calm. Very calm. *Too* calm."

A pause. "Bring her to emergency. She may need to be admitted."

"Where? How?"

"Bring her to the E.D. at St. Ann's. I'll meet you there."

"You'll run interference?"

"Yes. There's a good trauma psychiatrist on staff here. I know him. I'll call him for an emergency consult."

"No drugs. Tell him no drugs."

"What?"

"No drugs. None. She may be pregnant." I was watching Clare's face but she didn't seem to hear anything I said.

"Oh, Sam, now?"

"Save it. Call Philip first. We'll bring her. Andy's with me." I heard him come back into the apartment.

"Do you want an ambulance?"

"Oh God no."

"All right."

I heard water running in the kitchen as I hung up and went to stand in the corner of the dining room where I could keep my eyes on Clare while Andy and I talked in low voices. He had his shirt off and he was washing his hands and arms.

"All set? Any trouble?"

"Yes, trouble." Andy's voice was shaking. "I killed him."

"You what?"

"The tough-guy act was too good this time." He was getting control of his voice. "I thought he'd run for it, I *wanted* him to run for it, but he *jumped* me! I had a gun and a knife and he fucking jumped me!"

"Keep it down, damn it. What happened?"

"I didn't even move. He came right at me and the knife was in his chest—there was blood all over my arm!" He turned off the water and stood there letting his hands drip into the sink.

I handed him another towel and said, "I'll get you a clean shirt. Where is he?"

"Both of them are behind some trash cans three doors down, behind that white apartment building. He sighed deeply and shuddered at the end of it. "I see you got her dressed."

"Sort of. I called Catherine. She'll call Philip to get Peter and Mike over there and then she'll meet us at St. Ann's."

"Okay."

"Can you drive?"

"Yeah, I'm okay now. You'll have to hold onto her though. I don't want to be fighting her for the wheel at forty miles an hour."

"Right. Let's go." I went back into the bedroom. "Clare, we're going out." I found her sandals. "Shall I help you put these on?"

She was still sitting on the bed and she stuck her feet out and I carefully slid the sandals on. Once my hand touched her instep and she flinched, but she let me finish and stood up unbidden. I threw on a shirt, made sure I had wallet, watch, phone, and keys, went to the closet to grab a shirt for Andy, then turned to face her. She was watching me warily.

"Come on, Clare," I said, and she stood and walked toward the door. She stopped when she saw Andy, but stood quietly while he put on the shirt. Then she followed him out the door and onto the porch. We got her to Andy's car and I opened the door. Andy stood outside the driver's door and we waited. After hesitating a full minute or more, she got in. As we got in on both sides of her, she moved toward the middle but was stopped by the console and seemed to be trying to shrink from both directions at once.

"Please don't touch me," she begged. She was shaking visibly.

I twisted to face her. "Darling, I have to touch you now. I won't hurt you. No one will hurt you." Carefully I put my arms around her waist and pulled her onto my lap, held her arms against her body, and got my left hand around both her wrists. Andy reached over and fastened the seat belt around us.

"Please don't touch me," she said in a small pleading voice.

"Go, Andonios," I said through my teeth, and Andy started the engine.

Several times she asked me, in that same pleading voice, not to touch her, but she didn't struggle or try to pull away, just sat rigid and shivering in my arms. I touched her as little as possible, kept as far away from her as I could, and thought hard about holding her close, like somehow, wherever she was, I *would* be holding her close and she would know and know that it would be all right, she'd be safe.

3

Andy put the car into some doctor's reserved spot next to the door labeled "EMERGENCY DEPARTMENT" with some bright fluorescents above and called Catherine's phone to tell her we were there, and I waited until he came around to my side and opened the door before I took my arms away and backed out, moving her from my lap onto the seat as carefully as I could.

"Come on out now," I said, and after a minute she got herself out and standing next to the car. I was ready to grab and grab hard if she made any moves, like trying to run, but she didn't. By using our bodies and holding out our arms, we guided her in the door of the E.D. and then she stopped, blinking in the bright lights and looking a bit wildly at the people moving around.

But Catherine was there, wearing a white lab coat over a blue scrub dress. There was a man with her, tall, good-looking, very intelligent face, broad-shouldered, sandy-haired, about fifty, also in scrubs and lab coat, and another nurse, also in scrubs but no lab coat.

The man came toward us and Clare stopped. "Please don't touch me."

Andy and I came up behind her and her face changed from blank to frantic.

I said, "Catherine's here. Will you go with Catherine?"

She turned to Catherine who, at a nod from the tall man, held out her hand to Clare. Clare hesitantly gave her hand to Catherine and walked with her and the other nurse down the corridor.

The man turned to me and held out his hand. "I'm Ford Maxwell," he said.

"Sam Alexandros. Our cousin, Andy Alexandros."

We all shook hands.

I asked, "You're the psychiatrist?"

He said, "Yes. Specializing in trauma psychiatry. Catherine called me. Mrs. Kamariotis. The young woman is Frances Russell?"

"Yes. We call her Clare."

"Was she raped?"

"No. Well, not tonight. But she was… grabbed by someone who planned to rape her."

"I understand from Catherine—Mrs. Kamariotis—that there's no family member who can be responsible for admitting her."

"Right. No family."

"She's your fiancée?"

"Yes. I'll take care of anything that requires a responsible party."

"Good. I expect some admitting clerk will track you down before long. I'm going to see Miss Russell now. You'll be here?"

"Yes. Is she alone?"

"Someone is with her at all times. I'll need to know whatever you can tell me about her history, any other psychotic behavior or episodes of withdrawal, unusual emotional responses to events, anything, and I want as much as I can get as soon as I can get it."

I said, "Right. There's just one thing. Absolutely no drugs."

"Yes, Catherine told me. We'll keep it in mind but I can't promise that until I've completed an initial assessment."

"What can you do to replace using drugs?"

"Hypnosis."

I nodded. "Okay."

Maxwell left and Andy produced a tin of cigars.

I said, "Man. He takes no prisoners."

Andy said, "Let's step outside for a few minutes."

We stood where I could see Maxwell or Catherine reappear. "What the hell were you doing at Clare's apartment with a goddamn gun?" I asked as I lit my cigar.

"Well, I went to Jenneky's and you weren't there, which didn't concern me much, and about eleven-thirty I overheard Leo Graff on the phone saying, no, he isn't here but go anyway, and that did concern me, so I exited quietly out a side door and went to Clare's. It seemed the most logical interpretation of Leo's conversation. I had my gun in my car. The front door was standing open, so I brought it in with me."

"Man, I owe you on this one. Are you okay?"

"I'm good. Bastard surprised me is all. I don't like being surprised."

"You're sure—"

"You got some worrying to do, save it for Clare."

"Well, just let me know if you need me to fit you in," I said and glanced over and saw Andy grin crookedly.

After a minute I said, "Mrs. Kamariotis."

He said, "That would be Catherine."

We both laughed softly.

"Do we tell her?" he asked.

"We do not." I yawned, then said, "So Leo and Kevvy. Kevvy and Leo. And where did Paul fit in?"

"Someplace worms come out of," said Andy bitterly.

"Paul *wanted* status and money, Leo *has* status and money."

"Yeah."

I said, "I dunno if Paul had chosen up sides, if that's even what's going on. He was just following the money."

"Well, he was also doing what he could to hurt you without doing anything that would leave him out in the open."

There didn't seem to be much to say to that. "Is Andrea okay?"

"Yeah. I got to say, Andrea is a mink, but she's a natural." He blew smoke thoughtfully. "She has some bad bruises, and she had them before I got there."

"Really?"

"Leo Graff."

A woman in a blue smock came through the door with a cup in her hand. She said, "No smoking!" and held out the cup and I looked into it. It was half full of water. "In here!" she said.

We deposited our cigars in it.

"Sorry," I said.

She went away without replying.

"Why no drugs?" he asked.

I hesitated, then said, "She may be pregnant."

"Congratulations." He smiled. "Your timing is interesting."

"The timing is Clare's."

"But you were there."

"Uh huh."

"God, but she's beautiful, Sam."

We were silent for a while.

I said, "We'll have to cover the ratty duplex."

Andy nodded.

"And we need to talk to Philip and Uncle Nick."

Andy said, "I'll go there now, clean the place, and I'll call Philip and Uncle Nick in the morning. Maybe we can talk there? About noon?"

"I'll be there by then, or I'll call you. Philip's probably waiting to hear, phone in hand. Call him now."

"Okay. Give me a key. Should I place an anonymous phone call about the litter in the alley?"

"No. I'm sure they can trace anything these days. They'll get your breath print off a payphone that you used two months ago."

"Have you tried to find a payphone lately?"

He went to his car and drove away and I stood in the air and breathed.

A few minutes after Andy left, the admitting clerk found me and I went back in with her and answered all her questions about Clare. She was anxious about the lack of insurance, but I dug into my pockets and gave her three thousand dollars and signed my name to an IOU for another three grand and she gave me a receipt and went away, startled but satisfied.

It was a hospital form with a hospital name on it, but I know an IOU when I see one.

4

Philip came and Uncle Nick with him and Andy and by God Lillian My family backs you up and doesn't back down and never leaves you in trouble by yourself, and I was damn glad to see them.

Catherine and Dr. Maxwell appeared from the other direction.

Lillian was in her usual state of just-on-the-edge-of-drunk, taking my arm and not hanging but definitely in need of help to stay upright. Catherine showed us to a semi-comfortable private waiting room nearby for the families of critical patients. We all got seated in one corner after the usual commotion that obtained when more than three of us were in the same room. Lillian moved herself into a central position and smoothed her skirt and said, "I have to tell you, Sam, something important about Paul."

What could I possibly not know about Paul and need to know and now? But I listened.

She loved having the audience, but she played it straight. "The other day—I'm sure you know—we had a little girls' tea party—just us four—the Zandros sisters—to get to know Clare a bit more—without all those children running around. Clare really is so sweet. I see things in her—well, I think we will be good friends and I just feel so terrible—well, that can be later. There were no men, of course, at our little party, but Paul came in for a few minutes to pick something up in his study." She shrugged and rolled her eyes. "That's what he calls it. And while he was there Clare went in to use the bathroom and when she came out she…"

Suddenly I thought Lillian was going to cry, but she just sat silent and still and bit her lip for a while and started up again.

"When she came out she looked, um, embarrassed? Or maybe ashamed? I don't know. I wanted to say what's wrong, but I didn't.

And Catherine and Sofia had their backs to her and didn't see." And then Lillian did start crying. "I wanted to take care of her but I didn't," she said in a wavery voice. "I'm so sorry."

She put her hand over her mouth and looked at me while tears ran down and over her hand and dripped onto her large bosom.

I was totally missing her point, but I squeezed her hand and said, "It's okay."

After a minute Uncle Nick helped her to her feet and we all stood. She hugged me sort of desperately and then Nick and I went out with her. Nick had a taxi waiting. I knew the driver and gave him a good tip to help the security guard at her building get her to her apartment.

As she was getting in she threw her arm around my neck and finally said what she'd come to say, whispering it harshly into my ear, "There was a big black smudge when she came back, on her shirt, her white shirt, over her nipple!" and then scrambled awkwardly into the cab. Nick and I watched them drive away. The sun was coming up, about halfway over the horizon.

He said, "She insisted on coming. Very much insisted."

I rubbed my ear, said, "It's fine. It *was* something I needed to know."

5

In the waiting room Dr. Maxwell had organized coffee and Philip set out a box he'd been holding. Cookies from Sofia. We sat around a low table and munched and sipped.

Maxwell swallowed his last bite and put down his cup. He sat back and said, "I realize I'm a stranger to you, so let me tell you in more detail why I'm here. I'm Chief of Psychiatry here at St. Ann's and my specialty is emergency psychiatric care. I'm often referred to as a trauma psychiatrist. Besides being on the staff here, I consult in many of the hospitals in the metro area." He leaned forward and poured himself more coffee. "St. Ann's is not large and Catherine Kamariotis and I have both worked here for several years, so we know each other fairly well and she can vouch for me."

He drank and continued. "Dr. Frank, who is for the moment Clare Russell's attending, asked me in to consult. I was already looking at the case, as department chief, but we had to go through the formalities, so we did. And I am now officially a part of the Care Team. Miss Russell, so far as we can see has no physical injuries, except some minor bruising on her arms. However, she has not regained her normal state of consciousness and the reason for that is not immediately apparent. That concerns us. In a case of this sort, there is almost always a psychiatric component. That's why I am here."

Uncle Nick refreshed the coffee cups and Maxwell took another cookie.

"These are delicious," he said.

Philip said, "My wife Sofia's."

Maxwell said, "Please thank her. I've read the chart and talked with Dr. Frank. Now, about authorizing her care. I've had several cases where there was no natural guardian available and she needs someone to look after her interests. We need to get a guardian appointed by a judge. The judges are often reluctant to appoint a member of the family, and anyway your standing as family is, in legal terms, nonexistent. But so is your standing as not family in what, social terms? You are just too close. You all have your own agenda." He took another cookie. "Is there any one else who could and would represent her interests? I believe we can get a judge to hear a petition yet today."

We all looked at each other.

I said, "Jim Cochran." Everyone looked at me. "He was her photography professor at the university. She lived for a few years with him and his wife. I'm sure they'd agree. They and Clare are quite close.

Maxwell said, "I suggest the hospital legal department contact Cochran and get the petition underway post haste."

Uncle Nick said, "Can we pay Clare's bills here whatever happens with the courts?"

Maxwell said, "I don't see any problem there."

Philip said, "Okay, Nick and I will go back to the office and get things rolling with the Cochrans and I think we'll get Tim Christides involved, as an observer at least."

Nick nodded, and said, "Family's attorney," to Maxwell.

Everyone stood and milled about and then Philip and Uncle Nick and Andy left. Catherine disappeared into the working part of the hospital. Maxwell and I looked at each other. I was blank.

"What now?" I asked.

He gave me an assessing look. "When did you eat last?"

I tried to think. "Yesterday. Lunch."

"I remember a breakfast some time back. I suggest we walk six blocks, for our health, to where there's a sign that says Rosie's—"

"Yes, Rosie's. I feel better already."

Rosie's was always crowded but no worries. There was a rear dining room that had no signs saying reserved but nevertheless seemed to feed only hospital people and their guests. I'd never eaten back there before. Ordering was fast, service was fast, the food was excellent, and we each drank a small glass of beer. A small beer or a small wine were the only alcohol allowed in that room, and only one of either to a customer. A basket of sourdough bread was sitting between us and was replenished twice during the meal. Just as we finished the lentil soup and I had drunk a tall oj, doctor's orders, there was a large Caesar salad to share and then two pieces of apple pie. We ate silently and hungrily. Maxwell signed the check and we were out, well-fed, in under an hour.

At the hospital Maxwell led the way to an office on the psych floor and pointed to a long couch with a folded blanket and a white-cased pillow in place.

He said, "While Clare's condition still warrants having you close, you may use this room, day and night. Bathroom over there, towels, extra blanket in there. If there's any change, you'll know immediately."

"Is she alone?"

"No, there's someone with her all the time."

I slept. I didn't think I would but I did, for almost four hours. When I woke up there it was late afternoon light coming through the window.

I looked around and found a cabinet with some giveaway toiletries and I was able to comb down my hair and brush my teeth. When I opened the door and stepped out into the corridor, I could smell coffee. I also damn near stepped on Tim Christides' toes.

We shook hands and patted shoulders and I invited him into my new lair. I had folded my blanket and put it and the pillow into the closet. Everything was neat and tidy. Now I opened a couple of drawers and found some yellow pads. On the top sheet of one I wrote "In cafeteria, Sam" and left it in the middle of the desk blotter. We stopped at the desk, got directions, and left messages as to our whereabouts.

We found the cafeteria, got coffee, and took a table in a corner.

Tim said, "I've just come from Family Court… Judge Winchell. He appointed James Cochran as Guardian ad litem for Clare Russell until such time as the judge deems her to be a fully functioning adult and vacates the order." He was carrying a leather portfolio and he took out several papers and handed them to me. "Copies for you, and a note from Dr. Cochran. He and several doctors and a social worker will be meeting tomorrow morning to discuss Clare's condition and treatment."

I said, "Will you be there?"

"I can be. Representing you or Clare?"

"Both?"

"No."

I said, "Clare, then."

He said, "I can do that with Jim Cochran's okay. He'll have to hire me on her behalf. I'll phone him. He can hire another attorney, you know. It's his decision."

I said, "Good. Fine. Bills to us. To Cy."

I saw Maxwell come through the door from the corridor and waved him over.

Tim said, "Do you need legal representation at this time?"

I said. "I don't know. The cops may think I shot Paul. They may think I killed some other people. They may think I knocked Clare around. All sorts of people may think all sorts of things."

He took out his wallet and extracted two cards from it. "If they start saying things like 'you're under arrest,' call one of these two guys."

I said, "I know them. Played with both of them."

He said, "Did you win?"

"Of course."

"Good. They can get something back in fees."

Maxwell reached us and sat and introduced himself to Tim, who told him the judge had signed the order.

Maxwell said good, excellent, and wrote down all of Jim Cochran's contact info from the copy of the paperwork that Tim had given me. They left but I stayed where I was, stifling the urge to go to a bar, thinking about Clare. My head was feeling like there was too much stuff in it. Finally, three nurses asked if they could use the other chairs at my table, and I apologized for taking up space and took Maxwell and Tim's cups to the conveyor belt along with mine.

6

I went back to the office he'd given me and sat in the desk chair. Sat and dozed. Waited, dozed, waited. Then Ford Maxwell returned and invited me into his office, down the same long corridor that Catherine and Clare had disappeared into.

"How is she?" I asked as we walked.

"Asleep. For at least eight hours."

"Is she still… gone?"

"Yes. She's unable to face it, whatever it is, so she shut down that part of her mind to protect herself. She needs to have that comfort for now."

"Comfort?"

"Hold that thought."

He ushered me into a large, pleasant office—not the usual bookish den-and-clubroom decor but instead pale, sturdy, wooden furniture with plump, green cushions, pale-green walls, and a large, dark-green rug—and sat with me, at the other end of a long couch.

I was starting to feel some bruises and stiff muscles, and I winced and grunted as I sat.

He noticed.

"Want some coffee? Cream? Sugar?"

I nodded. "That'd be great. Black."

He ordered it by phone.

I didn't want to ask but I had to. I asked, "Will she stay like this?"

"No. This is a temporary condition, if we treat it immediately."

Relief went through me so hard I shivered. "Is someone with her?"

"Yes, Catherine—Mrs. Kamariotis is there."

"I know who Catherine is."

"Yes." Maxwell paused, seemed for a moment to be deciding what to say, then said, "I would like it if we could keep someone with her for the next few days. I don't entirely know yet what her state of mind is."

"If you're talking about money, make whatever arrangements you want to make."

He said, "That's what, uh, Catherine said. Tell me about Clare."

"Aren't you supposed to ask her?"

"One, she's not available to answer, not yet, and the more I know before I talk to her, the faster I can get to what she needs to talk about. And two, this is not psychoanalysis. I'm proposing to treat a mental break, like I'd treat any other traumatic injury. I need to know who she is—her history—and what happened to her."

"Jesus. Where shall I start?"

"At the beginning. We have seven hours."

Another woman in a blue smock brought a tall thermal pot and two mugs. Maxwell thanked her and poured coffee.

I leaned forward, elbows on knees, holding the mug in both hands and warming them, letting the steam rise into my face, and thought about Clare.

"She's from San Diego. Came here when she was sixteen. She graduated early from high school and got an art scholarship to the university. She's a photographer and one of the professors here, James Cochran, fixed up the money. I didn't know her then. I was in prison." I looked at Maxwell, a challenge. The first of many, I figured. "For manslaughter."

Maxwell was unperturbed. "Tell me about her family."

"I don't know much, and I'm not sure she knows any more. She had a father who died when she was five, and a young mother who said good riddance when Clare left to come here. Irish both sides, I guess." I flexed my fingers, one hand at a time. The hot mug helped. "And she thinks her father had a brother in the Navy. I found that out today. Yesterday. Whenever. And that's all I know."

"No childhood memories she's shared with you?"

"One. Two. She was raped. Twice. I think she was maybe three the first time and fifteen the second."

"When did she tell you that? And why?"

I described the nightmare and the ride in the car, and then the conversation at the Stardust.

"She's never told you about friends or pets or places she went?" I shook my head. "Or high school? Boy friends? Was she sexually experienced when she left San Diego? Other than the rape?"

"I think... not. But she had some... experiences after she got here. Not many. I'd say fewer than ten. Most of them before I knew her. But then Harry and I started playing guard dog, and there was one I knew then. He bragged about it."

"How did you feel about that?"

"I decked him."

"Did she have other partners? And did you treat them the same way?"

"Yeah, I did, a couple. Till the word was out. Hands off."

He smiled. "Did she know that?"

"I don't know."

"How old was she when you first met her?"

"Twenty. But I thought she was younger. She was just a *girl*. She looked about fifteen. And more than just looks. She was so *innocent*. I'd seen her around. She worked in a coffeehouse near campus and we had mutual friends. One of them—Harry Parker—introduced us. Then we were at the same table in a bar and she started laughing at something I said, and that was it for me. Seriously."

"You wanted her? Sexually?"

"That and every other way." I drank coffee. "I wanted to own her. Protect her. Possess her."

"And you—did what?"

"Nothing."

"Nothing?"

"She was so young and so… breakable, and I was the next best thing to a street fighter. I had to back off. Wait."

Should I tell him about Harry and his guardian-angel plan? Well, yes, I should. I did.

"And you both felt bound to take care of her, you and your friend, and not advance on her sexually. How long did you wait?"

"Months. Most of a year."

Maxwell tilted his head, raised his eyebrows. In disbelief? "During which time you wanted her, sexually, and you were aware of it—"

"Aware?" I laughed. Ha. "Oh, yeah."

"And you didn't touch her?"

"Right. I didn't. Well, once. But I backed off when she pushed back."

"Did she know this, that you wanted her?"

"No. Yes. I don't know what she knew. About me."

He said, "You sound confused."

"She confused me."

"You were friends?"

"Close friends." I could hear the pain in my voice. Roughening it. "Most of her relationships didn't get as far as getting into bed. They were hardly even relationships. These guys I'm talking about were just chatting her up in the coffeehouse and getting shut down fast. She's not a prude, by any means, but… Harry once called her sexually fastidious." I cleared my throat. "For which I was… thankful." I put the empty cup on the tray and leaned back, flexing my fingers. "She didn't always have very good judgment. She could have had lots of guys who were far better choices than the ones she made."

"You were in her life for a year? Was she seeing a lot of men?"

"No. Just them trying to see her."

Time to tell him about O'Connell.

I said, "Is this talk privileged?"

"Technically, no. But I will hold confidential anything you tell me."

"Even about a crime?"

He hesitated, then said, "Yes."

I told him about O'Connell. The Irishman that Harry and I took out of her life. Now a bog man.

"She stayed fully aware?" he asked. "No breaks with reality?"

"Right. None."

"Your friend Harry's cleansing ceremony was a brilliant idea."

"Yeah." I smiled. "He said better than hypnosis."

Maxwell laughed softly.

"Her other partners or potential partners. What was wrong with them?"

"They were losers. Drunks, some of them, but mostly just losers. One was a junkie. I'm not sure Clare knew that."

"But you did."

"I made sure I knew."

"But you didn't tell her."

"I knew a lot about her that she didn't know I knew. But she didn't belong to me. She's an extremely private person. I couldn't hang out in her bedroom. And that was part of it for some of them— that they were man enough to challenge me." I had to take a deep breath. "There was no way I could win *that* game. But I had to know what was going on."

"And you think she didn't know what was going on. What you wanted."

"I know she didn't. Everything she thinks is on her face."

"But then you did become her lover." He paused. "Will you tell me how that happened?"

I stood up and moved around the room. "I tried leaving. I went to L.A., stayed for four months. But I kept thinking about her. All the time. And then she anted up." I told him about the text message and coming back to St. Paul. "She was right. Something was happening. But events were in motion before I got here." I told him about Gordy Terrell. "And now that I'd seen her again I couldn't wait any longer." I laughed. "So I courted her."

"You *courted* her."

"Uh huh. Dinner, dancing. And then…" I waved a hand. "New Year's Day."

"Did she say yes? Did you ask her?"

"Of course I asked her, and she said yes." A flash of anger. "I didn't rape her."

"Did you push her?"

"Only a little. Persuaded. Maybe 'coaxed. '"

"What would you have done if you'd finally asked and she had said definitely no?"

"I think I'd have walked away. Completely. No more half-measures. It would have been a close call. Even money."

"And you and she have a successful sex life? She enjoys it?"

"Yes." I cleared my throat again. "Yes, she does."

"Did she go to bed with you to keep you around?"

"No, just the opposite." I laughed. "I mean, she was afraid that becoming lovers would break up our friendship, but she did it anyway."

"And are you still friends?"

"Yes."

Maxwell yawned. "Tell me what happened tonight. This reaction of hers was sudden, just tonight, never before?"

"Right." I leaned against the desk, looked at the rug. "We went to bed, made love, early in the evening. I was planning to go out later."

"Without her?"

"A card game."

"Right."

"It was especially… pleasing. Exciting. Especially exciting. Afterward I talked to her about making her pregnant. She knows how much I want children. We talk about them, the babies. She told me she had stopped taking her pills a month ago because she decided it was time for her and that I had no right to tell her when. Well, maybe I'm oversimplifying that last part."

"How did you react?"

"I was fucking *furious*. But I was also incredibly turned on and we made love again."

"Did you hurt her? Were you rough?"

"No, damn it. I was making her pregnant, for the first time, for the first time ever for either of us. It was not rough. It was fantastic." I felt a little prickle of tired ill-humor. "I am not a caveman."

"No, you're not. You're a man of extraordinary self-control. But you live at the outer edge of being domesticated. You are—you have *been*—a very violent man."

I said, "Mrs. Kamariotis. She talks to you. Professionally?"

He grinned. "No, personally." He picked up the phone and asked for more coffee. "Then what happened?"

"We went to sleep, woke up about midnight. I decided not to go out. About half past twelve we went into the kitchen. Two men came in. She had her back to the door. I saw them, she didn't. One of them grabbed her from behind and tore off her pajama top, which was all she had on. The other one had a gun and getting myself shot was not going to help her. I had to wait."

"Would he have shot you?"

"There's a certain kind of face. The ones who have it shoot."

He nodded, but like he already knew, not like I was telling him anything he didn't. "Right. Go on."

"The one who had hold of her tried to drag her out of the room and she started to fight, like crazy. It surprised the hell out of me She got loose and ran into the other one which gave me a chance to jump him. I did and knocked her down in the process. The first one got his hands on her again and she went berserk. Then Andy dropped in unexpectedly and took over the shooter and I got my hands on the one who had hold of Clare."

"You tell this very clearly."

I asked, "If the cops ask you about tonight, will you talk to them?"

"This is not legally confidential, but I'll undertake to make it so. I believe it should be. In fact, if I identify myself as your doctor as well as Clare's, I will be legally bound to hold your communication confidential."

"Are you my doctor?"

"Yes." He grinned. "If you will accept this as family therapy. Otherwise it would be a conflict of interest."

"All right." I paused. "I killed him."

"In the heat of the moment?"

"It sort of turned out that way, but I knew what I was going to do, heat or not."

"And she saw you do it."

"Yes."

The coffee came and a plate of Oreo cookies, and I walked over to refill my cup. I took a couple of cookies.

I said, "And I turned around and she was gone. She said 'don't touch me' and that's all she's said since. Don't touch me. Sometimes she says please. And her face—there's nothing. I don't know if she knows who I am." My throat was getting tight but I held on.

"She was calm?"

"Oh God yes."

"Did she dress herself to come here?"

"No, she let me do it. I didn't touch her."

"She walked to the car?"

"Yes, and then I had to touch her. We didn't want her going crazy in the car. I put her on my lap, held her arms. She didn't like it. She *shook*, and she *begged* me." I turned away from him. After a while I said, "If I ever hear that again—*don't touch me*—God!" I turned back. "Was it what I did? The killing?"

"That put her into this state? I don't know." After a while he said, "If she is pregnant, it's perhaps just a matter of hours."

"She said it was today, that she gets a pain in her side."

He nodded. "Mittelschmerz. Some women get it at ovulation."

"She was talking about it, being pregnant, when that gorilla grabbed her."

Maxwell nodded. "I assume you want to know what I plan to do. For her."

"Yes, I do."

"She seems to trust Catherine. I can use that. I'll use hypnosis. I think it wasn't just the trauma of being attacked and watching you kill her attacker. You say that she fought and that you were surprised."

"She did. She went wild, and I was amazed."

"I think two things about that. I think it was at least partly because she believed she was vulnerable, reproductively, and partly because it reminded her of something."

"Something in her past."

"Yes."

"When she was raped?"

"Maybe. She had told you about that, dealt with it to some extent. Do you know if she ever had any rape counseling?"

"No, I don't, but my guess is not. She really is intensely private."

"To be reminded of it in such a way would be horrifying for her, of course, but my hunch is that there's more going on than that. However, all these possibilities need to be brought out for her, *with* her, carefully, in a controlled environment, so she can deal with them. And it needs to be done soon. I'll be working with her very intensively for a few days."

"Whatever she needs. And money is not a problem."

"Good." He stood up and hesitated. "I know you want to see her, but I don't know when you can."

"Could I just look at her?"

"If she's asleep."

Maxwell led me a short way down the corridor, past a nurses' desk and dark patient rooms, to a door at the end. He opened it slowly. The room was dim but not dark. Maxwell stepped in, then held the door open and beckoned to me.

Clare was asleep in a hospital bed, curled up on her side as usual. She looked completely normal. Catherine was in a chair across the room with a tiny reading lamp next to her and a book in her hands. She stood up, walked over, and put her hand on my arm and squeezed. I took her hand and held it. Maxwell watched us intently. I took a long look at Clare, then left the room. Maxwell followed me.

"I'll need to talk to you again," he told me as we walked back down the corridor. "After I've had a session with Clare. You call her Clare? Does she ever use the name Frances?"

"She uses it professionally. I only call her Frances when I'm being hard on her. Everyone calls her Clare."

"I should know by noon when I'll want to see you. Call me." He fished a card out of his breast pocket and gave it to me. "I'll be here in the hospital. If I'm not in my office, they'll page me."

Saturday, May 12

1

I went out of the hospital building. It was dark. I wondered what time it was and what day. I was almost too tired to care.

I took a cab to the ratty duplex. Standing on the porch I looked around, up and down the street, trying to look as if I weren't looking. I rang the bell and Andy let me in. He was fully dressed except for his shoes, but he'd obviously been asleep. The extra comforter and pillow from the closet were on the couch. We went into the kitchen. He had straightened up the disorder. I started to make coffee.

"Go back to sleep," I said. "I don't remember the day or date, but I did sleep in the recent past."

"I wondered what you were doing when Dickie and his friend arrived."

"Cutting oranges."

"Good thing you had your pants on. You didn't hear them come in?"

"I was distracted by my fiancée's legs. Good thing I didn't cut my thumb off."

"They got in pretty easy. I looked around. I think they used a blade to jimmy the lock on your front door. I could do it in twenty seconds."

"Okay, so I'm an idiot. I haven't had the security upgraded here. I should have had all the locks changed. I should put fucking bars on the fucking windows. Familiarity breeds carelessness. Did anyone come?"

"Yeah, they came, couple of hours after I got back here. They collected the garbage, hung around a while. There's still a car there and the alley's blocked off. I put the knife back in the kitchen. It's clean. I washed it good and bleached it and put it back by the oranges. Don't know if you actually want to use it." He picked up an orange and put it down again. "So you and Clare are making a baby." His tone was ever so slightly wistful.

"Maybe. It's still very much maybe."

"Do you think we've strung out adolescence long enough?"

"None of your cheap psychology. I've been talking to the real thing. And so by God has Catherine."

"Catherine's in therapy?"

"No, she's in something else, I'm not sure what, with Ford Maxwell. And I don't think it's just good friends."

"Good for Catherine."

"And I am now officially in family therapy with Clare. Takes care of the confidentiality issues."

"Will he rat us out if the cops come?"

"Nope." I said, and he laughed.

"About time you got into therapy. I guess you trust this guy."

"Catherine does. So do I."

We were silent for a while. The kettle whistled and I poured boiling water over the coffee grounds. I asked, "What happened to Dickie Jordan's gun?"

"Left it with him. Just pushed it out of my pocket and dropped it. Never touched it. Now that I think about it, I think we should get rid of that knife. And that towel. I'll do that today. And my shirt. And maybe even my pants and shoes. They can find DNA in the damnedest places. I'll take care of it. This Ford Maxwell. Is he okay?"

"I think so."

He said, "I'll check him out."

"Do that. But don't let Catherine know. Are you going back to sleep?"

"Hell, no, I slept for over an hour. I can take it. I'm tough." He found a coffee cup. "So what shall we do with this bright morning?"

I looked at the kitchen clock. Six-forty. Well, it would be bright soon enough.

I said, "I want a shower, then we can stop at your place—I want that shirt back, by the way—then we can check up on Pete and Mike and the kids. I guess we'd better put at least Stephen in the picture."

We went into the dining room to sit at the table. The room was still in shadow except for one narrow bright beam coming in from a front window.

He said, "And Ioulia and Thomas, or you'll worry Thomas to death."

"Well, a suitably censored version, then."

I set down my cup. My hands had started to shake and tears started coming and I couldn't stop them. Andy moved his chair next to mine and put his arms around me. I leaned into him and kept on weeping.

Finally I was able to say, "Right in front of her!"

He said, "Doesn't matter where it was. Doesn't even matter why. What matters is you did it."

"Killed him."

"Yes, killed him. That's what you deal with. And she deals with her part."

He held me until the tears stopped.

Before we left, I bundled all of Clare's jewelry, plastic and pearls, into a little leather purse sort of thing she had, and stuck it in my jacket pocket. Then I rifled her shoulder bag for phone, keys, wallet, and checkbook. Her wallet contained driver's license, library card, three dollars, and photographs of me and Thomas, both separately and together, and one of me and Andy. I took her address and appointment books from her desk, and at Catherine's I put everything in my safe except the books and her keys. I kept her keys to use and told Andy to keep my house keys for now.

As we were leaving, he said, "For what it's worth, it was the right thing to do."

I said, "And Dickie Jordan? Are you okay?"

His face was tight. "That one was different," he said.

I opened my mouth, then shut it again. Maybe later. Maybe ask Uncle Nick to talk to him. Andy had always been special to him.

2

At noon we were back at the ratty duplex in our living room. Philip and Andy were on the couch, Uncle Nick was in one armchair, and I was in the other. Earlier I had given Thomas, Ioulia, and Stephen a truthful though very carefully expurgated explanation and now I had just finished giving Philip and Uncle Nick an equally truthful more complete story, but leaving out what had passed between me and Clare in bed.

Uncle Nick nodded. "Can I smoke?" he asked.

"Sure," I said.

He passed around his tin of little cigars and we all lit up.

I said, "Someday when you stop scaring her to death, and it occurs to her, she'll have you visit officially."

Uncle Nick smiled.

Philip asked, "Is she all right?"

"Damn, I have to call. Excuse me."

I went into the bedroom, called Maxwell, and agreed to meet him at four. Maxwell wouldn't say anything more than she was awake and better.

"Awake and better," I went back and told them. "And what about Kevvy Smith?"

Philip gestured. "We can't just let you go and tear him to little pieces, although that would be satisfying. Someone else even worse would take his place."

"Why does he insist on believing that we have any interest in his agenda? Or that we should be on it?"

"Dickie and I had a short conversation in the alley," Andy said. "Kevvy still thinks Black wants to move in here and he also thinks that you're on Black's team. Which I guess you are but not how Kevvy thinks you are. And he wants to push Black back to Chicago. Cutting you off from Black was going to be his first step. The attack on Clare was going to be a bargaining piece. How many times could Clare be raped before you said yes to Kevvy? And I hate to bring even worse news to the table, but Kevvy's going to start going after the rest of us."

I said, "I can't lock Clare up and I'm not anxious to leave town with her. And she'd never do that anyway. But Philip's right. There are two of his people that might take over from him if he goes down and they're even scummier than Kevvy. He at least keeps a certain amount of order."

Philip said, "Kevvy's been around a long time. I think he's getting tired and maybe a little scared. Maybe having trouble keeping a tight hold."

Andy nodded. "Yeah. I played with two guys last week who got chatty. There's more stirring than there should be. Guys telling him they're too busy to do a job for him. That sort of thing."

I took a deep breath and said, "Black."

They all looked at me, waiting for the rest. I said, "Kevvy thinks Black wants in here, let's get him in here. He takes out Kevvy and movesinto Kevvy's spot. He's not stupid, he has an organization, he'd probably leave us alone to run our business. And he'll keep the rest of them away from us."

"If we pay," Andy said.

Philip said, "We're going to pay someone. Do you want to put an ad on the Internet?"

Andy grinned. "Mob management dot com?"

"He knows us, who we are," said Uncle Nick. "You think we could work with him?"

I said, "Yeah. I think we could."

Uncle Nick sucked on his cigar. "Is Clare safe where she is?"

I said,"This morning I got the security people to send someone over."

"Will the hospital sit still for that?" Philip asked.

"They'll have to, or I'll move her. We can donate a fucking wing or something."

Philip smiled. "Well, maybe an x-ray machine."

Uncle Nick said, "Philip and I will go to Chicago to see Black. Sam can run things here. Leave Peter at Catherine's and Mike can stay with Sofia. Tell Lillian to get out now and take Andrea with her. Suggest we might call in the cops if she doesn't. She'll be scared enough to leave. Andonios can do that."

"Me?" Andy grinned. "What an insult. She'll be expecting at least Philip."

"You think she'll be expecting it?" Philip asked.

"The way Lillian's brain functions? Yes, I do."

"All the better," Uncle Nick said. "She'll have started packing."

I said, "Make sure you get Mama's jewelry. There'll be a list in the safe at the office. And get that damn gun." I turned to Philip. "Andy and I will stay here, in case Kevvy wants to find us. I don't want to be at Catherine's if he gets an idea in his head. And tell Black I want Kevvy."

Philip frowned. "That'd give Black one hell of a handle on you."

"I don't care. I want some satisfaction."

"The children will have to stay inside," Philip said.

"Yes. I don't like that part, but yes."

"And get the guard service beefed up a bit. Can you run the office for a few days?"

"Of course."

"Okay." Philip stood up. "Andy, call the airline. We should be able to get down there tonight. And call the Hilton there."

I said, "No, stay at the Clark. If Black's in Chicago, that's where he'll be. And it's very high-end."

"Okay, the Clark. Get a two-bedroom suite. Sam, you call Black first and set up a talk. May I see where Clare takes pictures?" he asked.

I took them all up and showed them the studio and workroom, and Uncle Nick examined at length the photographs she had hung about, nodding to himself. "If you could read faces like these do," he told me, "you'd never lose again."

As they were leaving I put my hand on Philip's arm and held him back to let Andy and Uncle Nick go down the stairs ahead of us.

I said, "Maggie Jenneky has become a menace, and you damn well better do something about it."

"You think she had something to do with Leo Graff setting you up for Black?"

"Maybe, but that's not what I'm talking about. She took Clare to lunch to tell her that I was a killer and that if Clare wanted to have a portrait business, to forget about marrying me. If Clare hadn't known about my record, Maggie was all too eager to tell her and there would have been hell to pay all around. As it is, trying to frighten Clare into choosing between me and her work is something I'll be happy to discuss with Maggie but I thought you might want first crack at it."

Philip was silent.

"So help me, Philip, I might do her permanent damage."

"All right. I'm sorry. I let my tongue go. I'll talk to her. You stay away. We have enough problems. It'll have to wait until I get back from Chicago, but I'll talk to her."

I said, "I'll count on it."

3

Maxwell was now in a lightweight dark suit and pale blue shirt, but no tie. The tie was a colorful blue and yellow pile of silk on his desk. We shook hands and Maxwell gestured in the direction of Clare's room down the corridor.

"I suppose you sent the guard?"

"Yeah. She won't have to know about it."

"Yes, she will, but not yet. Sit down." I sat on the couch and Maxwell opened a small refrigerator. "A beer? I have some Bell's."

"Excellent. Thanks."

He brought bottles and glasses on a cork-lined tray, set them on the low table in front of the couch, and sat down.

"I don't tell the hospital administration that I keep beer in my office," he said. "And they don't ask. So it's sort of legal. I spent two hours with Clare this morning and two more this afternoon." He opened both bottles and poured his own. I poured mine. He went on. "She's a very good subject, very trusting. Catherine stayed with us and that helped a lot. Clare held onto Catherine's hand through the whole interview." He leaned back and drank down half his glass of beer and sighed. "I'm getting too old for these all-night parties."

I grinned briefly.

"First we went over what happened last night. I had her start with when you and she arrived at her house. Do you still call it her house?"

"I guess we still do. Am I supposed to be hearing what she told you?"

"I have her permission to talk to you about what she tells me. She told me about your brother Paul, and your cousin Andy, and the young woman in the bar. The au pair. She told me how upset you were. 'Heartsick' was the word she used. Not a clinical term, but very descriptive."

I watched the wall opposite, in case it moved.

"She told me how the two of you made love and about your talk afterward."

"I hope Catherine was entertained."

Maxwell smiled. "She—Clare—said you made love again and went to sleep and woke up, all essentially as you told me. Then she was able to tell me most of what happened in the kitchen, though of course how she experienced it was a good deal different and more confused than what you saw."

I poured the rest of my beer into the glass and stared into it.

"She remembers the man with the gun fairly clearly and she was very frightened by his face. Then she remembered the hands of the man behind her. The look of his hands was very important. They were very hairy— heavy coarse black hair." I nodded. "And that was what set her off. She became very agitated and I had her stop talking about what happened in the kitchen. We talked about you for a while, and about your family, and about her work, and then I asked her whether she had been physically attacked before, and she told me about being raped when she was fifteen. As I thought, she had that moderately well sorted out. You played a crucial role in that because when she finally did tell someone about it, told you, you allowed her to be as hurt and frightened by it as she was. You didn't argue or suggest she had done anything wrong. That and the passage of time and the thinking she'd done about it over the years had let her move forward from that incident about as well as I would have expected without therapy. On the other hand much of her dealing has depended on not dealing. Stuffing it back into the dark."

I said, "Denial?"

"Of a kind. I think her memories are accurate, just enormously painful. And she can't deal with the traumatic events any further until she can acknowledge the pain and face it. And there are two major traumas to navigate and the pain from each gets mixed into the other."

"When she told me, I didn't ask for details. I was afraid to. But maybe I should have."

He finished his beer and held up the bottle and looked the question. I nodded and he got two more bottles from the little refrigerator.

"It's hard to say. Just telling you was somewhat therapeutic. More pushing from you might have had the opposite result. And you are not a therapist. That's not where your responsibilities lie." He drank some beer. "Then I took her back to the attack, but she got very distressed again, so I told her she could sleep some more but that we needed to think and talk about it again later. She agreed to that and I let her sleep until lunchtime."

I stood up and started walking around the room to stretch some muscles that were still stiff.

He said, "Catherine ate lunch with her and at one-thirty we started again. I got her into a deep trance very easily—she wants to do this—and she described, in detail, the rest of what she saw last night. She remembered almost everything and was able to talk about it, tell me about it, both when she was in the hypnotized state and after I brought her out of it. The last thing she remembers is you killing her attacker. But that wasn't what drove her to withdraw."

I stopped walking. "I was afraid it might have been what I did."

"No, it wasn't. She wanted you to hurt him, though she was ashamed of the satisfaction she felt when you did it. But she'd never seen anyone die before. She started crying when she talked about it."

I shook my head.

He said, "And she and I still need to talk about the Irishman."

He was silent then for a long time. He had a wall clock and I watched the second hand sweep the face three times.

He said, "After that she was able to remember what this man's hands reminded her of. I think it must have been rather near to the surface, for some reason, because ordinarily these memories—the ones that are this disturbing to the patient—can take days to emerge. I wonder whether she might have been about to remember without such a shocker of a reminder. Though that in itself would probably have precipitated some kind of psychiatric event." He leaned back and suddenly looked tired. "When you've been doing crisis intervention for a few years, you begin to believe you'll never be surprised or shocked or angry again. But then you are."

I leaned against the desk and listened.

He went on, "However, we've reached the limit of my narrative. I have now heard her story. If you're willing, and she is, I want you to hear it from her."

I said, "Of course I am. Anything. I told you. Whatever she needs."

"Yes, you did."

"Can I just ask—why?"

"Of course you can. My answer is this. You and Clare have what I would describe as a more than usually complex relationship. You have defined your role very clearly and definitively. No doubts, no uncertainties. She has not yet defined her own role with that same clarity. Moreover, you have very good boundaries. She does not, so you have extended yours to enclose her. The two of you are courting disaster."

I didn't say anything. I couldn't.

"She needs to find, within that relationship, her own autonomy. Her own boundaries. Her own clarity. Before it all goes nuclear. That means no hiding behind the past. No equivocations. No he-said-she-said."

"Right. When do we do this?"

"Now."

"Christ. You don't fuck around."

"No. It's best for her to get it done. It's out in the open and I don't want her reburying it before she tells you."

He stood and went to a closet in the corner and exchanged his suit coat for a long white lab coat, then went to his desk for a worn, black-bound notebook made fat and misshapen with sticky notes and miscellaneous pieces of paper between the pages and slipped it into his coat pocket.

He said, "But remembering everything with you in the same room may be too much for her to handle. If I ask you to leave, will you go?"

"Of course."

Maxwell grinned suddenly. "I wonder if there is ever any such thing as 'of course' where you're concerned. You're being extraordinarily open, transparent even, but I'm guessing it's very deliberate. That's what she needs right now, so that's what she gets." He stopped by the door. "I really shouldn't be on this case, you know, because I'm personally involved. I have every intention of marrying your sister."

"Mrs. Kamariotis," I said as blandly as I knew how.

He smiled. "Yes. So perhaps I should have referred Clare to someone else. But I knew something about both of you, and I couldn't resist taking you on. Besides, I'm the best." He opened the door. "Someone else might not pull it off and I will. And Catherine wanted me to take it, even after I explained the ethical considerations, which she already knew, of course, but I had to convince myself."

We walked down the corridor. "I told Catherine you spotted us last night. She said you'd have Andy checking me out by noon today."

"I told him to be tactful."

"I'll give you a copy of my vita," Maxwell said dryly.

"That should make it easier," I agreed.

A uniformed guard was just outside the door to Clare's room and Catherine got up from a chair by the bed when we entered.

"Jesus, Catherine," I said. "You're still here?"

"I'm leaving at eight." She patted my arm and smiled at Maxwell. "I'll be outside, Doctor," she said demurely. Christ. I'd never seen her demure before.

Maxwell stayed by the door as I went toward Clare. She was sitting up, cross-legged, in a hospital gown that was only slightly whiter than her face. She looked like she would spook if I moved too fast.

I sat down on the edge of her bed, very carefully.

"Hello there, cupcake," I said.

"Hi, Sam."

"Can I touch you now?"

"Oh, yes. Please do." Her voice sounded almost normal.

I took her face between my hands and kissed her. She turned her head to kiss the inside of my wrist.

"Are you angry?" she asked hesitantly.

"What for?" I let both hands slide down to her shoulders.

"About the baby."

"You know what I was angry about."

"What?"

"I didn't get to have my own way."

Some of the tension went out of her face. "Do you think we did it?"

"I gave it my all," I said, and she laughed shakily. I leaned over to mutter in her ear, "I won't be able to have sex again for a month. Can I hug you now?"

"Yes, please."

"God, you're so polite." I gathered her in close.

Behind me Maxwell said, "Clare, are you still willing to tell Sam what you and I talked about today?"

"Yes." She took a quick breath. "Yes, I am."

"Good. Start whenever you want."

I moved toward the foot of the bed and settled in against the footboard. Maxwell leaned, half sat, on the wide window ledge.

She started. "Do you remember the bad dream I told you about when we went out driving in the middle of the night and had breakfast in Hastings?"

"Of course I do."

"I told you that in the dream I was very little. Young. I told you that I was two. Maybe three."

I said, "Yes, you did." *That's still a baby!* I thought.

She nodded. "I didn't tell you some real things that happened that weren't part of the dream. They were real. And they were never part of the dream, but they were real life and they were connected." She took a deep breath. "Sometimes my mother would get angry at me and she would take me someplace, like a big store or a park, or the beach, and she would—she would—lose me. Leave me." She sucked in another breath. "And then later—hours, I think—sometimes it was after dark—she would come back and find me again. Sometimes she would hug and kiss me and say how worried she'd been, and other times she would say how bad I was and how good she was to find me, but if I was too bad she wouldn't come back. Sometimes there were lots of people and I would hide."

I said, "You don't like crowds."

"Right."

"Where was your father when this was going on?"

"I don't know. And I don't know how long this went on or how often she did it. But when I was still little—I think three—a man found me. He saw my mother doing it, watched her. Maybe he followed her. I don't know. He knew my name, but I don't think I'd ever seen him before. He took me to his house and kept me there. I don't know how long. But it was days, because sometimes it was dark and sometimes light out."

She had her eyes fastened on my face and mine were on hers and I couldn't look away.

She said, "He did—everything, and he hurt me a lot. Over and over. There was a lot of blood. I couldn't talk about it because I didn't know any of the words for what he did. And there wasn't anyone to tell anyway. Do I have to say now what he did?"

I said, "No. I know."

She nodded. "Then he took me home and stayed overnight in my mother's room. And the next day her face and arms were bruised and cut and—and bitten. What I remember after that is more—continuous. I was getting older, I suppose, and it was where I lived. Anyway, after that he came often, to spend the night with her. Usually he locked me in my room, but sometimes he made me come to bed with them. That was just for—for oral sex. If I had to pee when I was locked in my room, I just had to go on the floor. And in my clothes. I was afraid to take off my clothes. And I often had to wear those clothes then for several days. She made me. I smelled bad all the time. Other kids called me Stinky."

She stopped then, was silent.

Oh, Clare. I started to say, "That's—"

"I think my father was in nursing homes all that time. Maybe I saw him once or twice. I think I was almost five when the man stopped coming to our house. Just disappeared. Never came again. My mother stopped losing me. My father died. After that, whenever my mother went places, I had to stay home alone. Sometimes she cooked food. Sometimes she washed clothes. But by the time I was ten, I had to do those things for myself."

Another long silence.

She said, "The man had very hairy hands."

I tried to swallow but my mouth was too dry.

She said, "She didn't talk to me very often. But three or four times after he'd been there, to our house, she said 'This is all your fault.'And she hit me."

She started to cry.

4

Ford Maxwell went to the door, opened it, waved a hand, and Catherine came in. She went straight to the bed, put an arm around Clare, sat on the edge of the bed and let Clare cry into her shoulder. Maxwell gestured to me and we left the room. Neither of us spoke until we were back in his office and sitting on his long couch.

He said, "She couldn't bear to remember it last night, but his hands were there, real, undeniable, so she opted out to a place where she didn't have to remember. A place and time before it happened, I think. Except that if anyone touched her, she would remember. The danger was in being touched. And you, thank God, didn't throw your arms around her and say there, there."

"I wanted to." My voice was harsh, hoarse.

"Of course."

I stood and walked to the window, stared out into the park-like grounds of St. Ann's. I felt stiff and sore. "How did Clare ever manage to grow up at all? Let alone be who she is." I faced Maxwell again, leaning on the windowsill. "She's smart and funny and talented and she's sweet and loving." I folded my arms across my chest and clenched and unclenched my fists. "I told her once—Jesus, what an arrogant bastard I am! —I told her that Andy and I were survivors. But all we faced were the streets. In our gang—and our families—somebody fucked with us and they fucked with our brothers and cousins and friends. And Catherine was safe. Always out of bounds. Protected."

"Yes, I know."

I just breathed for a while, then asked, "How is she now?"

"I had her remember the whole story when she came out of the trance. That was very hard for her, extremely hard, but it's essential and it has to be done as soon as possible, before she can become entrenched in her hiding place. And she did it and came through it, and she's back in the same reality as the rest of us, as nearly as any of us can ever know that. She and I will have more sessions, both with and without hypnosis, and I'll use it to help her sleep as much as possible for a while. But I think the hardest part is done. I've arranged for private-duty nurses on all shifts for a few days. I don't want her to hurt herself. Has she ever tried to kill herself?"

"Kill? I don't know. A couple of days before Paul's funeral, she took some pills. And drank some beer. The doctor said fast-acting barbiturates. They let her go without admitting her."

"Can you tell me why she did that?"

"I can. I don't particularly want to." I stopped talking and Maxwell waited. "I bullied her in bed. I was feeling violently jealous, of Andy, and I wanted to have sex and she didn't."

"Were you physically violent?"

"No. Well, maybe. Maybe she saw it that way. I was not out of control but coming close." I dropped into a chair. "When I found her, late that night, and got her awake, she said—she *yelled*—that I used her in anger. That it was unnecessary and that all I had to do was ask her. And she couldn't work. She told me all this when she was crying . Maybe I didn't really understand all of it. Then she fell down the stairs."

"Did you push her?"

"No! No, I did not! She lost her balance. She hit her head. She was unconscious. I called 911 and they took her to County Medical. They wanted her to stay but she refused."

"A lot going on in her life lately."

"I suppose you already know about Paul."

"Yes. She's going off the scale on stress." He paused. "Is that the only time you've been violent? Toward her?"

"I grabbed her wrists once when I was mad at her. I didn't hurt her. Startled her, maybe. Startled both of us. Maybe I pulled her strings a bit."

"I expect you're good at that."

"Yeah."

"And it's tempting."

"Yes, but Clare—she'd be so hurt. And maybe so hurt that she'd never come back to me. I have to resist it. Control it."

"You seem to have seen from the beginning how easy it would be for you to hurt her. How necessary it is to use the control."

"No more necessary for me than for anyone else."

"Oh yes, it is, because you don't hide from yourself just how good you can be at hurting. How frightening. Knowing about it isn't a taboo for you the same way it is for most of us. Most of us control the violence by being afraid of it, denying it. For you it's just another tool."

I didn't know how to answer that.

5

We went back down the hall and Maxwell went into Clare's room. After a minute Catherine came out.

"What shall I call him?" I asked her.

"Call him Ford."

"He's good."

"He thinks you're good too."

"Has he met the children?"

"No. Tonight. We're taking them out for pizza. We decided it's time and we can't—meaning I can't—avoid it any longer now that you and Clare and Andy are in the mix."

"I talked to them about Clare this morning. I told them some, not all, of what happened. Will you check out Thomas for me? Until this situation is more settled, I don't want to go near your place. Maybe you could tell them again why I'm not there."

"I'll tell them and yes, I'll take a special look at him."

"Does it bother you that he adores Clare?" I asked, curious.

"No. Should it?"

"Some mothers would be jealous."

"I know who I am to Thomas. He adores you too. I hope he likes Ford. I hope they all like him."

"I think they will. You do. They'll worry about being disloyal to their father, but I expect Ford will know what to say."

Ford came out of Clare's room and we made a date for the next afternoon. He assured me that Clare was doing well, and I went back to Clare's. Andy came back from driving Philip and Uncle Nick to the airport, and we ordered a pizza and played gin. I won eighty bucks.

Sunday, May 13

1

Andy and I went to the office early. Friday and Saturday had been busy—baseball, soccer, and horseracing—and I spent the morning looking at the numbers and the receipts while Andy tallied bets, until I set him to postponing all the appointments in Clare's book and calling the ones she'd missed to spin them his sweet tales and apologize.

Midmorning I got a call from Karen. She jumped right in with, "I've been trying to call Clare and I think she forgot to charge up her phone or something. I want to get her to go to a movie tonight. That new chick flick that you and Harry disdained."

I said, "Didn't I tell you never to call here? How did you get this number?"

A moment of blank silence, then, "You idiot."

"Can you keep a confidence?"

"Not from Harry, but he's the only one."

"She's in the hospital."

"Did you beat her up?"

"Well, that was quick. You jump a conclusion well, lady. I read a novel about China and all the women were named after flowers. Henceforth you are Dillweed. No, I didn't beat her up. Maybe she can tell you about it someday, but she's flying incognito for now."

"What's wrong?"

"She had a little… psychotic episode."

"My God! Can't you tell me? No, you can't. Forgive my pushy-pig persona. My apologies and you may call me Dill. I can't visit her?"

"I don't think so. *I* can hardly even visit her. You can call St. Ann's, but I'm pretty sure they'll say no."

"Okay. I am now officially backing down. Hey, I'm sorry."

"Thanks. Say hey to Harry."

Andy finished with Clare's calls and started backtracking Ford Maxwell. For lunch we went to the gym for a short workout and then to a deli. After lunch Andy went to see Lillian, refusing my offer to go with him, and I went back to the office and called four doctors I had played cards with, one of them a psychiatrist, to ask about Ford Maxwell. Only one didn't know him, and the three who did, which included the psychiatrist, gave him very high marks. Then I tracked down Leo Graff, finally got him on the phone, and made a date for a drink that evening.

Andy and I connected again at a trendy little brew pub near the office.

"Well?" I asked. We were leaning on a corner of the bar, having a quick glass of ale, watching a tall dark-haired young woman in a skimpy summer dress make her way among the tables more slowly than was necessary.

"Just a minute," he said.

"Do you know her?"

"Slightly. Her name is Sue."

Andy got her attention and beckoned her over just as she was about to sit down at a table with three other young women, and I leaned on the bar on the other side of her and watched in the bar mirror, amused. Andy entangled her, giving her sips of his beer while he held the glass, moving her hair, facing her squarely and standing half again too close to her. I also watched the three other young women stare furtively at Sue and the fascinating strangers.

Finally Andy squeezed her knee gently and regretfully, brushed his lips across her cheek, and sent her on her way, reeling and swooning, as deftly as he had taken her in.

"Well?" I asked again.

"Lillian, Andrea, and Nicky leave tomorrow, by limo and driver, sent for her by her father. She's angry but she's also scared, I'm not exactly sure who of. You, I think. I don't know why. Far as I know you've never knocked a woman around. Maybe it's the cops. I told her we weren't telling them what Andrea said, but hell, she knew that without my saying so. Anyway, they're leaving. I feel sorry for Nicky. He's a sweet little guy."

"Yeah. Maybe she'll let him visit."

"Lillian didn't make any confessions, but she didn't make any denials, either. Losing the money was a blow, I could tell, but she took it like a man. I got the jewelry and the gun and left all of it in the safe at the office."

"And do you have a date with Andrea tonight?"

"You know me too well."

"You're getting set in your ways. Probably an age thing. We see Leo at nine. I'm going to the hospital first."

"Where shall I meet you?"

"Carson's. In the bar."

2

Ford Maxwell was in his office when I knocked on the open door, and he waved me in.

"A beer?" he offered, and I accepted and we sat on the couch. The office was cool and lit only by the late sun through the blinds, making stripes across the room. There were no diplomas on the walls but there were three traditional Chinese prints that I'd been admiring.

"How is she?" I asked.

"Jumpy, tired, sad."

"Why?"

"Well, she's tired because she's been working very hard here, confronting this horror. She's jumpy because she's afraid of being ambushed by herself again, and she's sad because she's grieving over the harm done to that little child who was Clare. She's also angry at the people who hurt her and frightened by who she is and worried about whether she has to change and how to accomplish that and wondering where she stands with you and what she did as a two-year-old to deserve what happened. And she's afraid that she's fatally flawed and that there must be something wrong with her relationship with you because of that flawed nature and maybe something wrong with you, both because you want her and because she wants you."

"Jesus H. Christ. How many years is this going to take?"

He laughed softly. "Many of these cases we treat with an initial period of heavy sedation to provide a period of relief from the pain and an opportunity for the healing to begin. With Clare I'm attempting the same thing with hypnosis, and it's working, but of course the physical effects of hypnosis are not the same as those of drug therapy and I think it's harder on her. Her brain is more active when she's asleep and so she's working harder. On the other hand, the work she's doing seems to be unusually productive. Whether or not that's true will become apparent in a few days. All in all I'm pleased so far."

I was thinking maybe my idea of taking her away someplace was not such a bad one.

He said, "And you can't do any of this for her or protect her from any of it. If you tried it would be very bad for her and you wouldn't succeed."

"You know just where to hit, don't you?"

"Yes, I hope so. It's my business."

"I want to take her away from this."

"And she'll want you to and she'll be angry when you refuse. And you have to absolutely refuse, no wishy-washy stuff, no evasions."

I said, "I don't do wishy-washy."

"Just be natural."

"Is there anything I can do for her?"

"Just the usual. Except, of course, the usual."

"It's not easy to see her in a bed and not be able to join her."

"I imagine so. Today we talked about the fact that she was entirely blameless in all that happened to her as a child. The mother, of course, blamed her for attracting the abuser and bringing him home, and Clare, of course, believed every word of that and still does."

I got up and walked to the window, pushed apart two slats of the blind to peer out, turned away, and walked back.

He said, "This afternoon we talked about her childhood. She doesn't remember much about it. It's not just not wanting to talk about it—she's erased a lot of it from the places that would ordinarily be accessible to her. Some of it can be gotten at through hypnosis, some of it may actually be gone. And she's very resistant to digging in it. She says, 'That child is dead.'"

I said, "Once we found a photo album that she had from her childhood, and there was a picture of her as a baby and she called herself 'their baby.' I didn't think anything of it at the time. And she only let me see a few pages."

"Can you find it, bring it here?"

"If she tells me it's okay." I thought for a minute, about what I was doing there. "You're letting me pretty far into stuff that she's kept private for a long time. And I've told you things that were just between the two of us and I didn't ask her permission."

"And you think you've betrayed her?"

"Maybe. I don't know."

Ford reached up to turn on a floor lamp. "Being a doctor involves hurting people, betraying their secrets, invading their privacy, humiliating them in their nakedness — all in the name of curing them. We get used to it."

"I'm not her doctor and I don't want to be. I don't want that kind of advantage over her."

"Yes, I can see that."

"I want to talk to her. Now."

"All right." We went to the door and Maxwell stopped with his hand on the knob. "Are you planning to ask her permission?"

"I don't have a plan. I just want to see her, talk to her, touch her if I can. Talking about her here in this room, I lose her."

There was a nurse with Clare, and Maxwell asked her to wait outside. Clare was leaning against her pillows, a magazine face down on her lap, and she didn't move when we came in, but when I took her hand from the bed she gripped my fingers hard. I sat on the bed, put my other hand behind her shoulders, and pulled her up to be kissed. I kissed her for a long time and felt some of her stiffness ease.

"Can we be alone?" I asked without turning, and Ford said, "Ten minutes," and left the room.

She said, "Okay, Sam, you brought me here, now take me home."

I laughed and put both arms around her and pulled her close. "Don't be silly. Time to play the hand out."

"I hate this."

"I know, but it'll be better for you later."

"I was fine, everything was fine. You had to change everything."

I let go of her, pushed her back onto the pillow, and glared down at her. "Oh, drunks who hit you was fine? Being afraid of your own fucking shadow was fine? And I forced my way into your bed and ruined everything. Can we at least stick to the truth here? And don't for God's sake start crying or Maxwell will have my head."

"I'm sorry." She turned her face away. "You're right. I'm wrong, I'm wrong."

"No. You're not." I took a hard hold on my temper. After a few moments I said, "Shall we start over?"

"Okay." Still not looking at me.

"Hi, Clare."

"Hi, Sam."

"I've been thinking about Christos. The traditional method is to name the child for the grandfather. My father's name was Christos."

"You want me to stay here for little Christos' sake." She sat up and wrapped her arms around my waist. "You're afraid I won't be a good mother."

"Damn it, Clare, cut the hysteria. That's not what I think at all. This is for *your* sake."

"It hurts."

I said, "Yeah. But it's also healing."

"You won't take me home?"

"No."

She said, "I could just go home by myself."

"You could."

She sighed. Resignation. "You have always been such a rat."

"But, as rats go, a great rat, right?"

"Well, Mr. Rat, you could bring me some things. I'm here with nothing but old magazines from the nurses' lounge and a novel that Catherine lent me."

"What do you want?"

"My point-and-shoot that's on my desk. And be sure it has a card in it."

"How do I do that?"

She sighed again. Exasperation. "Just bring it. And some books. Two or three books."

"Any books? M, N, and O of the Britannica?"

"I finished the Britannica. Just check that towering stack next to my side of the bed."

"By the way, are you baptized?"

"I don't know."

"Father Elias will not be pleased. I had better go talk to him and find out what you need by way of documentation. You people in the art game call it provenance."

"I need papers to marry you? Just tell him I'm pregnant and we have to get married."

"Good idea, why didn't I think of that?" I rubbed her back. "I've been talking a lot to Maxwell."

"Telling him secrets?"

"I don't know. Some things that were just ours. But I don't know if they were secrets." I was rocking slightly from side to side with her and she was relaxing against me. "He knows what he's doing. He's very good. And what I've told him has been useful, I think."

"Mmm."

"So I want to keep talking to him. For you. How do you feel about that?"

"If you want to."

I wondered if she was falling asleep. Her voice was muzzy.

"Can I show him the old photo album in your little trunk?"

"No."

"No?"

"No."

"Can I bring it here for you to show him if you change your mind?"

"Someone might see it."

"I'll wrap it up with sealing wax and string and seal it with my signet ring."

"You don't have a signet ring."

"A lot you know. It's very old and has a quite beautiful alpha on it."

"Why don't you wear it?"

"I don't wear rings."

"Does this mean you won't wear a wedding ring?"

"I'll have to think about it." Behind me I heard Ford come into the room. "I have to go, Clare."

"I hate sleeping without you."

"I know. Same here." She looked up at me. I said, "Shut those eyes or I won't be able to walk out of here." She shut them, squinched them tight. I said, "I'll see you tomorrow."

3

Ford said, "Cup of off-duty coffee in the cafeteria? Just us guys?"

I said sure.

We sat alone at a small table in the corner and Ford said, "It's interesting how many women watch you. And I know some of these women to be happily married."

I grinned at him. "Not always a reliable criterion," I said.

"True. So—" He cleared his throat. "I met the children last night."

"Oh man, I wish I'd been there."

"Ioulia was very cool, very like her mother."

"All a ruse," I said.

"Stephen was very correct."

"*Noblesse oblige*. And he's very shy. It's easier for him just to follow all the rules."

"You're stealing all my best lines. Then, Thomas. How can I describe Thomas? He was very challenging. He wanted to know about Aunt Clare and I think I told him more than I meant to."

I was grinning happily.

"And I promised he could see her soon, though I'm hoping he won't be too aggressive about how soon. And after he had established his rights and prerogatives with regard to Aunt Clare, he recited several lines of the Iliad in Classical Greek. He told me he's learning it on his own from a book."

I was laughing. "I believe him. I can't wait to hear his description of this meeting."

"They were very close to their father, weren't they?"

I said, "Yes, very. Of course. But—they know that they can love and be loved by more than one person. Thomas adores Clare, but I think he'll be able to love Clare's babies without feeling any doubt about his place in Clare's affections. And mine. There's always enough love to go around and then some." I drank coffee, swirled the liquid in the cup. "It hasn't been easy for Clare to deal with being so suddenly and totally loved. Of course, they wouldn't love her if she weren't lovable. They would accept her, for me, but... but maybe she never knew how lovable she is." I moved restlessly.

He said, "I'm keeping you from something."

"Not yet. Sorry." I paused. "I thought she knew. Maybe I was wrong." I cleared my throat. "I've never told her that I love her."

Ford said, "Intriguing."

"I *do* love her."

"Yes, I know."

"But does *she* know? My experience in love is from my family. But she doesn't have any family. So it took me a while to figure out that she has none of that experience. So does she *feel* love? I mean, *being* loved?"

He smiled. "I think she's learning. It's really hard to know the answers to these questions until she basically tells you the answers. And she won't know that until she knows and trusts the answers herself."

I asked, "How long will she be here?"

"Maybe a week. But it could easily be more or less."

"What will she be like?" I asked. "That's hardly her in that room. She's always been afraid, but she's always been... brave. She's had fight... spirit... guts. You call it. But today I yelled at her and she fell apart. Will she be the same?" I looked at him. "I wish I could kill that bastard *again*."

Maxwell sat solidly, calmly, in his chair and drank his coffee. "She'll be back. You're asking her to walk on a broken leg. Yes, she'll have a scar, but it will be a scar, not a gangrenous wound sapping her strength from the inside. Sorry about the metaphors. Some things might be different—you'll never be the same again, either, after that night." He paused. "You want to know about sex with her. It may be hard for her for awhile, but you have a tremendous home-court advantage here. She loves you so much. Damn it, Sam, I'm a jaded fifty-year-old trauma psychiatrist and it stops me in my tracks. She must glow in the fucking dark."

My eyes went shut for the length of a blown-out breath.

He said, "I think she'll give as good as she gets, in bed or out, same as before. My guess is she never allowed any oral sex."

I nodded stiffly. I felt hot.

"I don't suppose she ever will. But you can live with that."

"Of course I can live with that. I just hate any barriers or hesitations between us."

"Just think of it as hurting her, which it would, if she did it for you, which she might, if you pushed her."

"When can I see her again?"

"Tomorrow evening. Can you see me at six? Then you can see her after we talk."

"For more than ten minutes? This is driving me crazy."

"Half an hour."

"I need her. She needs me. You don't know."

"Oh, I do. But she needs every minute of good sleep I can get for her and she needs not to be distracted, even by you."

I blew out a breath. "Play the hand," I said.

4

Andy was in a booth in the bar at Carson's when I got there. He already had a beer and I got one on my way through.

"How is she?" he asked.

"Better. Hurting. Wanting out." I slumped against the back of the booth and looked darkly at Andy. "Leo Graff thinks he can walk in and out of this game and not even have to wipe his feet."

"And you want to prove him wrong?"

"Yes. I'm looking for someone to hit. Hard."

He said, "You know, I'm all for doing society the occasional favor and all, and doing the honorable thing, of course, but maybe you shouldn't let this become a habit. You aren't Captain Marvel, you know."

I said, "I am too."

"And you could get caught."

A pause. A silence. A drink of beer.

I said, "I'll think it over."

"Yes, do that. You in prison would not be good for Clare at all, although I promise you, I would see that she lacked for nothing. And beating up Leo in the alley would probably be risky. He's the type who complains and gets listened to."

I said, "You're taking all the fun out of it."

"I know this is something of a role reversal here, but I don't like the look in your eye. I think you should pull up a bit."

"Here he comes."

Leo Graff was a few years older than his brother, the late Bobby, suaver but just as poisonous. He looked around, found us, and walked over to stand by our booth and drop an envelope on the table in front of Andy.

He said, "You left rather suddenly the other night. I cashed you out." He laughed. "No fee."

Andy opened the envelope, flipped casually through the money inside, and stuffed it in his pocket. "Thanks. Join us." He moved toward the wall.

Graff sat down. "Sam. You said you wanted to talk about something." A waiter appeared and he ordered a scotch and water. "What about?"

"Kevin Smith," I said casually.

Graff looked startled.

I said, "I don't know what the fuck you and Kev are to each other, but you helped him set up Clare Russell the other night."

Graff said nothing.

I leaned forward on my elbows. "Luckily for Clare, I was there and Andy showed up to help save the day. Even so, she's in the hospital."

Andy brought out two cigars and handed one to me.

"I hear he lost two men," I went on, "but that's okay, because he won't need them. He won't need anyone, will he, Andy?"

"No, indeed." Andy lit his cigar.

I said, "Kevvy's going down."

"Is that so?" said Graff.

"You have my word on it," I said. I lit my cigar. "So maybe you should send Clare a get-well card. You might need a friend."

Andy blew three perfect concentric smoke rings.

Graff said, "What the hell does that mean?"

"It means that Kevvy's going to pay for what happened, but far as I know, you just answer the phone, so you get to stay in one piece this time. However, Clare Russell and everyone else in my family are forever off limits to you. If you come *near* any of us again, certain rumors will start making the rounds. Stick to selling condos."

Graff looked irritated. "Zandros, you are just a small-time card player. I could lock you out of this town."

"Really?" I grinned. "What're the odds, Andy?"

Andy shook his head. "Jesus. A thousand to one easy. Maybe more. Not my kind of bet. Too easy."

I stood up and Graff stood and moved aside to let Andy out of the booth.

"I can understand that you're upset, Sam," said Graff. "I'll try to keep that in mind and forget about these threats. Stick to poker."

I put my cigar between my teeth, and stuck my hands in front of Graff's face, palms out. "These hands aren't clean, Leo. And they say each one gets easier." I grinned around my cigar and Graff looked away.

"Good luck, Leo," said Andy.

He and I left the bar and began walking. "Want a ride?" he asked.

I said, "No, I need to walk. I'm going to the Stardust. What about you?"

"A dalliance with Andrea. I'll drop by the Stardust later."

"That's not a dalliance, that's a quick trick."

"Leave me alone, Sam. Except for this temporary setback, you have your sweet Clare in your bed every night. Kori won't budge until we're married, and she won't get married until her mama says it's okay, and all I have are whatever quick tricks I can scrape up. Andrea's not sweet, but she's round and very willing."

"Do you want me to talk to Kori?"

"And say what? No. Here's my car."

5

I found a game at the Stardust and played silently, breaking even. Andy showed up shortly before closing and drank a beer but didn't play. He said, "I see you're channeling Heathcliff tonight," and made me laugh. We left in Andy's car, parked two blocks from Clare's apartment, and walked silently down the alleys to stand in the shadows between two houses across the street from hers.

"In the car by the tree," Andy murmured after a couple of minutes.

"Uh huh."

"He's alone."

"Let's check out the back."

We went back to the alley and walked to the end of the block. The superette was still open and we went in. I greeted Mr. Salmon, and we went to the back of the store and out the back door. Andy flipped off the outside light as we went out, and the alley was dark. We drifted carefully up the block toward Clare's. Finally Andy put his hand on my arm and we stopped and I saw a vague figure on the back porch of Clare's house. Andy had cat's eyes. We stepped closer to a garage and waited. After ten minutes, the car that had been in the street drove down the alley, collected the watcher from the back porch, and drove away.

"Cops?" Andy said.

"Doubt it. Why would they? They're done here."

"Who, then?"

"Somebody's been keeping tabs on Clare. Don't know who."

"That's why we've become alley crawlers?"

"Uh huh."

"Does she know? Have you told her?"

"She told me. She saw them outside the Stardust."

He laughed.

We walked back down the alley, around the end of the block, and up the sidewalk to the front of the house. The street was quiet, dark, and empty. We let ourselves in, stood for a moment in the hall, went into the apartment, and stood just inside the doorway. Satisfied, we turned on the lights and looked through all the rooms and closets, including upstairs. We ended up in the downstairs kitchen and I opened the refrigerator.

I said, "Beer?"

"Sure."

"Was I too forthcoming with Leo?" I asked.

"It's a thought."

I leaned on the counter and wanted Clare. Felt the wanting move through me and threaten to steal my breath. "Have you been blabbing to Andrea about what happened? She could possibly put one and one together, if not two and two."

"No, I have not. My entire conversation with her has consisted of take off your clothes and the usual endearments with which I won't bore you."

"They leave tomorrow?"

"Yes."

"Good." I poured the last of my beer into the sink and ran the cold water. "I'm tired. I'm going to call Philip in the morning and get the news."

Clare's pillow still smelled faintly of her cologne and I held onto it all night.

Monday, May 14

1

I called Philip in Chicago and he told me that they had made a deal. Black was furious about the attack on Clare and sent her his regards and best wishes and I was to call him if she needed anything he could help with, anything at all. I raised my eyebrows.

Philip said, "Maybe I'm wrong about Black, but I think he is strongly pissed off about more than Clare. Someone else is reading his playbook. And maybe he's feeling a little guilty about Clare."

Then I called Black. I asked, "Do you have a plan?"

He paused, then said, "Philip, Nick, Cy by phone, and Carl and I have made a list. Top twenty-four in Kevin Smith's outfit. Of that list, count off nine. Then ten through twenty-four are offered the option of leaving town within forty-eight hours. After which they are prey. Most of them will leave."

I said, "And one through nine?"

"We discussed them and decided four of them are perhaps open to conversion and smart enough to work for me. So Carl and two others who I employ will see those four, separately, and offer a job. Probationary. In Chicago."

I said, "That's not a job, that's a sentence."

He laughed softly. "That leaves five. Smith, Davey Glenn, Leo Graff, Art Murphy, Brian Smith. They go."

I said, "Go."

"Yes."

"Can I put in a clemency plea for Davey Glenn?"

A long pause.

He said, "I'll talk it over with the others."

Another pause.

I said, "I want in."

He said, "The reason we have entered into this agreement is because Zandros brothers doesn't have the resources that I have to handle problems like Kev Smith."

"I'm talking about being a part of *your* resources."

"Can you take orders?"

"Depends on who gives them."

He laughed. "Philip will tell you what we decide."

2

Philip called me. "Black told us about your phone call."

"And did you approve my application?"

"Yes. Are you at the hospital?"

"Yeah."

"Come over to the office for an hour."

"You there clearing up the mess Andy and I made?"

"There were two paper clips out of alignment."

3

Andy and I dropped off books and camera for Clare, then spent the morning at the office and the afternoon at the gym, where we got in the ring and sparred three rounds. We were pretty evenly matched but Andy went down once and ended up with a sore jaw. We went to the Stardust for an early supper or late lunch. Then Andy went to see that Lillian had indeed left. He came to the office and told me that four guys with very big muscles were there packing all their stuff and putting it into an unmarked moving van. The foreman was very cordial. Lillian, Andrea, and Nicky were gone. I went to the hospital.

Catherine was drinking coffee with Ford when I went into his office. She stood up to put her hand around my wrist and squeeze it. "I just saw her," she said. "She's taking pictures of everyone and it's become a status symbol. She's doing so well. She asked me when she could know for sure about being pregnant and I told her she would have to be patient another two or three weeks."

"Be patient, be patient. That's all I hear around this place."

"And you just want to hit someone. You're all in a knot. Go to the gym and get a massage."

"I've been to the gym. I knocked Andy down, but it didn't help much."

Ford put his arm around Catherine's shoulders. "Pick me up at six-thirty," he said. "Out front."

She nodded and patted my arm and went out the door in her quick way.

"We're taking the children to a movie," Ford said. "I'm on the campaign trail."

"Running for stepfather?"

"Yes. Sit down. I'm out of beer but I've ordered more coffee." He looked at the paper-wrapped package I was holding. "A present for Clare?"

"Her photo album. The one I mentioned. But you can't have it. I told her I'd give it to her and she can decide whether to let you see it." I set it on the coffee table. "How is she?"

"Better. Working hard. We spent five hours together today."

The coffee tray arrived and I took my cup to the window and leaned on the sill.

He said, "She told me that she's been getting more and more frightened in the past few weeks."

I thought about it. "Longer than that. Maybe she didn't notice. Her crowd phobia's been getting worse for several months. But maybe she's right. The last few weeks there's been something new. She's afraid to be alone at night. She used to want to have a lot of time alone. She always seemed to need it."

He said, "She may have always been afraid, but her stronger fear, of people, overrode it. With you taking on this new role in her life, helping her to deal with people, shielding her from many of them, all her feelings have been working, after some years of being stabilized, and perhaps that let the other fear start to show itself."

I was staring at the wall.

He went on. "She's bullied herself into handling crowds, to some extent, but now she needs to figure out some new mechanisms for being alone."

"I'm gone at night a lot. I always will be."

"I think she'll figure it out. She has, obviously, some very good coping mechanisms. And with you around, she can be safe while she figures it out."

"If I have my way, she'll never be unsafe again."

"Yes, I know."

"You think I can't do it."

"It's true, I used to think that sort of thing, before I knew you. I thought Catherine was exaggerating. In another time I would have had to turn you over to the local Inquisition."

I said, "In another time you would have *been* the local Inquisition."

He said, "History was your subject, wasn't it?"

"Uh huh."

"Did you have a specialty?"

"If I'd gone on for the doctorate it would have been the Medieval Byzantine Empire."

He said, "You could have stayed in the academic life."

"Too much like a harness. And very little action."

"You could go back to it. Your motivations will have changed somewhat. It would give Clare a lot more security."

I said, "I'll give her security."

"You'll surround her, all by yourself, and keep all the hobgoblins and troglodytes at bay."

"Exactly." I smiled. "You still think I can't do it."

"I'm skeptical."

"So when are you going to do the honorable thing by my sister?"

"She only just allowed me to meet the children, and I'd like their approval. Why the hurry?"

I straightened from the windowsill and stretched my back. "Catherine. She was twenty when our mother died. Then she became the mother—mine and Andy's. Philip and Paul were older. She went through nursing school and met Stephanios and they loved each other, but they had all the usual hard times. She wasn't resigned to his being a gambler. Three children and then he's in prison and then suddenly he's gone, dead. And she's still the one we all go to. She'll never want for anything, and we all love her and she knows it, but who does *she* go to?" I turned to the window and looked down on the lawns and terraces of the hospital. "I want to take Clare outside, just on the grounds. Will you allow it?"

"Sure. Can I tell Catherine what you said?"

"If you think it'll help. Do you sleep with her?" I turned around and caught Ford flushing red and laughed. "What I'm really wondering is how? When and where?"

"We, ah, skip lunch a lot. My apartment is near here. And we both have rather irregular hours. Perhaps we could get back to business here?"

"You have a very narrow outlook. All right. Clare. God, Clare. I want her back."

"You'll get her. Soon. And she may start talking to you about her childhood. We talked about it for a long time today. It's a long dismal story of neglect. No outright abuse—not after the man with the hairy hands—just neglect. Indifference. No care. No protection, no touching, no affection, no attention. She fixed her own meals and washed her own clothes. The mother seems to have done what she needed to do to keep the neighbors from calling the authorities and that was it. She didn't work but she had men around who gave her things. There was her father's life insurance and social security, Clare thinks, and they had food and clothes and a little house. But for herself, Clare started earning money when she was fourteen and she discovered photography, and that got her away from the mother. It saved her life. It was a great piece of luck or gift of providence or whatever it is that she has this talent. It protected her, gave her a focus—sorry—when she could have been floundering around, probably being victimized by men."

I picked up Ford's paperweight, set it down in the middle of a stack of papers. "They tried."

Ford smiled. "I'm going to do a paper on you and Clare. Come on, you can see her now. You aren't paying any attention here today."

4

We stopped at the nursing station and Ford wrote the orders on Clare's chart to allow me to take her out on the hospital grounds, then walked with me down to her room. I stopped outside the door to speak to the guard, to ask him to follow us, and Ford went on into her room.

"Where's Sam?" I heard her ask immediately.

Ford said, "He'll be here in a minute. He's right behind me."

She said, "Is he talking to that guard?"

The nurse came out and I went in. "Yes, he was talking to that guard," I said. She was standing by the window and I crossed the room to put my arms around her.

"Why do they have him here?" she asked.

"Who?"

"The police. Why do they have him here? What do they think I'll do?"

Ford said, "Is that what you think, Clare? That he's from the police?"

I said, "No, he's from the guard service we use." I held both her hands in mine. "I put a guard here to keep you safe, to make sure you don't have any more nasty surprises."

She looked furious. "You didn't tell me."

"I didn't want you to worry."

"Will you stop that? Stop not telling me?" She pulled away from me and I felt the anger rise. "I'm not a child!"

She turned away and I took her shoulders and pulled her back around.

"There were some things you didn't tell me!" I said hotly.

"You're changing the subject!" she shouted.

Suddenly the anger was gone and I just felt very tired. "Jesus, Clare, I don't know what to tell you while you're here." My hands were still on her shoulders and I squeezed gently.

She came forward and put her arms around my waist and buried her face in my shoulder.

"I don't want to be here," she said.

"I know, fruitcake. I didn't mean that. You aren't to blame."

"You should have taken expert advice," said Ford. "She's right, Sam. You've got to stop not telling her. Or I should have, this time. It was partly my fault, Clare. But if you don't tell her, Sam, she'll make mistakes. That can't have been a pleasant feeling for her these past few days. And it has probably interfered with the work we're doing."

I rubbed my cheek on Clare's hair. "And someday you or someone else would decide I wanted her to make mistakes."

"We might."

"You'd be wrong. Okay. I'll tell everything." I felt the desire for her in my belly. "I suppose there's some damn hospital rule against sex," I said, and heard her muffled laugh.

"I'm afraid there is. But she can have her treat now, if you two are done throwing sparks."

"What treat?" she asked.

"I get to take you out for a walk," I said.

"Out? As in outside?"

"Uh huh."

"Air, grass, stuff like that?"

"You remember it, then."

"Oh, yes. I do."

The day had been warm but dry, and now it was cooling quickly. We held hands and walked slowly around the wooded edges of the large lawn below the terrace. Then mosquitoes came out of the woods and we went back up onto the long screened porch where I sat in a large wicker armchair and pulled her onto my lap. Except for four elderly people in robes playing bridge at the far end of the porch, and the guard standing by the door beyond the card players, we were alone. She curled up comfortably and I rested my head on hers.

"I think I'll tell you something," I said.

"A secret?"

"Not exactly. No, not exactly a secret. Just—I mean, I hope I know what I'm talking about."

"So tell me."

I said, "Are you ready?"

"I think I'll bite you."

"I love you."

"Oh, Sam," she said breathlessly, and after a moment, "Oh, Sam."

"How does it sound, okay?"

"It sounds wonderful. Say it again."

"I love you, Clare."

"I love you, too Sam."

"I like the sound of that, too. You better come home soon, Clare."

"I will, I will, as soon as Dr. Maxwell lets me."

"Oh, oh, here's your dragon." Her nurse was coming toward us. "I'm off to cultivate the olives."

5

Ford and I met again in his office at six o'clock. I collapsed on the couch, my hands loose between my knees.

"You look tired," he said, getting beers and glasses from his little refrigerator.

"I am tired, but Philip and Uncle Nick are getting back tonight and I won't have to spend so much time at the office. Philip gets his charge from it, but I find it… burdensome."

"Incredible. You sound exactly like an acquaintance I play bridge with. He's also part of a family business, but theirs is restaurant management. They own the Pisces chain."

I said, "Yeah, well, that's what ours is, a family business."

"Where were Philip and Uncle Nick?"

"A short business trip."

"And mind my own business." He sat down at the other end of the couch and opened his beer.

I ignored that. "And I don't sleep very well without Clare. I've gotten used to that warm body."

"They can be habit forming. Well, I expect she can leave the day after tomorrow, or maybe the day after that. We like to get these patients up and out and back to their lives as soon as possible."

I sighed. "Good."

"So let's talk about what's waiting for her back out in the world."

"I suppose you know what is."

He said, "That's *my* business. My concern is that she should be healthy, both emotionally and physically. And those two items are connected. What does she do when you aren't around?"

"She works. And worries. She works hard, a lot of hours. She always has. And I don't interfere with that part of her life and I'm not starting now. That's her, that's a big part of why she's so special, that she can see things through a camera that way, and I don't want to tinker with that."

"Of course, but she needs to offset that, and I doubt that worrying is the best hobby for her. She needs some physical activity, not in bed, that would offset both the long work hours and the worrying. She said that you and she played tennis."

I said, "Yeah, a few times."

"Well, get her out there and bounce her around the court a few times a week. She'll do it with you, but not without you. It would be great if she would do it for herself, but I'm not as picky as some of my colleagues. I'll use you for her sake." He drank a long swallow of beer. "When you move around, I believe I see an athlete. Did you do any organized sports in high school or college?"

I said, "Swimming and cross-country in high school. Some boxing—at the gym, not in school. Some intramural boxing at the university."

"Do you work out?"

"Yeah, Olympian's Gym, near the office."

"Weights?"

"And the bags. Get in the ring now and then. Usually with Andy."

He said, "You must be well matched. Is it easy for you to stay in shape?"

"Pretty easy."

Ford sighed. "I have to fight the weight all the time. And the stress."

I said, "Catherine gives a mean backrub."

"Yes, I know. Anyway, wear Clare out a bit. She needs it."

"Check. Shall I take notes? That sounds like the beginning of a list."

Ford shook his head. "You know what to do with her, what to say."

"Does she need to keep seeing a psychiatrist? You?"

He said, "Need? That's for her to decide. If she feels she needs or wants to see someone, I'll help her find the right person." He drank off his beer. "My business is to get them functioning again. The issue most people in my profession would see here is her dependence. On you. Theoretically, and in most cases clinically, it's unhealthy for one adult to be dependent on another. And I believe she's very dependent on you and most psychiatrists would view this as a problem to be solved."

I said, "You don't agree?"

"It's difficult. First of all, if she's around you, she apparently will always actually need physical protection and you'll have to give it to her."

"She's totally careless about locks and things. And I—okay, this is wrong, I admit it—I don't want her to start worrying about people like Kevvy—like came into her kitchen. I worry she'd lose something, some way of seeing the world. It might affect her work, put some sort of block between her and what she sees. I won't let that happen."

He said, "Then you will always have to be there or be sure someone is, someone you can trust."

"Right. That's what I'll do."

He said, "But that's just first of all. Secondly there are her various fears and phobias. She's handled these things pretty well so far—very well, in fact… maybe too well. If everything goes smoothly for her, she'll be fine, or at least okay. We all have our problems, after all. But you are allowing her to be very dependent on you to see that everything does go smoothly."

"I've made it so she'll never have to worry about paying her rent again. No more than any man should do."

He said, "That's not all you do."

"No, I love her. And that *is* all I do. And I have time for her. Maybe if I were a doctor or a lawyer or a butcher, I wouldn't have time for her. But I'm a card player, so I do have time, and I like it that way. And when she doesn't want me bossing her around, she lets me know."

He said, "Listen, you and Clare have something that works and works very well. Speaking as a man, I envy you like crazy. Speaking as a doctor, her doctor, I'm warning you. The kind of responsibility you've taken on for her, knowing what you do about how vulnerable she is—that can't be set aside some day if you get tired of it."

I said, "You think I might just abandon her? You think I don't already know what you just said? Right from the beginning I decided that as long as she would let me, until she said no to me, I would be whatever she needed. I know what I'm doing. When she and I stand up in church together, it won't be the first solemn oath I've taken there for her."

A long silence.

"Well, there's nothing more I can say," Ford said. "Just two more pieces of information for you. She let me see the pictures, and she looked at herself as a five-year-old and said, 'That's a picture of me.' I don't suppose she'll ever be able to say, 'That's me', but maybe I'm wrong. Maybe it's a photographer talking."

"Can I ask her to let me see them?"

"Of course." He smiled. "She also told me that you told her you love her. She was so sweet and so happy. Do you want to see her now?"

"You need to ask? What kind of psychiatrist are you?"

Tuesday, May 15

1

I called Ford. "Uncle Nick wants to talk to Clare, before she leaves the hospital."

"What about?"

"Jesus, if you were any other doctor, I could just say none of your business, but I can't, can I?"

He said, "If he'll wait until she's released, I'll never know."

"He won't, and Catherine and the children are involved and you probably have a right to know. What are you doing for lunch?"

"I was planning to go to the weekly E.M. seminar at the U, but I'm open to other suggestions."

I said, "Can you meet me?"

"Sure."

"You aren't too far from the Stardust. Do you know where it is?"

"No."

I told him and we agreed to meet at noon.

2

Andy and I were at the bar when Ford arrived. Andy got a pitcher of beer and we all moved to the end booth. I sat where I could see the other booths and the rest of the room. Being a Tuesday, it wasn't too busy. And lunch wasn't their biggest draw, although the sandwiches were always excellent. We ordered.

I asked Ford, "Did you and Clare ever talk about her apartment being vandalized?"

"No, but I knew about it from Catherine. Last winter, early spring?"

"Yeah. Do you know why it happened?"

He said, "No, I don't think I ever found out. She told me about it—Catherine did—to explain how she had finally met Clare."

I said, "A man named Hugh Black engineered it. Black hired a guy with a grudge against Clare to do the actual dirty work, but the real target was me. He wanted a tame card player, and he got one."

He said, "Black's from Chicago."

I raised my eyebrows and Andy laughed, and said, "Did his residency there, Cook County Hospital, and then he was on the staff. Emergency interventions. Hostage negotiations, leapers, abuse victims. Crime victims. Gang warfare. Came here in 2002."

Ford shrugged. "One hears things."

I laughed. "I'll bet one does. What do you do for recreation?"

"The hospital has a small fitness center and I work out. Go to the races. Play some cards."

"Yeah?"

"Bridge. Very minor money. But it keeps me in good coffee."

"Can we get down to it?" Andy asked. "I have a date."

"Black," prompted Ford.

I said, "Right. He sets up games and I play in them. He stakes me and takes a cut."

"Of your winnings."

"Yes."

"What if you lose?"

"I don't."

Ford laughed. "Go on."

I said, "There's a local man, Kevvy Smith, who does a sort of general-store operation in drugs and women and so on. He saw what he thought was Hugh Black moving into his territory, and I was first on his list for pushing back. That's what Clare's visitors were up to. I wasn't supposed to be there at all."

Ford said, "I suppose before you had Clare, you weren't as susceptible to these tactics. And her life was a lot less dangerous." He poured beer for all of us. "And she doesn't live in some nice, high-security apartment building in the bosom of her family, like Catherine does."

I said, "No. But she'll have to start. At least for a while. We've decided Kevvy Smith is more than we can handle and we've invited Black in. He's agreed to take over this territory, such as it is, and set up a local organization. And take Kevvy out. Naturally we pay a management fee."

Ford said, "You set this up?"

"*We* did. Yes."

"For Clare's sake?"

"Yes."

He said, "So she can live in a nice safe place and take pictures and have your children, you've engineered a hostile take-over? Black's not Miami or Las Vegas, but he is nonetheless a player."

Andy said, "Clare's family."

Ford kept his attention on me. "You'll climb into Black's pocket for her?"

"I would treat with Satan," I said, and out of the corner of my eye I saw Andy trace a small cross on the tabletop. And I saw that Ford had seen it too.

"And this is what Uncle Nick has to tell her."

"What he *will* tell her, whether or not you're in on it, but it would be good if you had her back."

"Yes."

I said, " And he'll be telling her that she and I will be living at Catherine's for a while. Andy's Kori and Philip's Sofia and my cousins Mike and Pete and their girlfriends Dani and Jackie and all the children are going up north to a resort for a few weeks. Black owns the resort."

He said, "But you're not sending Clare out of town."

"No."

"Why not?"

I shook my head. "I can't. Unless she wants to go. Then I will."

Ford said, "All right, he can see her. Better now, while she's still in. When can he come? This afternoon?"

"Four o'clock?"

"All right. Will you bring him to my office?"

I said, "I expect Catherine will want to do the honors."

"She'll be on duty. We can call her down. So. One more question. No one in the family said forget her, she's too much trouble?"

Andy shook his head, an unbelieving look on his face. "Everyone would know he'd choose Clare."

I said, "But they'd never say it. I'll go money they've never even thought it. They'd be totally shocked at the idea. She's been family for longer than she realizes. Ask Catherine."

"I think I will." He drank the last of his beer and looked around. He said, "I used to go to a bar like this one when I was at Cook County. The Astor. I didn't know there was a place like the Astor in St. Paul. I've been asking the wrong people."

I laughed. "Andy owes me ten bucks."

Ford smiled. "I grew up in Chicago. Lincoln Park. University of Chicago, Magna, then Johns Hopkins. I was Illinois Golden Gloves light-heavyweight two years in a row. I was in the marines, small-arms instructor."

"You blew it, Andy," I jeered.

"I haven't gotten back that far. This is an old man here."

"Would you like to meet me in the gym?" Ford offered.

Andy said, "Too much reach and too many pounds on me. Perhaps if you'll tie one arm behind your back."

Ford laughed. "I have to go. I'd like to see you two in the ring." He stood up and reached for his wallet, but I put up a hand. He said, "I'll see you at four. Thanks for lunch."

"Why isn't he married?" I asked when he'd left.

"He was. No children. Wife died five years ago, cancer."

I threw some money on the table. "I think we can stop worrying about Catherine."

3

Andy, Uncle Nick, and I arrived at Maxwell's office at four. He greeted us in the corridor.

Catherine arrived a half-minute later, wearing a scrub suit with a stethoscope draped around her neck and a preoccupied expression. She paid no attention to Andy and me.

"Can we go into your office?" she asked Ford.

He opened the door and she took Uncle Nick's arm and entered. After five minutes she came out and sailed off. Ford and Uncle Nick came out smiling.

"She's waiting for you," Ford said. "I told her you were both coming."

When we entered her room, she was sitting cross-legged on the bed wearing a robe over her hospital pajamas, pillows behind her, her hands on her lap. Uncle Nick leaned over to kiss her cheek, then waved me away.

"Please leave us alone, Sam," he said, and I backed out and closed the door.

Andy sprawled in a chair and I walked up and down the corridor. Ten minutes. Another minute. Another. Two more. Another five. Another three. Four more. The door opened and Uncle Nick came out.

He said, "She'll be fine."

Andy said, "We didn't even hear you yelling."

Uncle Nick said, "I don't need to yell at women."

Andy and I grinned at each other.

He said, "I want to talk to Dr. Maxwell if he's available."

I said, "I can call," and I did and he was free for a few minutes. He came down the corridor and we all went into his office and sat down.

Uncle Nick said, "You'll want to know what I said to her. I told her that Sam told us what happened. I said we took certain steps and they have to be explained to her."

Ford nodded. Today he didn't look like a guy who drank beer at the Stardust.

But neither did Uncle Nick look like a retired bookie. He said, "Things aren't as simple as they used to be. Used to be, we made a few bets, paid a few cops, that was it." He paused. "No cigars allowed in here, I suppose."

Ford said, "No, sorry."

Uncle Nick sighed faintly. "Well, the whole world is more complicated, but our problem is Sam."

I stayed quiet. Ford smiled and Andy grinned.

"He's good. If he stopped being lazy, he'd be better. And that makes other people see money. Do you know about Kevin Smith?"

Ford said, "Sam told me some things about him."

Uncle Nick said, "Those were his men in Clare's kitchen. Smith will keep bothering us. He's greedy and he deals in crap—drugs for school kids, low-class whores, stolen cars. Bashings. Protection. He's dishonest. He's got no sense and no sense of honor. He's dangerous and we can't handle him. That's not our kind of business. Some might think it is, but it's not. But we have to do something about him."

"I can see that you do."

"Good. You know Hugh Black."

"I know *about* him."

Uncle Nick nodded. "Right. Philip and I went to Chicago and talked to Black, made a deal with him. He's going to come into St. Paul and take over from Kevvy. He's got good sense and he's smart and we can work with him. Mostly he'll leave us alone, but if we need protection, he's our insurance company. I told her all this."

Ford laughed a bit and shook his head. "Hugh Black."

"You don't like him."

"I don't know him."

"Yeah, well, he's not an altar boy. But he's smart. Clare says he's scary. But I told her, he likes her and he wants her to like him." Uncle Nick was smiling.

Ford said, "Why?"

"Because Clare has it in her to be famous, and he wants to know her and tell his friends he knows her, tell his customers, offer to introduce her. And of course that will keep Sam in his court. And that will turn into money for him. It's always about the money."

"Hugh Black as a patron of the arts."

Uncle Nick shrugged. "Maybe the Medicis were the Hugh Blacks of their day. That's business. But I think he also likes *her*. And Sam. So he's willing to move in up here."

"He'll live here?"

Nick said, "No, I mean put his people in here. She said that before she and Sam were lovers… " He looked at me. "It embarrassed her to say that to me."

I should damn well think it would. I nodded.

"She said she didn't even know people like this existed, not here in St. Paul, not real gangsters, and now they want to hurt her. And Sam. They're always there. I told her that. They're always there. Then I told her she'll have to live at Catherine's for a while. To keep her safe. I said it might be even more dangerous for awhile, until things shake out. She said no."

I'll just bet she did.

"I told her, after Black's in, it'll be safe again." His voice went hard. "I said, do you want more men in your kitchen in the middle of the night? Or maybe in your bedroom? Sam not there and two or three of them in your room? Scum?" A pause. "She thought that over and said all right, she would go to Catherine's. Then she said what about her work. I have to work, she said."

He looked at me. "I knew she wasn't talking about money, and I didn't insult her by saying that."

I made an of-course gesture.

He said to Ford, "I said, in the daytime. With someone there." His face softened. "She does have to work, I see that. I saw her photographs. I told her that." He smiled. "I told her, you're a very unusual woman and Sam's very lucky to have found you."

Odds on tht made her blush.

"So then I said, what happened to you, the reason you're here… I understand these things can come out because of some strong unhappy event a long time ago, when you were a child."

Ford said, "Very accurately put."

Uncle Nick said, "And I said you're all right now. I said you're no longer a child and soon you'll have your own child. You'll be all right now."

He stood up. "I'm happy to meet you, Dr. Maxwell. Happy for Catherine and for you. She's another unusual woman." He gave me a very bland look. "But then, she's Greek." He looked back at Ford. "Most doctors we would have had to work around. It's good that we can talk to you. Thanks for your time. Andonios can take me back to the office," he said to me.

He and Andy shook hands with Ford, said goodbye and left.

Ford said, "I've been handled."

4

She was standing by the window when I went in. The hospital robe was a washed-out blue and much too large. If it hadn't been for the curves underneath the robe, she'd have looked like a waif.

"You look good enough to eat," I said.

"All the men in your family are wizards," she said. "You throw magic dust on us poor defenseless women and we melt like butter in the sun. I suppose Christos is learning how even as we speak."

I said, "When it comes time to teach him about similes and metaphors, let me do it."

With Ford's permission we went to the long, screened-in porch and walked back and forth in the slanting light. We talked some, but mostly we just held hands and walked from one end of the porch to the other.

Then she said, "I have something to tell you."

"What?"

"I remembered something."

"Really."

"Remember when we were at the Stardust and those two guys were threatening us outside?"

"Uh huh."

"And I told you about those two people sitting in the car?"

"Uh huh."

"And one was that blond girl."

"Uh huh."

"And I told you I'd never seen that man before."

"Uh huh."

"Well, I did. After that. He—the man with the scar. On his face."

"Really." I stopped walking.

She said, "I'm sure."

"I know. I trust you completely on faces. But I'd sure like to know how this fits in."

"Too bad you can't walk and think at the same time, like I can."

She was silent while we walked the length of the porch and turned to walk back.

Then she stopped. We were alone.

She said in a fierce, raspy whisper, not looking at me, "You killed that man."

I said in a low voice, "Yes. I did. He was going to rape you. And beat you. Beat you bad. Hurt you bad. It was going to make O'Connell look like a walk in the park." Tears were rolling down her cheeks and my voice went up a little. "Did you think I was going to let that happen?"

"But that other one was going to shoot you!"

"No. His orders would've been no killings. Kevvy wanted me alive."

Now her voice went up. "Did you *know* that?"

"No. Well, sort of. But it didn't matter what I knew. I was getting you out of there as intact as possible. He might have put a couple of peripheral bullet holes in me, but... " I shrugged.

She said, "Peripheral!"

I grinned. "You know. Foot. Shoulder. Kneecap."

"Don't patronize me!"

"Sorry. But while he was trying to think out his best target, I'd be taking him down. I was just trying to get it done before—"

"Yes." She moved into me and I held her while she sniffled. Then she wiped her face on the sleeve of her robe and we walked to the end of the porch. It was dark there, inside the screens, except for a small yellow light over the door.

She stopped again. Without looking at me she said, "Thank you."

I said, "Anytime."

Friday, May 18

1

They let her go. We went to her place and she puttered about the studio and workroom, making sure all was well and still there and packed clothes to take to Catherine's. I had all new locks installed by Pete and Mike, and she noticed them, but just accepted the new keys without comment. I told her I was having a top-of-the-line alarm system put in on Friday, all the windows and doors, and she accepted that too.

She did say, "In the Ratty Duplex. And it isn't even yours."

I said, "It'll never be mine. Might be yours. Anyway, the alarm system goes in even if we move out next week."

"My cameras…"

"Yeah. Pack them up in that bombproof case and we'll take them with us. Pack up everything valuable and portable. For now, you'll have to bring stuff back and forth that you need. In a few days I can probably get one of the cousins to stay here at night."

"That is so restricting!" she said. "I hate this!" and she stalked back into the studio.

2

In the corridor outside Catherine's apartment, while I dug for my door key, I said, "You have your choice. You can move into my old room with me, or you can move into the guest room and have your own space and more of it, and it has its own bath."

"I think my choice is already made. You just don't want me messing up your room."

"You can come and play with my toys whenever you want to."

"Do I have to sleep in the guest room too?"

"Well, I was hoping you'd sleep with me."

I finished setting her bags in the entryway and pushed the door shut. "In fact, I was hoping we could start now."

She said, "But I'm not sleepy."

"Ha."

We went to my room and I sat down on a chair to take off my sneakers and I watched her kick off her sandals and drop her cotton dress to the floor to stand in front of me wearing a little pink bra and pink bikini panties. I reached for her and she sat down on my knee and began unbuttoning my shirt. I ran my fingertips over the curve of her breast, then put my hands behind her to unhook the bra and slip it off her shoulders. She pushed open my shirt and put her breasts against my chest and said, "Hi," and kissed me.

3

I propped myself on my elbows and looked down at her face.

"Welcome home," I said. I put my fingers into her hair. I loved her hair. "I was... afraid you might be afraid."

"To make love with you?"

"Uh huh."

She said, "I love you. And you love me."

"Well, that explains it, doesn't it? Silly me."

She sighed. "I'm not a simpleton. I was afraid too. But now I'm not."

We showered and dressed and I lounged on the bed in the guest room, now her room, while she unpacked and surveyed her new surroundings. The bookcase had become a staging area for photography equipment going back and forth to the studio, and I promised

her a large corkboard to pin up pictures she was looking at. She drifted around the room, moving things a few inches, then putting them
back, fixing the pieces of her universe into new places.

"Just think of it as going to summer camp," I said.

"I never went to summer camp. Did you?"

"Andy and I went once. I think they asked my father not to send
us back."

"Are you planning to teach your son to be a hellraiser too?"

"I'll teach him to be a man. The rest of it he'll figure out on his
own."

"I've never even held a baby."

"Don't worry."

"You always say that." She sat down on the bed cross-legged,
next to me. "But I happen to know that you worry."

"Then you don't need to, do you? You'll have Catherine and
Sofia, and even *I* remember which end to hold up. The baby knows
what to do with the tit."

"I'm hungry."

I laughed and said, "Good timing. I hear Catherine."

Catherine knocked on the half-open door, put her head in at my
invitation, then came in to collapse into a chair. She was wearing
scrubs and her makeup was gone and her hair was falling out of the
bun she wore at the hospital.

"Twins," she said.

"Oh, my," Clare said.

"Both healthy and she did fine. But a busy day." Her expression
changed. "I'm going out to dinner."

I said, "Good. Take advantage of the gang being gone."

Catherine looked defiant. "And I won't be back tonight."

I laughed and Clare gave me a confused look.

Catherine said, "Oh, Sam, you haven't told her, have you?" I
shook my head. "And I can't believe I'm being so rude. Welcome
home, Clare. It's good to have you here again. I just wish the circumstances were happier."

I said, "I'm happy."

"I'm sorry to keep barging in on you like this," Clare said to Catherine.

"Please consider this your home, really. Sam's home, your home. I'm sorry I won't be here for dinner with you."

"We'll manage," I said, still grinning. "Go on, get dressed. I'll explain to Clare."

Catherine left, looking flushed, and Clare said, "Explain what to Clare?"

I said, "Catherine has a lover."

"That's wonderful!"

"And you know him."

She said, "Dr. Maxwell."

"How long have you been reading minds? Can you read mine?"

"That's too easy."

I said, "Come on, how did you know?"

"I didn't know, but one day he called her Catherine and then looked embarrassed, and another time I saw them smile at each other."

"And on that flimsy evidence, you concluded that they were lovers?"

She said, "You know I didn't, but when you said that, I guessed. Who else would it be if I know him? Is it a secret?"

I said, "Not any more. I busted 'em the first night you were in the hospital. But he's only just met the children and started his campaign for their approval. And I don't think they've ever spent a night together."

She said, "Poor things. I love sleeping with you. I love waking up and finding you there. And you're warm in the winter."

"Same goes. Anyway, you can call him Ford now."

"How strange that will be." She went back to hanging up clothes.

I said, "I'm not sure about asking this but I have to. Are we okay? You and me? I… don't want to have lost you in all this turmoil."

She said, "Is that what this is? Turmoil?"

"Is there a better word?"

She said, "Turbulence?"

"Ruckus?"

A second. She said, "Distress?"

I said, "Clare—"

"So. Boy meets girl, boy gets girl—and vice versa, I might add—then girl loses girl. But girl finds girl. And there's boy, waiting. And girl may have a few stitches in her, but everything is there. Is that okay with boy?"

I said, "Girl is better than ever."

She said, "Girl hopes so."

I said, "And boy loves her more than ever. And boy is in awe of girl."

She said, "As it should be. Maybe girl is now woman."

"Yes. Even better."

"Okay. We're good."

Tuesday, May 22

1

We seemed to be back to our usual ease with each other, but I wasn't sure. So I was being careful, and I thought she was too, a little.

I was leaning in the bedroom doorway watching her dress. I liked to do that and she let me. I thought she was getting used to these small intimacies. She was putting on what she apparently considered appropriate to visit a lawyer—pink collarless cotton shirt, dark red linen blazer, pink linen skirt, high black flat-heeled boots, and her sapphire ring—and asked me, "Do I look like business?"

I said, "You look perfect. Do I look like money?" I was wearing a crisp new blue shirt that I'd taken out of the package that morning, indigo-blue straight-leg Levis that were just barely broken in, tan suede low-cut work boots in which I had never done a lick of work that required boots, and a slim-cut navy-blue sports coat, Italian.

She said, "You do, you know. You always look exactly right. You lack only the Stetson."

I said, "Must have left it in the car. We're due downtown in forty minutes."

The appointment was with the family attorney, Tim Christides, who was also a cousin by marriage. Married to my cousin Mary. One of the cousins Mary. There were three. Same age cohort, just four years older, as me and Andy. He had an office with two partners, names on door, not far from the Zandros brothers' office. But Christides, Pappas & Stavros was several steps up the hill. Tim's clients were a lot more interested in decor than the Zandros'. I explained all this in the car.

She said, "Do I need to write this all down?"

"I think Stephen has a family tree. They had a school project. Ask to borrow it."

I greeted the receptionist and introduced Cousin Tim's secretary and then "Timothy Christides, Clare Russell," and they shook hands. There was small talk. He said, "I saw you at the funeral but we didn't actually meet." We all sat down. Tim moved a pile of documents to the center of his blotter and handed the top one to me. While I was reading it, Tim spoke on his telephone and two women came in.

"We'll need witnesses," he told them. They were introduced to Clare—they already knew me— then waited quietly until I finished reading. I signed my name and they signed their names next to it and they left the office.

I handed the document to Clare, and she held it in her hand and looked at me.

"It's my last will and testament," I said. "I leave some personal items to Philip and Sofia and Catherine, and all the kids, and Andy, and Uncle Nick and Uncle Cy, and some cousins, and then everything else to you and our children. Whether or not we're married."

"Are you sure?" She glanced at the top page, then handed it back, still looking at me, maybe frowning a little.

"Yes, I'm sure." I handed the will to Tim who cleared his throat and handed me the second document, a somewhat thicker one.

I said, "This one is already signed and executed. What it does is in the works. It creates a trust fund for you and any children we may have, whether or not we're married, as of last Friday. It will be administered by Capitol Hill Bank. Very conservatively. They're totally reputable and my family has banked with them for years. And Uncle Cy will be watching over everything. I've turned over a sum of money to be invested, and all the income goes to you and the babies. And it's irrevocable. I can't take it back. It's done. You have to take it."

I handed it to her and she looked at the first page.

"This must be a mistake," she said.

"What?"

She pointed. "It says five hundred thousand dollars."

"No, that's right."

I was enjoying this like crazy.

She said, "And I was buying you beers?"

Cousin Tim grinned.

I said, "We'll go into that later. Are you done reading that? You've seen the relevant part."

We drove to the bank, which wasn't far up the hill on Rice Street. When we'd passed the capitol building and a few blocks more, she pointed and said, "There's that bar. The Stardust."

Four blocks farther on was the bank. I parked in the lot and we walked around to the front door.

"Did you use to live in this neighborhood?" she asked.

"Didn't you know?"

"Not exactly where. Just Rice Street."

I stopped walking. "See that Sally Army store? That was a grocery store. Uncle Nick owned it. He ran a few bets on the side. Andy's father, Uncle Steve, owned a restaurant across the street where that parking lot is. But they lived in our building. Uncle Cy didn't have a business here but he lived in the apartments over the restaurant, and so did Aunt Ekaterina. I think Cy was an accountant for a CPA firm after Viet Nam and before we got the book going. My father was Christos. He was a tailor and owned that dry-cleaning shop on the corner. It's still owned by a distant sort of cousin of ours, and he owns a small chain of laundromats to go with the dry cleaning. We lived upstairs and so did Andy and Uncle Steve and Aunt Danielle. Everybody lived upstairs. Except on this corner. This was already the bank and there were offices upstairs."

"And then gambling became the family business?"

"Right. And we moved across the tracks."

"Were your parents—when I met you? Were they gone?"

"Both my parents were. Mama had a stroke when I was twelve. And my father had a heart attack when I was seventeen."

"So young when you lost your mama? You never told me that."

"It's hard to talk about, even now. Even to you. Andy and I found her." A pause and a breath. "Catherine was our mother then, after that. She was twenty. But mostly Andy and I ran wild. Andy lived with us. I told you that. After his parents were killed. Then he and I lived with my father until he died, and then Andy and I kept on sharing the apartment until Catherine's husband died and I moved there and Andy moved to Uncle Nick's carriage house."

"Good heavens, what a time for you all."

"My father died when Stephen was two. He held him, played with him, his first grandchild. Families go on." I cleared my throat, took her hand, and opened the door into the bank.

Our entrance was noted by an older man in a banker's dark suit who stepped from his glass-fronted office to greet us and shake hands. I introduced him—George Christides, the bank's president and Tim Christides' father.

"Good to see you, Sam. It's been some time. Except at the funeral, of course. Very sad about Paul. How's everybody? I see Cy fairly often, but of course he's always the same."

I said, "Philip said to say hello and we appreciate it that you were able to come to the funeral. I'm here to look in my boxes and change some signature cards. Miss Russell and I are getting married."

"Congratulations! Wonderful news! Life goes on, doesn't it?" He shook hands again. "Jo Anderson is out of town. Why don't you use her office? More comfortable."

"We won't be long."

"Well, you have until Monday, then she'll kick you out." He laughed and so did I. Clare smiled.

Christides ushered her into an office, and I followed a little later with a bank clerk, each of us carrying a large metal deposit box.

"I'll bring in the new signature cards," Christides said and left us alone.

We sat on a small couch, the two boxes on a low table in front of us. I took one of her hands in mine.

"This is my life insurance policy," I said, "or what I fall back on the day I forget which are the hearts and which are the diamonds. And after today you'll be able to open these boxes so you can get a new black dress if I walk in front of a bus."

I took out his key ring and showed her the two small keys for opening the boxes, and from his jacket pocket I gave her a small brown envelope, which contained copies of the two keys. Then I lifted the cover on one of the boxes. It was completely full of hundred-dollar bills in neat packets, each labeled "$5000" on its paper belt.

She looked at the money and then at me. "Is it real?" she asked.

I burst out laughing and closed the cover. "Yes, it's real, and when you run away to Belize with Andy, don't forget it."

"You said there are alligators."

"Country's full of 'em."

"So I'm not going."

"Good." I opened the other box. The contents were an assortment of boxes, leather bags, and papers, and I showed her each item. There were stock certificates and bonds, savings certificates, and several bank passbooks. There were three small leather bags containing cut and uncut gemstones, mostly diamonds. There was a box of gold coins in velvet nests. There was a box of six gold bars, each stamped with "1 kilo" and other numbers, each wrapped in a bit of silk. There were two worn black velvet-covered jewelry boxes that I put in my jacket pocket. "For later," I said.

When I closed the lid on the box, she asked, "What is all this?"

"I told you. My insurance, my nest egg, my pension plan. And yours. The olives."

"All this time... you never said..." I think she actually was angry. Her eyes were wet. "Have you been trying to... trying to..."

"Bamboozle you?"

She sniffed. "Yes."

"No." I gave her a handkerchief. "Never then, never now. It's all real and I never mentioned it because, not to put too fine a point on it, it wasn't any of your business. But now it is. I waited until now because I figured it might scare the bejesus out of you."

"I suppose it would have. It does."

I laughed. "I've made you... well, not rich, but secure, and you didn't have a thing to say about it."

"You *always* get your way."

"And a good thing too."

There was a knock at the door and George Christides came back in. He had a handful of old signature cards for the boxes and the passbook accounts and two money-market accounts. She watched me arrange to cash in the old passbook accounts and transfer those funds to one of the money-market accounts, and we both signed new cards for the accounts and for the boxes.

Finally we were done and we stood in the warm sun in front of the bank and I looked around at Rice Street at store fronts and passing cars and buses; at three boys on bikes, an old man getting off the bus with groceries in a cloth shopping bag, and two teenage girls in tight pants getting appreciative looks and comments from four teenage boys following them.

"Come on," I said, "we'll eat lunch at the Stardust."

2

It was cool and dim and we sat in silence and ate roast-beef sandwiches with hot mustard and I drank a dark draft ale and she drank a small glass of lager and a tall glass of water and I felt like I was restarting.

"Alive again?" I asked.

"Yes. May I have another beer, please?"

"Are you asking my permission?" I asked unbelievingly.

"Of course not, I'm asking you to get it."

"I suppose that's best. Only fast women get their own beer at the Stardust."

She said indignantly, "And I'm not fast enough?"

I said, "In this neighborhood you are Miss Clare Molasses."

She was still grinning when I came back with the beer.

I said, "You may laugh, Miss Molasses, but this is still a rough neighborhood. Perhaps rougher now than then, now that drug dealing has gotten here."

"Was it rough when you were growing up here?" she asked.

"My dear young lady, Andy and I, and Philip and Paul before us, lived in the streets here and we saw people die in them, from no money or from no friends or from guns or knives or fists. And we didn't survive by being charming, either. Well, sometimes Andonios did, but he's a special case."

She smiled. "He *is* special."

I finished my beer. "Next item on our order of business—"

"There's more?" she wailed.

"The next and almost last item on our order of business is by direction of Catherine. We are to proceed to Brewer & James and order wedding invitations."

"When are we getting married?"

"Four p. m. , October twenty-ninth. It's a Saturday. Buffet dinner and dance to follow, six p. m. , at the River Club. If this meets with your approval. Catherine stressed this most strongly. She made these reservations for the church and the club, but they can be canceled in a trice. Although, I think she had to call in some favors at the church, and there was a cancelation at the club just yesterday. These things usually have to be nailed down years in advance."

She drank off the last of her beer and looked regretfully into the empty glass, then leaned on her elbows and looked at me across the table. "I said I would do this and I will, but I don't know the first thing about what to do or how to do it, and Catherine does, so why not?"

"Why not indeed? Catherine says they'll know what to tell us at the printers."

The printers did, and after some discussion we settled on "Clare Russell and Sam Alexandros request the pleasure of your presence at their marriage…" and so on. I wanted to say "the honor of your presence," but she said "the pleasure" means something to people, something about us and them, but "the honor" is just something they skip over. Then the clerk asked how many and I said, "Three hundred." And she said, "You have two hundred and ninety-six people to invite?"

"You have four? Maybe we'll need some extra."

When we got in the car, I asked, "Who do you want to invite who isn't going to be on my list too?"

"I don't know many people that you don't. Jim and Nan Cochran," she said, naming her photography professor and his wife. "Ellie Bragg and Angie Lee. We were at the U together. Five or six others from the art department. Anson and Maureen Greeley."

"Anson and Maureen are on my list. No clients?"

"No. But I think I'll invite Mr. Salmon, at the deli. He's been very kind to me. Now where are we going?"

I said, "One more place to visit."

3

It was the building I'd shown her the day my life started up again. I produced the large brass key that opened the front door, and we went into the shadowy interior. I'd had it cleared of all the debris and more or less cleaned, and now it was a large empty space. We stood in the middle of it and looked around.

Finally I said, "This is the main room."

"Of what?"

"A club. A night club."

"Someone's opening a night club here?"

"I am."

"You're opening a night club here?"

"Yeah. Well, maybe more like a bistro. A joint. A saloon. No ambience. No tablecloths or candles. Or maybe candles. Maybe a couple of bar snacks. Good beer, good wine, good drinks, good jazz." I pointed. "*Good* jazz. Stage over there. Top-of-the-line sound system. Two dressing rooms behind. Bar there." I took her hand and led her to the small hallway at the rear of the building. "Restrooms that way, kitchen this way. Office here. The basement is finished and in good—well, reasonably good—shape. I'll put in a climate-controlled wine cellar and beer storage. Lots of imported beer, microbreweries, that sort of thing." I stopped talking and stood looking at her. "What do you think?"

I had never felt so vulnerable before.

Her smile was incandescent. "It's wonderful! I can't think of what to say, not yet, but it's definitely wonderful."

"So you're okay with being married to a bar owner?"

"Of course I am. I don't care what you do, you know that."

4

We went to Catherine's for supper. I was relieved that only she and the children were there. We ate on the glassed-in sun porch, and after the ice cream I motioned to Catherine and the children to bring their chairs closer as I took the two jewelry boxes from my pocket.

"Before our father died," I told Clare, "he gave each of us a portion of our mother's jewelry, and I am now giving my share to you, which is what he meant for me to do with it. And if any of the babies are girls, someday they will have it. Ioulia will be getting hers from Catherine someday and Meli from Philip, after Sofia. And Paul's will go to Nicky."

I opened the first box and lifted out a necklace of three strands of pearls and a pair of earrings that were clusters of small pearls. I set the earrings in Clare's hand and reached around to fasten the necklace on her. The pearls glowed against her pink shirt.

"Remember?" I murmured in her ear. "I promised you pearl earrings for your wedding?"

"You did, didn't you?" She touched them delicately with her fingertips. "I've never worn pearls before."

"Now you have pearls." I carefully removed her dangling, plastic-bead earrings and she put the pearls in their place. "How do you suppose my father knew how lovely you would look in them?"

Catherine smiled. "He had his moments, didn't he?"

"You have to wear them a lot," said Ioulia, "so the pearls will stay healthy from the oil in your skin."

"Don't Thomas and I get any of your jewelry?" Stephen asked Catherine.

"Mine, yes, that I got from your father, to give to your wives, but only Ioulia gets my mother's. That's what we were told by our father."

"And in no uncertain terms," I said. "He could be very emphatic."

Catherine smiled.

I picked up the second box and noticed Thomas quivering with excitement and craning to see past Stephen. I reached out and drew him around to sit on my knee, inside my arm, and opened the box. It held a pair of earrings and two finger rings.

"Your birthstone is the sapphire," I said to Clare.

"Yes, I know."

"It's also mine, of course, which you also know, since we were both born in September. What you might not know is that it was my mother's too, and these were her sapphire earrings." Two clusters of tiny blue stones set in gold tremblers. I reached for her right hand and laid them in her palm. "And to match your blue eyes, of course." She picked one up, so carefully and tentatively. It did match her eyes.

"I wish I had blue eyes," Ioulia sighed.

"You could get contacts," Stephen said.

"Mama won't let me."

"Can I have some attention here?" I said sternly. "I don't suppose Clare's even noticed that I haven't gotten her an engagement ring, but I haven't because, if it's all right with her, I want her to wear our mother's. And her wedding ring, too." I opened my hand to show the two rings, a plain gold band and a matching gold band with a diamond. The diamond was square cut and not very large, and both rings were somewhat worn. "Help me out, Thomas. Hold this one for a minute."

I put the wedding band into his hand and he closed his fist tightly around it.

I picked up Clare's left hand and took her sapphire ring off her third finger and gave it to Thomas to hold tightly in his other hand and slipped the diamond ring onto it. It fit loosely and I closed her fingers to keep it in place. Then I looked up into her face and saw the smile that always made my heart jump. I leaned past Thomas and kissed her softly. "Is it all right?"

"I might lose it or hurt it or something."

"You can't hurt a diamond, and we'll have it re-sized so it doesn't fall off. I want you to wear it and my mother would too."

"Oh, she would," Catherine said. "Sam was her baby and she truly would want you to wear it."

"Then I will."

"We could have it reset," I said.

"No, I want it just the way it is."

I picked up her hand and looked at the ring. "It's not large, but it's real and a very good stone, actually. Not that I'm a gemologist but I had someone look at it once." I took it off her finger and took the other rings from Thomas and the sapphire earrings from her other hand and put them all in the box. "If you don't mind, we'll put these in my safe. We'll take the rings to be sized, first chance." I laughed. "And so ends the betrothal party."

Catherine opened her mouth to speak, but stopped herself and only laughed.

5

In the car she kept her left arm stretched out toward me and I held her hand when mine wasn't busy, but she said nothing. She looked dreamy and tired. In her bedroom she removed the pearl earrings and necklace and laid them carefully in their box. The little box fit nicely into her replacement jewelry box, a red, lacquered, wooden chest that she'd gotten at a thrift shop. She said antique store, I said thrift shop. In bed she lay flat on her back, staring at the ceiling. She hadn't said a dozen words since leaving Catherine's.

"A penny for your thoughts?" I suggested.

She said, "A penny? Ha. I am a woman of substance. You'll have to sweeten the offer some."

"I know just the thing. Move over."

She scooted sideways.

"Not that way, this way."

"Was today real?" she asked.

I laughed. "I guarantee the whole day. Did some of it strike you as unusual?"

"Oh, no, I acquire jewels and vast fortunes quite often."

"Not vast, perhaps not even a fortune, but you'll never have to worry again, not about money. You do understand that, I hope."

"I can pay the rent every month, on time," she said. "The gold standard of poverty."

"Fruitcake." I moved down in the bed to kiss her belly, then lower, to kiss the inside of her knee. But when I moved back up her inner thigh, she pushed my head away. She would never let me touch her there with my mouth and she would never tell me why, or perhaps couldn't, even though she let me move into her with my fingers and let my mouth touch every other part of her body. I never pushed, never asked. Although, since our night ride down the river, I thought I now knew.

I kissed her breasts and moved up to kiss her mouth while I guided myself into her wet warmth with my fingers. I felt her shiver and heard her make a sharp little noise and in a matter of seconds I felt the contractions of her orgasm around me. I let go and lost myself.

As I became aware of her again, she began weeping convulsively, almost hysterically.

"Clare! Did I hurt you?"

She shook her head, apparently unable to speak, so I held her firmly until she became calmer, then wiped her face with the sheet.

"What happened?"

"I don't know! I couldn't stop crying. Don't know why."

"Okay, I know why. Hush now. I piled too much on you today. And right after the funeral and… other stuff that's been going on. I'm sorry. You need some time off. I'll be out of town this weekend. Two nights. You can rest up."

She struggled out of my arms and sat up. "You'll be gone?"

"Chicago."

"No, please don't."

"Why not?"

"Just don't. Please."

"This is new. I can't just not go. I'm committed. You have to tell me why. You never minded time alone before. Hell, you demanded it."

"I know, but…"

A hesitation.

"But what?"

"I don't know. Please?"

"You have to tell me what's going on."

"Sometimes lately…" She hesitated again. "I'm afraid. At night."

"Of what?"

"I don't know."

"Phone calls? Someone hassling you?"

"No, really, nothing like that."

I shook my head. "I'll get Andy to stay with you."

"No. That would be a scandal. Forget it."

"You can stay at Catherine's."

She shook her head stubbornly.

"Well, then, come with me."

"Come with you?"

"Yes."

"Would that be all right with Mr. Black?"

"He's got nothing to say about it."

"Would it be all right with you?"

"Yes, it would be all right. It'd be great. I'll buy you a bauble and seduce you in a hotel."

"Vivian Maier."

"The photographer."

"Yes. I'll see some of her work. Chicago is where she did most of it."

Baubles couldn't really compete, could they?

Wednesday, May 23

1

We were drinking our coffee on the front steps, and she said, "Flash! I have a great idea!"

"What?" I was reading the sports pages and not really listening.

She said, "Let's take Thomas."

I said, "Take Thomas?"

She pushed the paper aside. "To Chicago. Let's take Thomas."

"And what about my seduction in the hotel?"

"Is that essential?" She slouched a little, looked up at me, opened her eyes wide, and used her most innocent voice. "Please?"

I grinned at her. Knowingly. "I suppose you think I'll fall for that."

She said, "We can get two rooms and close the door."

I said, "Do you really want to do that?"

"Yes."

"Okay. Call Catherine. She's not on duty today."

She said, "See, you fell for it. Here comes Harry."

2

With Harry as my trusty assistant, I brought in and installed two large window air conditioners, in the bedroom and the studio. Then we turned them both on high and pretty soon the entire apartment was icy.

She said, "I'll have all my clients bring jackets." And she kissed me.

Harry said, "Jesus, I helped and you get a kiss and I don't even get a handshake."

I shook his hand.

3

While Clare went around adjusting blinds and air-conditioner settings, I asked Harry down to the front porch to smoke cigars and talk about the men who'd shot up the Hmong's. Who were they?

He said, "Don't know, not yet, but my cousin Craigie has been playing at undercover detective and thinks he has them identified But the point is which party they're associated with. Which could just be nine or a dozen boyos who like to shoot guns. But maybe they're the gunslingers of an actual party. We'll find out."

Thursday, May 24

1

Harry and I had just done a six-mile round-trip run on the river path while Karen and Clare did two miles walking. They were waiting back at the starting point, sunning themselves on a small patch of sand. At the car Harry and I changed into dry T-shirts and we all went to a sandwich shop nearby and stood in the deli line.

Karen said, "Clare said you're going to Chicago for the weekend."

I said, "Uh huh."

"And you're taking a child with you."

"Uh huh."

"You do know what a child is, don't you?"

"One of those short people," I said. "Sort of like you."

Harry said, "Thomas?" and smiled when I nodded and said "Uh huh."

I said, "Her idea," and jerked a thumb at Clare.

She said, "I need *some*one intelligent to talk to."

Karen said, "Is this for practice?"

Clare said, "He's a bit old to be practicing on. He's five. And a half."

Karen said, "Does he look like Sam?"

Clare laughed. "You name an Alexandros male, he looks like Sam. Only this one is smaller."

We carried our food to a table.

Harry said, "Have you introduced him to the manly art of poker?"

I said, "His mom won't let me."

"Teach him gin. Tell her it's a variation of go fish. There are some similarities."

I said, "I think she'd know better."

Clare said, "He plays chess."

Harry said, "There's very little money in chess."

Karen said loftily, "Is that all you two care about?"

Harry and I said "Yes!" simultaneously and bumped fists.

Clare said, "He's very sweet and smart *and* well-behaved."

Harry asked me, "Is he adopted?"

Karen asked Clare, "Do you do any sports?"

"No. Well, I used to play tennis."

Karen said, "What do you do now for fun?"

"Take pictures."

"That's what you do for work. Do you do any other art things?'

Clare said, "There are others?"

"No painting or pottery or anything?"

Clare shook her head.

I said, "She draws sometimes."

Karen looked at me. "What do *you* do?"

"Me?" I shrugged. "Go to the gym. Hit the bags. Jump rope. Lift weights. Get in the ring sometimes."

"A *boxing* gym," she said.

I said, "No girls allowed."

"What did you do in college?"

"In what?"

"I know you went to the U. That's where Harry met you."

Harry and I laughed and I said, "True. But we didn't exactly meet in the library. We played poker in the Union and fleeced undergrads."

Karen said, "You *cheated* them?"

Harry said, "Didn't have to."

"So," Clare said, "what about Karen?"

"Me?"

"Uh huh."

"I'm a librarian."

"And as an undergraduate?"

Harry was grinning.

"Teaching physical education."

"And for fun you?"

"Mostly I swim. I blew out a knee a few years ago. This walk today is about my current limit."

Harry said, "Tell them how you did the knee."

She said, "Ski jumping."

I said, "Boy howdy! They let girls do that?"

Harry said, "Our Karen was a gold medalist in the Norwegian national competition."

Clare said, "I'm so impressed! It looks so scary!"

I said, "Why didn't you go into coaching, or teaching, since you have the training?"

"I may yet. But I've been recuperating. And having surgeries. And recuperating."

Clare said, "My God, I'm officially a slug."

Karen said, "But you're an artist. It's allowed."

2

Clare and I went to her place and showered together and then sat on the front steps to drink a beer in the cooling evening.

After a few silent minutes I said, "When you went to the hospital, when I was an idiot—"

"When *I* was an idiot and drank beer and took pills."

"You were hurting and I hurt you, for which I beg your forgiveness."

She said, "Didn't we already have this conversation?"

"Don't close me off. Before you… fell, you said something. You said what I did before I left was rape." The word hurt my throat. "Was it?"

Now it was her silence.

Finally she said, "I don't know. Certainly it was *nothing* like what happened to me before, when I was young. You were pushy, you were angry, you wanted something you weren't getting and you didn't like that. Thirty-five centuries. All those Greek god stories are rape fantasies written by men. Greek men. But are they *your* stories?"

I said, "I guess they *were*. I'm sort of hoping I'm growing past that phase of my development."

She said, "I hope so too. It's hard for both of us when you're angry."

"Yeah."

"Maybe rape is part of a bell curve, and you were pretty far to the left end."

"Maybe not far enough."

"I don't want to be afraid of you."

"Oh God, no."

Another silence.

She said, "You didn't ask me for sex. You asked me for submission."

I had my arms folded across my knees and I dropped my head to rest on them. "I didn't even ask."

She said, "No. You didn't."

Another silence.

She said, "I don't know what forgiveness is. What it feels like to forgive. But I *think* I've forgiven you."

"Oh, God, Clare, I hope so."

Silence again.

She said, "Let's go in."

"Wait," I said. "Wait." I sat up straight. "There are women who want that. Want it rough. Or say they do."

She said, "I know."

"I've encountered them. It can be exciting. But if the man is angry… that's different."

It came out a whisper. "Yes."

I turned to face her. I said, "Here's my promise to you. I will never come near you angry. I will stay away or go away."

"Oh."

"Maybe this is just a band aid and not a real fix, but it'll do for now and I'll work on the fix. I promise."

She said, "Right. Okay. Thank you."

"Let's go in."

Friday, May 25

1

Catherine had said yes and on Friday morning I escorted Clare and Thomas through the airport terminal to our gate. I had my carry-on, which was a small duffel on a shoulder strap, and Clare was pulling an old-looking carry-on case on wheels. Thomas had a really shabby backpack that he used for school and I decided he needed a new one.

Thomas was so excited he couldn't talk, which I considered a blessing, and Clare was thinking about being in an airplane, shut in and surrounded. But Black had put us in first class, front row, no one in front of her. I put Thomas by the window, Clare on the aisle by Thomas, and me across the aisle from her. Thomas held her hand during takeoff.

In the cab to the airport she asked me if I worried about flying on this day. I said that that wasn't one of my superstitions and that I'd won a lot of money from guys whose it was.

During the flight we drank a quick glass of some very tasty Cabernet Sauvignon and ate little cheese crackers. Thomas asked for a sip of Clare's wine, but I said, "Only at home, Thomas." We allowed him to have a fizzy water with lime. The woman sitting on the other side of me tried to flirt but I politely blew her off. I held Clare's other hand during landing.

When we came off the concourse, Thomas was the one who spotted the young man in a chauffeur's cap holding a sign that said "Mr. Zandros." The driver also held a small posy of daisies, which he handed to Clare. "From Mr. Black," he said.

She was delighted, and said, "How sweet!"

I'd never thought of Hugh Black as *sweet* exactly.

Then the driver and Thomas examined Thomas's comic books together until our luggage came down. The driver snagged a loose luggage cart and escorted us to a new black Mercedes sedan and drove us to the hotel, which was downtown across Lakeshore Drive from the water. An assistant concierge showed us to a two-bedroom-and-parlor suite where an enormous bunch of red roses dominated the sitting room. The card was addressed to Clare Russell and said, "Welcome to Chicago. Hugh Black."

"How did he know I was coming?" she demanded.

I said, "Put your bag in your room, Thomas, and hang up your suit. I told him when I called him to cancel dinner tonight. Usually we eat dinner together before the game."

"Which is my room?" Thomas asked.

Clare said, "You eat with him? Like friends?"

"The smaller one. That way, I think. Yeah, I do. Maybe we *are* friends. We talk about history. He reads a lot."

We went into the master bedroom and I opened both bags, took out jackets, pants, and shirts from mine to hang up, and then some items of Clare's as long as I was in front of the open closet. She was still admiring the roses. She had pulled three from the vase and was carrying them around with her, holding them next to her cheek.

"Why is he being nice to me?"

"Because you have a nice bottom and he wants your good will."

"Why?" She started her unpacking procedure: taking out all her underwear and dropping it into a drawer.

"To keep me sweet."

Thomas yelled from his room, "Theo, I can't reach the hangers."

"Okay, I'll do it." I went into his room.

He followed me back to our bedroom. "Can I watch TV, Theo?"

"God, no, I want lunch. Are you two ready to go?"

We ate lunch at a place I'd found nearby that had great sausages and excellent beer. It also had a poker table in the back room that I hadn't mentioned to Black and didn't mention to Clare. Then we walked down Michigan Avenue to a men's shop I'd had good luck in, and I bought a dark gray oxford-cloth shirt, and an even darker gray cashmere pullover sweater, and some pale gray all-cotton handker-chiefs. They had a boys' department and I bought Thomas a yellow, cotton pullover sweater to wear under his windbreaker, and a palest yellow oxford-cloth dress shirt, and some black knee-length socks to wear with his suit.

I claimed I cared little for what money could buy, but I did like having good clothes. And I liked buying things for all the children. None of them were suffering any deprivation, but as parents my sib-lings were sensible and even-handed and frugal, perhaps more than they needed to be. It was a bit of a habit learned from our parents, who really had needed to be. So now I was making up for it, just somewhat.

A bit farther down the avenue there was a store for women that I'd window-shopped on earlier trips. I showed the windows to Clare and she liked what she saw there. I said, do you have a dinner dress and she shook her head, so I sent her in to buy one while I took Thomas strolling some more. When we got back she shyly modeled a long strapless number in sapphire-blue silk that had lavish gold em-broidery on the fitted top and a full skirt that swished nicely around her ankles. She got low-heeled, gold sandals, a very long, blue and gold silk scarf—the two ends went to the bottom of the dress—and a little gold purse to carry, and she was high as a kite. Then we sent all the packages by taxi to the hotel and spent the rest of the day at the Natural History museum. At the end of the long afternoon we let Thomas watch something silly on television and eat a small bag of potato chips in his room while we drank a beer and leaned against each other on the couch in the parlor.

She said, "Having a bunch of money could be fun."

I said, "That's not what you said on New Year's Eve while I was driving you home from Jenneky's."

"Were you taking notes? This trust-fund thing. Can I use that money?"

"Yes. It's yours. Weren't you listening?"

She said, "Well, how do I get it?"

"The income's in your checking account. The May deposit should be there now."

"It is?"

"First of every month starting this one. Your income will be a little over four thousand a month."

"My God. Do you think I could get a credit card now?"

"You don't have *any*? That's illegal, isn't it?"

She said, "I'm too poor."

"You were, but now you're not. Talk to Uncle Cy. He'll arrange it."

"Can I tell people about my money?"

"I think it'll be our little secret."

"Nobody's business but our own."

"Exactly."

"Not even Karen?"

"*Especially* not Karen."

"Where did you get all those things in the box at the bank? The coins and things."

"The stocks and bonds I inherited from my mother. They aren't worth much. I really only keep them for sentimental reasons. The rest of it I won in poker games."

"And all that money? The Black Dress Fund? And the money in the trust fund?"

I started laughing. "I'm a partner in a thriving family business. Plus I sometimes play on my own account, outside the family. And I'm not interested in the stock market or fancy cars or big boats or gold jewelry. Except for you. I like giving you baubles."

"Can we spend some money on dinner? I'm hungry."

"Let me shower first. Then I'll organize Thomas and me while you get ready."

2

I escorted them to dinner in the very posh hotel dining room. It was on the mezzanine level and had a lot of glass and we could look out over the lights of the city. Haute cuisine and haute décor. Me in my headwaiter's uniform, Clare in her new dress and her sapphire earrings and sapphire ring, and Thomas in his neat black suit and new shirt and a red tie. The suit looked like I should get him a larger one. He never looked like he'd changed size, but he must have.

"I feel like a queen," she said, standing tall and haughty in the elevator. "And all the other women will say, how did *she* get the two most handsome men in the kingdom?"

Thomas made a horrible face.

"All the men will know how," I said in a low voice next to her ear.

We were drinking coffee and Thomas was eating ice cream when Hugh Black walked up to our table with another man, someone I'd played with before. They were both in evening dress. I stood up, and, at a look from me, so did Thomas. Black introduced Franklin Clark to Clare and I said, "My nephew, Thomas Kamariotis. Thomas, this is Mr. Black and Mr. Clark." Thomas shook hands very smartly, and Clare gave him a very warm and approving smile.

Franklin Clark looked pleased. "Thomas," he said. "Miss Russell."

Thomas dived under the table for his napkin.

Black was beaming, which I found very amusing. He said, "May we join you for a brandy?"

I said, "Please do that," as I gestured to the empty chairs. We all sat. Clark ordered four brandies from a hovering waiter, naming a brand I'd only heard of, never tasted. Two more waiters rushed up to pour coffee and ice water and replace the cream pitcher with a fresh one.

Clare leaned forward slightly and said, "Thank you for the flowers, Mr. Black. They're so beautiful. I especially love roses." She did. She had carried four of them to dinner and they were on the table by her hand.

He smiled again and bowed slightly, his attention all on her. He had a very smooth voice when he wanted to. "I'm glad you like them. I always enjoy sending flowers to a beautiful woman, and I thought roses would suit you. The queen of flowers."

She went pink. For a man who had to do nothing more than snap his fingers to get a woman, he certainly had the moves, and I didn't think he'd learned them at his daddy's knee.

Clark said to Clare, "Is everything in your suite satisfactory?"

She said, "It's perfect. We're very comfortable."

The brandies arrived and Clark offered me a cigar, then turned back to Clare.

"I've seen some of your work, Miss Russell," he said. "I have friends in St. Paul. The Ramseys. And the Bookers. You did portraits of their grandchildren. I'd like very much to arrange to have you photograph *my* granddaughters."

"How old are they?"

"Two and three."

"Would you bring them to St. Paul?"

"It would be a lot easier to bring you to Chicago."

She smiled. "I usually use a large-format camera. Rather bulky. But I do have some other cameras I could bring here. Or possibly I could rent one." She looked thoughtful.

"You didn't bring cameras with you? I thought all photographers carried several hundred pounds of equipment at all times."

She smiled again. "I brought a point-and-shoot, for fun. But I stick pretty much to portraits and I think the results from a large-format camera using film can't be touched by digital."

"Could you come to our home while you're here this weekend? You could meet the children and my son and daughter-in-law and my wife. And Thomas could meet a litter of puppies."

I laughed. "You play dirty, Frank."

She looked at me, back at Clark.

He said, "Could you all come for lunch on Sunday?"

Thomas was bouncing.

She said, "Sam?"

I said, "Whatever you want."

"You'll come too?"

"Of course."

"Well, yes then." She smiled at Clark, and he all but blinked.

"Oh, wow," said Thomas. "What kind of puppies are they?"

"Poodles. Six of them. Eight weeks old and full of beans. My wife breeds them." He finished his brandy and stood up. "I'll see you Sunday then, Miss Russell. And Thomas."

Clare put out her hand and he took it and bowed over it. Then, with a hesitation so slight only I would see it, she put out her hand to Black, and he too took it, ever so gently, and bowed over it, a perfect imitation of Clark. And no mockery. He'd been studying.

Clark said, "See you later, Zandros."

He and Black walked away.

"Well," I said. "I was wrong about the good will for my sake. He wants it for its own sake. He wants to offer his friends and important acquaintances an introduction to Frances Russell."

"To me? Who's Mr. Clark? Is he important?"

"Haven't you ever heard of Franklin Clark?"

She shook her head.

"He specializes in being rich. He owns two popular nightclubs, which are just a hobby, and some racehorses, another hobby, and he inherited several boxcars of money from his father who owned some railroads and a bank or two. Or four. All of which Franklin inherited. He now also owns a liquor distribution company and two or three big trucking companies and a small chain of deluxe hotels. Like this one. And a gold mine in Canada and some other mining interests in South America. Copper, I think. Or silver. Maybe both."

"I'd like to see a boxcar of money," said Thomas. "Can I ask to see one when we go there?"

"Sorry, Thomas, it's only a figure of speech. Are you done eating?"

"Uh huh."

"Okay, you and Aunt Clare are off to bed. I have to go earn some olives."

He said, "You play for olives?"

"Another figure of speech. Come on, I'll see you two home, and Aunt Clare can explain figures of speech."

"Our TV has HBO," Thomas said wooingly to Clare.

"We'll see," said Clare, taking his hand. "I'll bet your mom is pretty strict about TV, and we have to follow her rules, even when she's not here."

"Well, *that's* not fair!" he said.

3

When we were in the lobby, Clare's hand in mine and Thomas's in hers, I said, "Oh, wait, before we go up…" I pulled Clare by the hand, and she pulled Thomas, and we detoured into the multi-level, sparkling glass-and-steel shopping concourse that was part of the hotel. All the stores were open still, and I led them into a jewelry store that I had window-shopped several times. A very superior salesman was at our side instantly. I introduced him to Clare.

"Ah, the bauble!" Clare said.

I said, "Thomas, hands in pockets."

He complied easily enough, and he'd keep them there until we left the store. We'd done this many times before.

We went to a case I had already cased, and I pointed to a pair of bangle bracelets. "May we see those, please?"

Another clerk appeared whose task seemed to be watching Thomas, and I grinned at him and suddenly wondered what it must have been like to go shopping, to go *any*where, with me and Andy when we were young. I think my mother once mentioned hand-cuffs.

The clerk took the velvet tray out of the case and laid the two bangles on another velvet pad. They were thin gold hoops set all around with impossibly tiny gold flowers with even tinier ruby petals and emerald leaves. He offered me a magnifying glass and I offered it to Clare. She looked up at the clerk.

"Do you have a loupe that I could use?" she asked.

"Of course, Ms. Russell." He handed her a small round magnifier and one of the bangles and she examined several of the flowers.

"My God," she said.

"Yes," he said, and smiled.

Then she picked up the magnifying glass and examined each bangle all the way around on both sides as it lay on the flat of her hand. I glanced over at Thomas. Hands still in pockets, he was absorbed in a display of men's signet rings.

She examined the second bangle and slipped them onto her wrist. "They're lovely," she said. She smiled at me. "The perfect bauble." She slid them off.

The clerk said, "I'm glad you like them, Ms. Russell."

She smiled at him.

I gave him a card and he took the bangles away to be wrapped and paid for. A couple of minutes later he presented me with something in a small leather fold to sign, and a minute after that there came a discreet receipt in a silver-colored pasteboard folder, just the right size, tucked under the flat silver-colored ribbon with bow around a flat silver box, and all handed to me on a silver salver by God. The name of the store, Argenta, was discreetly embossed on the folder and the box.

He made a delicate gesture toward Clare's earrings. "We have a very nice selection of antique jewelry, if that would interest you, Mr. Zandros."

I said, "Another time, I think."

He looked over at Thomas, who was now looking at men's bracelets. "That is the most well-behaved child I've ever seen."

Clare gave him another smile. "The most loved too," she said.

In the elevator Thomas asked, "Do men wear jewelry?"

"Sure," I said. "Many men do."

"You don't. Or Cousin Andy. Or Uncle Philip."

I stopped him before he could name every man he knew. "Your dad had some jewelry that I bet your mom is saving for you and Stephen. He had a signet ring."

"With a letter? Like the ones in that store?"

"Uh huh. And he had two really good watches and an engraved ID bracelet. Your mom is probably saving the bracelet and ring for Stephen."

"He gets everything," Thomas said bitterly as only a five-year-old can be bitter.

As we exited the elevator, Clare said, "He knew my name."

I said, "I don't know how they do that, but it's my guess that the staff of a hotel catering to money have a very efficient grapevine. Maybe even a daily newsletter from the management."

She asked, "Are two bangles one bauble or two?"

"Oh, two," I said.

"I think one. Definitely one."

4

I sent Thomas into his room to watch TV "so I can say goodnight to Thia Clare."

"And kiss?"

"Absolutely."

He made a face.

I pulled her down on the couch and she put her legs up on my lap. I put my hand under her dress and she pushed it away.

"Not in front of the child."

I took off her sandal and held her foot. "I want to buy you a bathtubful of blue stones. You will lie in it naked and your eyes will be the bluest of the blue."

"Are you sure you aren't Irish?"

I squeezed her foot. "If I don't get out of here now…" I pushed her legs off my lap. "One more kiss." Then I tore myself away.

Saturday, May 26

1

They were already up when I came in, watching cartoons and eating room-service scrambled eggs and bacon and French toast. I leaned over to kiss Clare and she said, "Ugh. Cigars and whisky do *not* go with French toast."

"No more kisses for you."

"I'm going to the science museum with Thomas," she said, "and he's going to a photography exhibit with me. Then we're going to the aquarium. Can you give me some money? We'll have to get lunch. And admissions. And souvenirs. And maybe taxis. And we may just shop a little. And I don't have much cash with me."

"A red-letter day. You asked me for money."

"You have some very strange ideas about money," she said.

I gave her three hundred in twenties. Then five hundreds. "Is that enough?"

She looked at it and said, "I came to Chicago once with a history-of-architecture class. I had forty dollars for the whole two days. And I thought I was rich."

"If you see the right one, buy Thomas a new backpack. Okay, Thomas. What's your name?"

"Thomas Kamariotis."

"And what's my name?"

"Sam Zandros."

"Or?"

"Sam Alexandros."

"Spell that."

He did.

"And what is Thia Clare's name?"

"Frances Clare Russell."

"And what hotel are we staying in?"

"The Clark."

"And what is your phone number at home? And my cell number? And the office number? And Thia Clare's cell number?"

He reeled them all off.

"Where's your ID card?"

He took his school picture ID from his backpack and showed it to me. "Carry it in your pocket," I said. "One with a zipper." He was dressed for an expedition—yellow T-shirt, khaki cargo shorts with zippered pockets, fleece-lined yellow wind-breaker. I took one of the concierge business cards from the desk and zipped it into one of his cargo pockets along with the ID card and then put one into Clare's pocket. "And you're planning to stay close to Thia Clare and do everything she says?"

"Yes."

"Take good care of her. Don't let her wander off."

He grinned. "Aye aye, sir."

"Do you know how to take a taxi?"

"I saw it on TV."

"If you get lost, you come right back here in a taxi and go to the front deskwhere we signed in when we first came here. Ask for the manager and tell him what's up. Then wait in the lobby for us. Or ask someone to call a cop for you. Like someone working in a shop. But don't take any rides with any other nice people who just want to give you a lift. Only a taxi or a cop." I put two twenties into one zippered pocket and three twenties into the other. "This is for emergencies. All your other stuff Thia Clare will pay for."

He nodded.

She kissed me carefully. "You're very bristly."

"Wake me up when you come in."

2

I was almost awake when they came in and I sat up in bed and listened to Clare order chocolate milk and coffee and a pitcher of juice and ice from room service before she came into the bedroom.

"Where's the child?" I asked.

"In his room, watching a show about dinosaurs. I hope Catherine would consider it appropriate. It's public television. Is dinosaur violence acceptable? We had a good time, but he's tired. So am I. We bought a book about rocks and a poster of sharks for Thomas' room, and we found him an excellent new backpack at a shop right near the hotel. Bright yellow. We'll never lose him."

I pulled her down on the bed and rolled over on top of her, dragging the covers with me. "Can we play the seduction scene now?"

"Absolutely not." But she put her arms around my neck.

"Do you want barbeque?"

"Yes."

"But no seduction."

"No."

"You are very hard hearted."

"Whereas you are just hard." She giggled, then laughed all out.

Room service came, which Thomas loved. Someone knocks on your door and hands you something you never get at home. He drank chocolate milk and we all had orange juice, and Clare and I drank coffee and they rested up from their day. Thomas fell asleep in front of the TV, and I showered and shaved.

We ate some excellent barbeque and went into a big bookstore and bought comic books and a chapter book about a time-traveling dinosaur for Thomas, and new mystery novels for Clare and me, then back to our rooms where she and Thomas sat on the bed watching me change into my evening uniform, business mode. Suit, charcoal gray, Italian. Shirt, pale yellow, with collar. Silk tie, gray-on-gray stripe.

"Where do you go?" she asked.

I stopped tying my tie and looked at her. "I didn't tell you?" She shook her head. "Damn! I'm sorry, darling. What an idiot I am." I took a card from my wallet, and handed it to her. "It's a private club on top of that tower of apartments next door. Give me your phone." I punched in the club's phone number. "Call me if you need anything. Anything at all. You look tired."

"Thomas and I walked *miles*. He was very polite about the photography." Thomas made a face. "Most of it *was* pretty boring. The whole gallery was boring. I didn't even buy the catalogue. However, we persevered. And the aquarium was interesting."

Thomas said, "Especially the sharks!" and he rolled on the bed in the throes of a shark attack.

Sunday, May 27

1

At two in the morning, my phone rang. I had just thrown in a particularly irritating hand. I had played a 2 4 of spades on the big blind, flop came 3 5 6, the 3 and 5 being spades, I failed to make the flush on the turn or the river, and ended up losing to some loud-mouthed ass in lousy position who thought he was brilliant for playing 4 7 off-suit. Fuck.

Clare said, "Sam?"

"What? What is it?" I stood up.

"Someone is knocking on the door and saying he's hotel security and that I should let him in."

Oh, Jesus, no. "No, don't! Call the switchboard and tell them to send security up right now. Don't let them make you explain, get hysterical if you have to. Just tell them *right now*. And don't open the door to *anyone* until I get there. No one!"

I was moving. I headed for the elevators. Without a word, Black's man Carl followed me, opened an elevator door with a key card, and there it was, waiting. We went down with no stopping. He had no trouble keeping up as we ran across the open plaza between the two buildings. In the hotel he said, "No, this way," and steered me to a service elevator that he also opened with the card.

In the corridor outside our suite, two police officers and three uniformed hotel security guards had two men, also wearing uniforms but not the right ones, spread-eagled against the wall. Two ski masks on the floor. I knocked on the door and shouted my name to Clare, and it opened on the chain. She shut it, then opened it all the way and came straight at me. I caught her. Caught them. Old as he was, she was carrying Thomas on her hip. I got both of them in an embrace. "Anyone you know?" I asked Carl past her head.

The police handcuffed the two intruders and turned them around. Carl shook his head and said no.

I looked again. "Well, fuck, I do." I moved Clare and Thomas aside, gently, and stepped closer. "Haven't I seen you? Working as a janitor, here in the hotel? I saw you by the front desk, early in the morning."

One of the hotel's real security guards jerked a thumb at the other intruder. "I think this one works here, too," he said.

An assistant manager and the head-on-duty of security, both looking like they'd dressed in a hurry, appeared with many *many* apologies. I demanded and got a security guard outside our door for the rest of our stay. Thomas wiggled his way to the floor and ducked out of my reach to stand in the middle of everything in his flannel pajamas, his dark hair all on end. After a short period of confusion, everyone but the guard disappeared and I herded Clare and Thomas inside. Almost everyone. Carl followed us into the sitting room.

He said, "You can go back to the game, and I'll stay here."

Clare said, "No!" and Thomas looked startled.

"I only do my job," Carl told me.

"Did Black set this up?" I asked him.

"No, nothing to do with us."

"Call him and tell him what happened."

I found a tin of little cigars in my pocket, lit one while Carl talked on his phone, and realized that Thomas was still in the room.

I said, "Thomas, go to bed."

"Now?"

"Yes, now. When else?"

Clare said, "Go on, sweetie. I'll come in a few minutes." She gave him a kiss and a pat to send him off.

Carl held out his phone to me.

"Not our affair," said Black. "And Miss Russell is reluctant to let Carl stay?"

"Do you blame her?"

"I suppose not. It would be for her safety, and your nephew's. Carl is an extremely capable bodyguard."

I said to Clare, "Carl would be here to protect you."

"All right, all right. Whatever you say."

She went into Thomas's room, and shut the door.

I handed Carl his phone and left.

2

I got back at eight. Carl was watching television and jerked his head at Thomas's door when I started for our bedroom. She was asleep with Thomas on his bed. I shook her gently and took her hand and she followed me into our bedroom. Carl was gone when we went through the sitting room.

I took off my jacket and pulled her down on the bed to cuddle. "See? You're okay, Thomas is okay, and I played like an angel. Hugh Black is happy, Frank Clark is not too unhappy, and several of his friends are poorer but wiser men."

"Mmm." She snuggled closer.

"Wake up. Time to feed the baby. And lunch at Clark's today, remember?"

"Clark who?"

Franklin Clark apologized up one side and down the other for *his* hotel having been the scene of a middle-of-the-night fright for Clare and Thomas. He didn't say heads-will-roll, but he may have had it in mind. I told him, as an aside, that we had purchased some expensive jewelry from the shop in the arcade, and perhaps someone there was also selling information. He looked grim for a minute, then cleared his expression to introduce his daughter-in-law.

By late afternoon, Clare had promised to return in several weeks with cameras. She sat on the floor and played with the two toddlers and her point-and-shoot, showing them pictures of themselves and their parents and grandparents, and they crawled onto her lap and snuggled in. And Thomas played with baby poodles and took pictures of everybody with a new little pocket-size digital that I'd never seen before. I had a talk with Frank Clark about night-club management, and had the offer of a minority investor, and Thomas wanted a dog. We flew home

3

Before we left Chicago, I had a short conversation with Thomas. "About what happened last night," I said. We were sitting on the master bed, waiting for Clare to finish packing. "Tell your mom about it tonight. As soon as we get home. It's very important that she knows about it right away. And I'll talk to her about it tonight or first thing tomorrow morning, whenever she wants, but I'll want to take Aunt Clare home first."

"Okay."

"You can talk to Uncle Philip about it, or Cousin Andy, or Uncle Nick, or Uncle Cy, if you want to, but no one else, okay?"

"Okay."

"No Aunt Sofia, no Jamie, no one at school, no Stephen, or Meli, no Ioulia. This is important. Now get your suitcase and check your room, make sure you didn't leave anything. Look in the closet and the bathroom." He dashed off.

Clare was in the doorway. "Tell no women?" she said.

"Philip will tell Sofia, and maybe Meli, as is his right. Ioulia is a total blabbermouth. Catherine can tell her, but I'm not going to be on the hook for that one. I'll be telling Philip and Andy and Uncle Nick and Uncle Cy. I would just rather they heard it from me."

"What will happen to those men?"

"The police have them. There've been four or five robberies from guest rooms here over the past six months, same MO. The hotel thinks they might be responsible."

"Wow, you talk just like those cops on TV."

"I know how to bring it, baby."

4

When we arrived at Clare's there was a black-on-yellow sign in her miniscule front yard.

"Are you moving?" I asked.

"It must be the guys downstairs."

I can take a hint from God as fast as the next guy. I went out the back door and down and stood on the back porch and called Clare's landlord. And while I was standing there, something that sounded like a horsefly hit the tree at the end of the porch. Simultaneously there was a semi-loud bang from down the alley. I stepped backward into the hall and shut the door and went halfway up the steps. No more shots. There was a small dusty window and I peeked out, very carefully. Nothing. No one. Quiet Sunday evening. After a while my pulse returned to normal and I went in.

Monday, May 28

1

I called Andy and he came over. We went out into the backyard—to smoke cigars, we told Clare—and I showed him two small envelopes I had found in Clare's desk. They were for holding little photos. On one I had written yesterday's date and on the other April 23. We went down into the yard and to the tree at the end of the porch.

I said, "As I thought, Watson. Two bullets."

"Yes, Holmes, you are correct."

I said, "Give me your pocket knife."

"No, you'll just cut yourself." He elbowed me aside and started digging at the bark.

I said, "Don't scratch it."

He said, "Do I *look* stupid?"

After a few minutes he gently extracted a spent bullet from the hole he'd dug.

A few more minutes and we had the other out.

He said, "Are you sure you know which is which?"

"Not totally, but if I'm right and they're from the same gun, and it's the gun I think it is, it won't matter. None of this'll ever be in a court of law."

2

Clare and I were on our way to eat with Harry and Karen at Tomato Red before he and I went to play at Elmore's.

I said, "You have a new downstairs neighbor."

She said, "Oh, is the sign gone already? I didn't even notice."

"I signed the lease today."

"What?"

I loved it when I said something and she gave me that nonplussed look. It always made me want to kiss her.

"I rented the downstairs apartment. It's ours as of tomorrow. Those two guys wanted to move out as soon as possible. They even sold me their furniture and all their household stuff. They've got jobs at some resort in Colorado."

"My God."

"Indeed."

"What a perfect idea!"

"You think so?"

"Why does everything always fall your way?"

"I'm a very lucky guy."

"Have you sold your soul to the devil?"

"I declined his paltry offer. But it's yours for the asking."

3

The restaurant was warm and smelled delicious. Their specialty was Italian dishes in casseroles of varying sizes, served family style. We four had long since chosen the four dishes we all liked and we took turns ordering when we came here.

Harry said, "Your family owns a dozen apartment buildings and you're moving into that ratty duplex?"

I said, "How the hell did you know about the buildings?" I waved at the waiter.

He said, "I pay attention to the gossip. Clare told Karen and Karen told me. Is it a secret?"

I said, "I guess not. I never thought about it."

Clare said, "I admit it's on the downhill slope, but it's not *ret-ty*."

He said, "You couldn't pay me to go into that basement. I've seen all those movies."

I ordered the food, the wine selection for the women, and mineral water for me and Harry.

Karen said to Clare, "You make movies in your basement?"

Clare said, "My own company. Rat Films. Whips 'R' Us."

Harry said, "Try to stay on task here, you two."

The two beauties bumped fists.

I said, "I've got a cleaning company coming in tomorrow. Want to help me paint?"

Harry said, "I already painted ninety percent of the upstairs."

Clare said, "Ten percent. Maybe."

The salad-for-four came with a platter of vegetables and dipping sauces.

I said, "Then you know just how to do it. You can show me."

Clare said, "You wouldn't want Sam to have all the fun, right?"

He said, "Oh God no, Tom. What time do we start?"

Karen said, "Can I come too?"

Clare took a little tomato. "Bring your whip," she said.

4

Harry and I both did well, as usual, and at four a. m. we were on our way out, feeling good, when a man I knew slightly, Davey Glenn, a sidekick of Kevvy Smith, stepped out of an alley and stopped in front of us. I already had my gun out of its holster, soon as we left the game, and resting in my pocket, in my hand, and I figured Harry for the same.

I said, "This is getting tiresome."

Harry said, "Indeed. Hey, Davey. You're up early."

"Harry." Davey nodded slightly. "Kevvy wants to see Zandros. Talk to him."

I said, "Tell him to give me a call at the office."

"He would like to talk to you now," he said carefully. "His car. Over there." He jerked his head.

Harry said, "Too much TV. It's ruining our civil society."

I said, "My thoughts exactly. Tell him he can get out of his car and come over here and we'll all talk. The walk will do him good."

"Not Parker."

"Yes, Parker. Am I crazy?"

Davey went to a Ford SUV parked a few yards away, and the window by the passenger lowered halfway. After a couple of minutes of vigorous head nodding by Davey and muttered conversation, the passenger door opened and Kevvy Smith got out and walked over to where we were standing.

His opening gambit was, "You're a pain in the butt, Zandros."

"As always," I said.

"Yeah." Kevvy Smith was a short, whippet-thin, sharp-faced Irishman, with black hair combed back and washed-out blue eyes. He'd lost three or four teeth and the remaining ones were brown. He wore a suit that hung on him and a white shirt and no tie. He looked like a harmless barfly but for twenty years he'd been running the biggest outfit that passed for organized crime in St. Paul. He said abruptly, "I didn't do your brother and none of my guys did. I'm sorry he's gone."

I said. "Thanks. Good to know."

A bus went by, all lit up inside, with two passengers.

He said, "You're working for a guy in Chicago."

"That's putting it a bit broadly," I said. "He's backed me in a few games."

"You don't need outside backers."

"And how is this your business, Kevvy?"

"It's in St. Paul, it's my business."

I said, "Not me, not my family." I was starting to simmer.

"Quit with Black," he said. "Or you'll be sorry."

"What's it to you, anyway?"

"I don't want Black here. At all. Not even just some hot-shot card player."

"Thanks for the conversation, Kevvy. Always a pleasure." I walked away, no hurry, Harry beside me.

He muttered. "My shoulder blades are clenching."

I said, "There's a picture."

5

Uncle Cy did not fail me. I asked if he knew a ballistics expert and he said yes and gave me a questioning look. I handed him the two envelopes.

He asked, "Do you have the gun?"

"I think they're from Paul's gun, which is in our vault at the office."

6

I took Clare to get the rings sized and when we picked them up we also picked a gold ring guard, set with baby sapphires, to wear with the engagement ring. She was going to balk, but I told her that as her affianced it was my right, nay, my duty, to buy baubles for her. I think the clerk was more impressed by my speech than she was, but she let me have my way. Luckily she didn't see the price.

7

Shortly after we got back from Chicago I got a postcard in the mail at Catherine's address. The front side was a picture of the Chicago skyline and it had been mailed the Saturday before. The message said, "Everything of which I die possessed I leave to Sam Alexandros, except the bauble from Chicago, which I leave to Karen Lund. Frances Clare Russell."

I put it in my safe.

Tuesday, May 29

Everything went according to my plan, of course. The cleaners, who were my cousins Mike and Peter, and Harry and I took out all the old furniture and junk that the two guys had left, and Peter and Mike paid a guy they knew with a truck to haul it all away to the thrift store. Then they scrubbed the place from top to bottom and inside to out and waxed and buffed the floors. And we all painted.

We decided on his and her bedrooms, hers upstairs and his down, for the convenience of clothes storage and for accommodating odd schedules and the occasional need for separateness. So Clare still had basically the same apartment, which was good, but she no longer had to use her waiting-room-slash-office for a living room—also good—not that this changed the furnishings in any way. We had a real living room and a dining room and a kitchen I claimed as my own. And a guest room. All good.

Clare and I did a lightning shopping trip at a store Sofia recommended—I don't browse—and bought the basic furniture and rugs for the living room and dining room and downstairs bedroom, and I brought most of my clothes and books and bedding from Catherine's, although my room there was still mine. For emergencies. Catherine gave us sets of dishes—breakfast, lunch, and dinner—that had been languishing in her storage room since her own wedding. They baffled Clare. Who needed so many dishes! Catherine also gave us three sets of glassware for twelve and two sets of flatware for twelve—one stainless, one silver—and Sofia furnished us with a complete set of pots and pans and bakeware and a bushel of kitchen utensils and gadgets. Karen busily measured all the windows for blinds and sent me and Harry off to the store to purchase what she assured us were 'window treatments. ' They were venetian blinds. Harry and I installed them and then we all drank champagne.

We slept in our new apartment for the first time and in the morning made love. While I got coffee and juice from my new kitchen, Clare examined all the new patterns of light and shadow in the bedroom. And when we finally got up she did a walk-through and came back to report. "Blank walls! This place is *full* of blank walls!"

Thursday, May 31

Before our next trip to Chicago, Franklin Clark called Clare twice to make appointments for other clients that same weekend. She told me after the second call that she was going to use some of my money.

I raised my eyes to heaven. "It's not mine, it's yours. Absolutely. You don't have to tell me or ask me or even mention it. The Black Dress fund, yes. You can tell me about that if you go into it, and you can tell me afterward if you're in a hurry beforehand. Unless you really do need it for a black dress. But the trust fund income is yours. Yours absolutely."

"Well, it still feels like yours."

"So what are you going to buy? I'm just curious. Not checking up on you or anything."

"Camera stuff. A carry-on case. And I asked Mr. Clark to rent some lights for me. And get some film. So I'll have to reimburse him."

I started laughing. "You've got Franklin Clark doing your gofer work? And on an expense account?"

"I'm sure he has an assistant," she said haughtily. "I don't know where to buy film down there and I want it fresh. And I didn't want to take the film through security more than once. You can talk to them on the way back, *Mr*. Know-It-All."

I called the airline.

Because she had shoots lined up for all day both Saturday and Sunday and she wanted plenty of time to set up and check out the space and lighting at the Clarks' again—some of it outdoors this time—we were flying down on Thursday at midday and staying until Monday. After much lobbying from Clare and Thomas, we were bringing Thomas with us again. He had the new yellow backpack that Aunt Clare had bought him, and in it he was carrying the camera Clare had given him on our last trip, his homework for the three schooldays he was missing, his allowed number of comic books, which seemed like more than I had allowed, two books from the Greek School library, and his sweater and windbreaker. Hanging around his neck on a lanyard he had a new cell phone, with games, that I had bought at a store where the clerk was probably twelve and made me feel like a geezer. Then I took Thomas for a haircut and he showed me how to use the games, and I felt prehistoric.

When we got into the cab to the airport Clare had a new black plastic hardcase with wheels and pull-out handle. "It's sized to be carry-on," she said. "And the inside is all foam. I think it will withstand atomic explosions."

"What's in it?"

"My Tachihari."

"So this is serious business."

"I was thinking of handcuffing it to my wrist."

"And what's that Nikon hanging around your neck?"

"My new DSLR." She colored a bit.

"And the one I saw going into your pocket?" I was laughing.

"My ultra-compact digital. I got it for kids to play with while I work. I'm shooting ten-year-old twins on Sunday."

"And that bag on your shoulder?"

"Lenses. Tripod. Laptop. Stuff. I sort of had to use that new credit card. Next month, after I pay the credit card bill, new tablet and some new apps for it. And the month after that, upgrade the desktop. They just upgraded the software I use and I need to upgrade all my hardware in order to use it. I think one of those paper-thin, desktop-sized laptops. And one of these months soon, a new printer."

She was looking like the cat just about to chomp down on the canary.

I said, "Wow. Did you upgrade your insurance?"

"I did."

"Good. Give me that shoulder bag. You're listing."

I resolved to get more money into her account. I would claim it was from the trust fund. Investments doing better than expected. Cy could set it up. I wanted her to have all the income her business needed.

All her shoots were successful and I was successful. Clare got another bauble from that same store, an estate piece this time, a delicate gold and amber necklace, to wear with a new black silk shirtwaist dress from the shop on the Avenue. Styled like a man's dress shirt on top and long plain flared skirt below.

The cops had found a recently hired employee at the jewelry store doing just what I had suggested. The store owner, who had waited on us our first trip, practically threw himself on the floor to be walked on when we appeared, gave me a fifty-percent discount on the necklace, and said the discount was on my account forever, for anything in the store. He said his reputation was worth every penny.

Thomas got a new suit and a tie with a diagram of the solar system printed on it, and he and Clare went to an art show, and I took him to the planetarium. He played with the puppies, and Franklin Clark and I chatted about my bistro.

And I had the privilege of watching Clare work, which didn't happen often. This time for some reason she invited me in. I leaned against the wall behind her, quiet as midnight, almost afraid to think loudly. She had a talent for dealing with children, talking to them, getting them to be themselves and open up to her. They all three talked while she worked, and they could see that she was both serious and friendly, and so they were too, because they wanted her to like them. And she did. She genuinely liked them.

Monday, June 22

1

Harry dropped me off and I went straight into the kitchen, grabbed the o.j. from the refrigerator, and chugged a half-dozen hefty swallows right from the carton. Clare hated that but I figured I was co-owner of the juice *and* the carton. And what she didn't know, and all that.

Then upstairs and into her office. The room was dim, blinds drawn and only a small desk lamp, and at first I thought she wasn't there, but she was, sitting at the desk, her back to me, her head down, resting on her forearms.

I said, "Hi. What's up?"

She said, "Hi." Her voice was muffled and she sounded congested.

"Have you had lunch? '

"No."

She sat up slowly.

I said, "Do you want something? Ham and cheese sandwich?"

"No. Not now. Would you sit down? Please?"

"Sure." I sat on the edge of the couch. All my spidey senses were tingling.

She said, "I have to tell you what I did this morning. It may take a while."

"Sure."

"So please don't interrupt."

I raised my eyebrows. "Sure."

She said, "I went for a walk. I crossed the river and went over to Seven Corners and down Cedar. There were a lot of people out, you know how it is. You get past Riverside and everybody's outside." She put her hands up to rub her eyes. "I couldn't walk fast because it was so crowded." Her hands fell to her lap.

I was making no moves past breathing enough to stay alive.

She went on. "Up ahead of me there was a woman pushing a baby in a stroller and carrying a smaller baby in one of those large shawls and calling out—not English, maybe Somali. She was wearing the long skirt and tunic and a headwrap. She was calling to a third child—maybe he was four. He was running around, bumping into people, pretending to be an airplane—you know how they do. Then I realized that the man walking behind her was with them. But not paying any attention to them. He was using a cell phone and calling out to some other men crowded around the front door of a store. One that sells phones and things."

I knew the place. I had the whole picture in my head.

"For some reason I was assuming he was her husband. I'm not sure why. I just did." She paused for a few seconds, then went on. "I had a point-and-shoot in my pocket, and I took it out and started taking pictures of the family. All of them. I was trying to be as unobtrusive as I could, and I don't think anyone noticed what I was doing. After about a half a block of this, the four-year-old child suddenly ran out into the street and was hit by a car. And flew. He flew through the air. And landed. In the street." Pause while she swallowed. "The mother stopped walking and started screaming. The father ran out into the street and went to his knees by the boy. The baby in the shawl started wailing. A bunch of men, maybe half a dozen, went out into the street and started shouting and waving their arms. Two of them were sort of directing traffic around the whole scene. The driver got out of his car. He looked Somali too, and he started shouting and waving his arms and it seemed like he was saying *it wasn't my fault* and the kid was lying all still in the street and the father was still there on his knees and now *he* was wailing. A bunch of women gathered and surrounded the mother and *they* were wailing and waving their arms. And then the sirens and the cops and the ambulance and flash-ing lights—and all the while—*all the while!* —I kept shooting."

Anguish was wringing the low tones out of her voice, pushing it up into another register. "I kept shooting!"

She found a wadded-up tissue on the desk and wiped her eyes and found another one and blew her nose. After a couple of minutes she started talking again. "The father jumped up and came back to the sidewalk and went straight to the mother and *hit* her, open-handed, *hard,* on the side of the head, and everyone else just watched. All the wailing stopped. He started shouting at her and pushing her. She al-most lost her balance but some women caught her. Then some of the other men in the street shouted to him, and he ran back to the street and got into the ambulance with the boy, and they drove away. I got it all. And right then I realized what I was doing and I put my camera back in my pocket and walked away as fast as I could. But I got it all."

She went silent.

I opened my mouth and she put up a hand to stop me.

After another interval she said,"First it was Donal O'Connell, and you and Harry got rid of him and I was really very glad you did. Then it was Gordy Terrell and I was glad about that one too. And Mr. Black. And those men in the hotel. And then your brother Paul. And Mark Morris in the bar. And the men in the kitchen. And the story about the frat boy. And the guns. When I put my arms around you, there's a gun." She shook her head. She wasn't looking at me. She said, "I think that's all."

Another interval.

Then she said, "You weren't to blame for all of it. And blame is probably not the right word anyway. But you were there. You didn't start them happening but you were in my life when all those things happened. Too many to be cosmic coincidence. Those things never happened to me *before*. And I'm not sure just how... how many more such events I can *take*."

More silence.

She said, "I guess you can talk now."

I said, "Good." I leaned forward and rested my forearms on my knees. "Are you looking for a solution here or is this just so far a description of a situation?"

She said, "It's been two years now, that we've been together."

"Uh huh."

"I thought it would be getting better. Easier maybe."

I said, "So you are looking for a solution."

"I think I am."

"Is there one?"

She said, "I think so. Maybe two or three. One is that we just say oh well and go on as before. One is that we don't go on at all."

I felt the anger start to fizz in my chest and behind my eyes.

She said, "I think there's a middle road. But you won't like it."

I waited.

"We back off. About six months or something like that."

"What the hell does that mean?"

"The wedding is—off."

I said, "Postponed?"

"Canceled."

I said, "No."

She looked startled.

I said, "No," again. Loud. I wanted to stand up and start wailing and waving my arms around.

She covered her eyes again and said almost as loud, "Why should *you* get *your* way all the time?"

I said, not as loud, "Why did you tell me that story?"

"Because I was there and no one saw me!"

I lowered my voice even more. "Isn't that how you want it when you're shooting?"

"No, I don't want to be absent! Or invisible. And I don't want the world to eat up my work!" I didn't know what that meant, but I didn't want to ask now. She was starting to cry again. She waved her arm at her desk. "Look at them! They're great pictures! *I got it all!*"

I did look at them. I stood up and looked at them, print-outs spread across her desktop. They *were* great. She *did* get it all. The family in sharp focus, the crowds and traffic and storefronts less so. The father just slightly out of focus but the mother and babies in, making an invisible bubble around them. The boy dashing away and out of the bubble. Still photos, but still you could hear the sounds and see the action. The mother's stunned look of horror. The boy in the street. The women crowding around the mother. The men around the father. The father striking the mother. The father gone. Five, maybe six, men getting into a big car at the curb. Then just the mother with two or three women, all the men gone. And it was true—no one seemed to have been aware of what she was doing.

I said, "You did." But I had to clear my throat to say it. "You did. You got it all."

I reached out a hand to her but she leaned back, away from me. I stopped.

I said, "The whole story is right there. You've gone right past the need for any words. The pictures are *outside* of words."

She said, "I'll tell you another story."

"Okay."

She said, "When those two men came into the kitchen, and you fought the one and he, um, died, then everything—the room, you and Andy and the two men—it all started to move away from me. The hairy man was on the floor and limp, not moving, but his hands were reaching for me. So I went backward and against the wall. It was cold. So I looked down and I was naked. Then everything was moving away faster and faster. It moved away, faster and faster and I was little again and I didn't understand anything. Then you were there and you put your hand out to me and I said don't touch me. That was all I knew, all I could think. Don't touch me. I don't know why I was saying that. *To you!* But it was all the words I had."

I didn't know what to say. Too bad she hadn't had a camera that night in the kitchen.

After a while she said, "I just kept on shooting."

I said, "And good you did. These are great."

"I was a ghost. I'm becoming a ghost."

I said, "No ghost took these pictures."

A silence grew between us and seemed like to go on forever if I didn't break it. There was something I should be saying and I didn't know what it was.

She looked at her watch and stood. "I have a client coming." And the air broke around us and fell to the floor in a thousand glittering bits.

I said, "I need to change."

"Okay."

"Can we talk more later?"

She nodded.

2

But we didn't. Not then. Her client came. I went downstairs and showered and dressed. Later I heard her client leaving and I went to the kitchen and started fixing ham and cheese sandwiches and a pitcher of grapefruit juice and ice. She came into the kitchen to fetch her tray and we went out to eat on the back porch where we had put a small table and some chairs by a big screened window. She asked how was the tennis and I said I beat Harry two out of three but he was pushing me. She asked where we played and I said the club and she smiled. She thought it was very amusing that we all belonged to a private tennis club, but she agreed that the public courts were broken and weedy and hard to play seriously.

I said I'd promised Philip I'd be at the office later and she nodded. She said she had clients until six and then she might go to a movie with Karen. I said I was going to play at Elmore's, so maybe I wouldn't see her until morning.

"Is that all right?" I asked.

"Of course," she said.

I did all that and I guess she did too, but when I got home the next morning, she wasn't there.

The End

Acknowledgements and Thanks

A large number of friends and relations have read this story, all or part, or helped in other ways during the writing of it, and have given me invaluable feedback. If you are one of them and I have not included your name in the following list, please get in touch so I can make corrections and amends.

Bruce Rubenstein
Catherine Parker
Gary Lindberg
Ian Leask
Alice Phoenix
Simba Blood
Ian Moore
John Buranen
Dave Garland
Gary Jenneke
Tom Gibbons
Mary Shapiro
Dick Shapiro
Natalie Marr
Toua Her

Thank you all.

About the Author

Jeane Moore writes books about families that are unusual, gamblers, cops, vigilantes, mercenaries, soldiers, crime, love that grows and love that doesn't, death, murder, friends, and friendship. She has written screenplays, won two major screenwriting fellowships, and had a workshop production. She is a long-time member of the Tornado Alley Writing Group, and an experienced earth-sciences writer and editor.